THE GIRLS'
BOOK OF
PRIESTHOOD

First published by Muswell Press in 2018

Typeset by e-Digital Design Ltd.

Copyright © Louise Rowland 2018

Louise Rowland has asserted her right to be identified
as the author of this work in accordance with the
Copyright, Designs and Patents Act 1988

Printed and bound by CPI Group (UK) Ltd, Croydon CR04YY.

"God Says Yes To Me" by Kaylin Haught ©.
Reprinted with the author's kind permission.

This book is a work of fiction and, except in the case of historical fact, any
resemblence to actual persons, living or dead, is purely coincidental.

A CIP catalogue record for this book is available from the British Library

ISBN 978-0-9954822-8-9

MUSWELL
PRESS

Muswell Press
London
N6 5HQ

www.muswell-press.co.uk

THE GIRLS' BOOK OF PRIESTHOOD

Louise Rowland

MUSWELL
PRESS

To Phil, Phoebes and Hellie – for everything

God Says Yes to Me

by Kaylin Haught

I asked God if it was okay to be melodramatic
and she said yes
I asked her if it was okay to be short
and she said it sure is
I asked her if I could wear nail polish
or not wear nail polish
and she said honey
she calls me that sometimes
she said you can do just exactly
what you want to do
Thank God I said
And is it even okay if I don't paragraph
my letters
Sweetcakes God said
Who knows where she picked that up
What I'm telling you is
Yes Yes Yes

Part I

The Stranger
in the Mirror

Chapter 1

5 July 2016
Twelve months to go

Dearly beloved, we are gath—
What is this? A Friday-night sitcom?
Hello, everyone. I'm thrilled to be here giving my first—
It's not the BAFTA awards, either.
In the beginning was the—
No.

It was 3 a.m. by the time she'd finally thrown herself under the duvet, fully clothed. The lights in the flats opposite had long since flicked off in a Morse of despair.

Sermon-writing was never like this when she was training at Wilhurst. Even her thesis, *Body Beautiful: Female Iconography at the Heart of Middle-European Medieval Christianity*, had tripped off the keyboard in comparison.

'Don't try too hard, Margot,' Jeremy had advised her in the Heron a couple of days previously. 'Just be yourself. Our job is to keep the gathered multitude interested. Or, failing that, awake. I know how you women like to connect through the personal stuff, real-life issues, et cetera. All fine, in my book. Just don't be flippant. Or too clever-clever. I'd skip any references to Julius of Norwich or the Gnostic Gospels. St Mark's isn't really that kind of place. The last curate fancied himself as our very own Simon Schama and

9

most people didn't love it, to be honest. Though the one occasion I tried to be a bit clever, I had some QC email me the day afterwards, telling me I'd misquoted Rilke.'

He'd chuckled and taken a long sip of his pint, eyeing her over the foamy rim.

'And not to unsettle you but, well, one or two individuals – OK, maybe a few – may be watching you quite closely on Sunday.'

'Willing me to fail, you mean?'

'Could I trouble you for the sauce?'

The brown splatter had covered the mash like a muddy massacre.

She glances sideways back into the mirror now, half-dazed with disbelief. Her fingers reach for the collar. Your entire identity summed up in eight inches of pliable white plastic. Say halo to your new life: curate of the parish, carer of souls.

She swallows.

The naked bathroom bulb picks out every blemish: the pasty cheeks, the violet bags, the streaky whites of her eyes. Black clerical shirt: perfect shade for a pale-faced redhead who's had three hours' sleep, tops.

She feels like a rookie stand-up at the Fringe, about to face a sweaty cave full of hardcores. Except this is life or death. Twelve months to prove she's got the mettle to do this, starting with her first appearance in front of them all in two hours' time. The past five years have been child's play compared to what lies ahead.

She rubs in a third layer of Touche Éclat, another whisk of blusher. Demure and discreet in all things, someone at Wilhurst warned them, reverence and restraint. This is an emergency. It's all she can do to resist downing the rest of the sherry from the vicar's welcome hamper. As it was, the Ferrero Rocher didn't survive the night.

The collar is chafing at the sides of her neck, even with the extra investment in the latest 'comfort' model, complete with inner band for increased air circulation. She should have stuck to the flick 'n' push version. Each of the four shank collar studs is grazing her skin, demanding, *Who exactly do you think you are?*

She steps back and searches the mirror for some vestige of herself. It's like pulling on a high-vis tabard bearing the words *Holy One*: black and white confirmation you're on Bible business. She walked underneath some scaffolding on the Holloway Road yesterday and one of the builders shouted down something she didn't catch, and then they all started cackling and catcalling.

Throughout it all, you have to smile, smile, smile.

She rummages in her make-up bag yet again and pulls out a lipstick in brazen carmine. At least it'll colour-pop against the funereal black.

She closes her eyes. She can do this. She's made it this far. Several of the other ordinands have already fallen by the wayside, not even making it to being deaconed.

She leans back against the towel rail and takes some steadying breaths. Her sense of vocation has never been greater. The transformative power of God's love is all around her all the time: she's never in any doubt about that. In some moments, a quiet, gentle grace; at others, a turbo-charged source of raw spiritual energy. And always, always, that sense of something – someone – greater than she is, cradling her in its care. She knows this is how she's meant to live out her faith, just as you know, when you fall abruptly, recklessly in love. When life can be altered in the flicker of a smile.

She opens her eyes and bullies some more colour into her cheeks.

Is she good enough, though? The stakes couldn't be higher. Anything might derail her. Maybe her father was right and she has lost the plot in pursuing this as her calling?

It's twenty past nine. She snaps off the light, snatches her bag from the bed and walks out of the door.

A short way along the pavement, she stops and retraces her steps into the tiny studio flat, hurries to the rickety bookcase and runs her fingers along the top shelf. She pulls down a small flat grey stone with a hole in the centre: it's travelled everywhere with her, since she found it all those years ago with her mother on the beach at Hengistbury Head. Its contours lie warm and familiar in her palm. She slips it into her pocket, takes another breath without glancing back at the mirror and rushes out of the front door.

Highbury Fields is muggy, drizzle-sodden, as she makes her way across, a drumbeat throb in her right temple. Her fringe is already kinking at the edges. The haters will take one look at the madwoman at the lectern and rest their case.

She crosses over, turns right and stops. St Mark's. The Georgian-Victorian mishmash in which she will make or break her career. She pulls the buckle of her shoulder strap higher. Something about the church's solid, burnt-fudge façade always reminds her somehow of the sea: the way it changes mood and tone according to the season or the light. This morning's moist grey gauze flattens the whole exterior, making the whole post-war patch-up more of a misjudgement than the seamless blend it sometimes appears to her to be.

One hundred and eighty-two years. How much joy and wonder, grief, loneliness, despair – ecstasy – have played out here, she wonders? And now, enter stage left, the clueless upstart.

She sighs, rolls her shoulders back and continues on past the huge magnolia tree by the porch, resting her palm briefly against its trunk.

As she steps inside the porch, however, the distinctive blend of over-the-hill chrysanthemums and Mr Muscle floor polish is like slipping into a second skin. The board by the front door displaying the photos of the church team, with a gap where her own face will be. The patchwork spread of notices below: the coffee rota, curling minutes from April's AGM, the plea for second-hand toys and books for the Kool Gang, the sign-up sheet for last week's summer fete, the Polaroid of Jeremy gamely holding a bored-looking salamander at the Pet Blessing service. She smiles at his open face, age indeterminate beneath the close black crop, the pronounced widow's peak above the unexpected yellow-rimmed glasses. The vicar is a one-man rebuttal of all those studies that have 95 per cent of clergy down as introverts, a statistic that probably still holds good, given the number of sociopaths she met at Wilhurst.

She glances up to the top of the board where the church's mission statement sits in large bold print.

Jesus was open to all. So are we here at St Mark's. Whoever, whatever you are, wherever you're from, we welcome you unreservedly to our worshipping community and Eucharistic table.

Her pulse slowly regains its composure. It's all so reassuringly offend-no-one C of E. Not a whiff of *Sturm und Drang*, no twanging electric guitars or speaking in tongues, no fairy lights on the altar or lacy accessories: just, for her, that profound sense of belonging, of coming home. The numinous bathed in the familiar, like stepping into a tiny village church and catching the delicate scent of candle wax, cloth-bound hymnals and well-worn hassocks; dust pirouetting in the shafts of sapphire, ruby and gold like sparkled stardust in the ancient air.

Just as I am, of that free love
The breadth, length, depth and height to prove,
Here for a season, then above,
O Lamb of God, I come, I come!

The organ's wheezy exhalations taper up behind the altar screen. A profound silence falls, punctured eventually by two or three psychosomatic coughs, then the soft swish of the choir's robes as they retake their seats.

Margot drags her head from the service sheet and stares fixedly at the decorated reredos across the sanctuary. She's aware of every single pair of eyes in the building. All the young families, the Highbury great and the good, the male couples, the older couples, the singles, the one-offs, the huge battalion of retirement-aged women, the lonely, the bored, the nostalgic, the devout, the loyal, the aspirational. The well-wishers. The ill-wishers. The expectant.

She swallows again. *Lord, help me. You chose me to dedicate my life to Your service, when sometimes I've no idea why. Help me to reassure them all that there hasn't been some hideous mistake in taking me on. Even those who don't want me here. I know this is a long journey and I've only just pulled out of the station, but I desperately don't want to fail.*

She gets to her feet. Out of the corner of her eye, she can see Jeremy discreetly holding up his thumb.

The air has thinned. She turns to her left and takes a few slow steps along the tatty crimson, hugging her surplice close, glad she decided against high heels. The scent of yesterday's lilies is overwhelming as she shuffles her notes on the lectern and arranges her face into poise.

Jeremy guessed about 1.45 this morning: they'd coagulated into a blur. She looks out over the top of their heads and focuses on the fire-exit sign above the door: Jeremy's last-minute top tip. Minutes pass, or so it feels. She fills her lungs and lifts her chin. Deep, authoritative. No high-pitched girly tones.

Someone smacks their lips in the front pew, right below the lectern. Margot can't resist glancing down. A father has his toddler balanced on his shoulders to get a better view, as though Margot's a new arrival at Rainforest Life in London Zoo. In front of him, the likely lip-smacker: an older woman with scrubbed red cheeks, snaggle teeth and an unfortunate mole, gazing up at her, as though witnessing a beatific vision.

Jeremy gives a small cough. Margot forces herself to focus back on the fire exit, fingers gripping the side of the lectern.

Her mother always used to quote that American film star's line about acting: it's all about standing up naked and turning around very slowly.

Do this for her.

Margot Goodwin. Priest-in-waiting.

'May I speak in the name of the Living God, Father, Son and Holy Spirit. Amen. So, hello, everyone.'

Chapter 2

Queasiness comes in waves as she watches the vicar flicking off the bank of lights in the porch. Two hours in and she's already given the antis enough fodder to launch an excommunication. Jeremy shrugs on his raincoat and shoos her outside, rattling the huge bunch of keys.

'Nice work, Margot.'

Her heart plummets five floors. Killing with kindness. Maybe he's saving the dressing-down for next week's supervision.

'I'm sorry, Jeremy. I don't think I quite nailed it.'

'Don't be silly. That whole "the contents of my handbag" number was fine.' He drops the keys into his rucksack. 'Who knew about the philosophical symbolism of mascara wands?'

The go-to emergency sermon of all trainee priests with ovaries. How could she have been so stupid?

'In fact, several people at coffee told me how much they enjoyed it,' he continues.

'Did they?' She hesitates. 'One couple I spoke to seemed a bit put out. Said how they normally like extensive scriptural input, how they always go home after a sermon and reread the relevant passage in the Bible and plan their week's witness around it.'

Jeremy sighs.

'I have a pretty good idea who that was. But you can't please all the people all of the time. Actually, we're all doomed to failure, if that makes you feel any better.'

He smiles across at her, brandishing a couple of bursting bin bags, and she waits as he places them on the pavement opposite.

Coffee had been hideous. Actors aren't expected to leave the stage and mingle with the audience the moment the curtain falls on a first-night production, catching the appalled whispers behind. Yet twenty minutes after she'd walked away from the lectern, she'd had to circulate around all the different clusters in the hall, a chocolate bourbon balanced in the saucer of her lukewarm coffee, smiling gratitude at the friendly welcomes, joining in the new-girl chat, dipping her head at the slightly too intrusive questions, trying to ingratiate without giving too much away, and all the time braced for someone to start yelling one of St Paul's clobber texts about how women should know their place and keep quiet in church.

Jeremy comes back alongside her.

'Penny for them?'

'Oh, you know, I was just thinking about this morning.'

'Don't be too much of a perfectionist, Margot. Canterbury wasn't built in a day.'

He nudges her arm. She looks down at her lace-ups and nods.

'In any case, I didn't spot anyone playing sermon bingo, so you've already bagged several brownie points. Come on, the Heron's calling. I bet you're in need of something stronger than Millicent's coffee. I keep telling her to add another scoop, but she's worried about overrunning the entertainment budget.'

Ten minutes later, she's sitting on a scratchy green banquette, watching her incumbent thread his way through the bar of the unreconstructed boozer opposite Highbury tube that doubles as their off-duty HQ. Jeremy's a head taller than most of the customers, but his rapid progress is still impressive. Brick-cheeked regulars make way for the man of the cloth. One or two even touch their temple as he passes, possibly confusing him with Father Joseph from St Aloysius of the Holy Redeemer.

Her gratitude for the gamble he's taken is now shot through with a deep unease. The jokes that had seemed reasonably witty at 3 a.m. had popped in the air one by one like silent soap bubbles. She'd been aware of several people nearby flicking through their orders of service, as though checking to see whether there was a complaints hotline. The Rainforest Life toddler had had two screaming fits before emptying an entire box of Lego into the aisle. One man in his early thirties had even taken out a copy of *Private Eye* and a packet of crisps, the synthetic smell of onion strong enough to overpower the lilies.

She leans back and closes her eyes, aware of a shuddering exhaustion in every inch of her body, as the clinking and chatter carry on around her.

'Oops, thought we'd caught you napping there, Margot.'

She jerks herself upright, mouth dry. Jeremy is holding two glasses of red, now joined by a man in his fifties, cream silk shirt undone a button too far, choppy silver layers on his collar.

'Too much partying, Reverend?' The smile is silkily suave, appraising.

Jeremy puts the drinks down and claps him on the shoulder.

'You two haven't met. Margot, this is Fabian Spence, rising star of the PCC.'

Fabian's hooded eyes are assessing her with the impersonal thoroughness of an airport scanner.

'Pleasure.'

The hand is cold and impeccably manicured.

'Can I get you something, Fabian?'

'Sorry, Jeremy, but I have to skedaddle, sadly. Family stuff.'

He hasn't taken his eyes off her.

'You're not what I expected.'

A joke – any joke – eludes her.

'I mean, you know, someone says "woman priest" and you think the whole grey-hair-bobbly-cardigan-house-full-of-cats thing, right?'

He's got the full cast of stereotypes. Just like how the cocky male crew at Wilhurst used to call the first floor corridor 'Death Row', because that's where the older women ordinands lived.

'Well, yeah, I guess.'

The vicar's smile rounds into a cherubic O.

Maybe it's because she has the energy of a limp balloon, but she can't tell whether she's being flirted with or insulted, or both.

Fabian glances down at her left hand.

'I kind of thought you'd be wearing a skirt.'

'Oh, Margot's very twenty-first century,' chortles Jeremy, slightly flirtatious himself. 'She's going to be a huge asset to the team. Full-time, to boot.'

'I wouldn't have taken a non-stipendiary job,' Margot shoots back.

Fabian tips his head.

'Sorry to have missed your star turn this morning. I'll have to catch it on YouTube.'

Margot glances at the vicar, but disloyalty wouldn't be his style.

'Jeremy says you've come armed with a Ph.D.' He juts out his lower lip. 'I hope we won't be too dull for you.'

The vicar beams, thrilled at this interaction.

'What was it about, this Ph.D of yours?'

She hesitates.

'Well, how the Church in the Middle Ages represented women as the counterpoint of body and spirit, a rendering of the eternal conflict between flesh and soul.'

A muscle flickers by Fabian's right eye.

'Looks like you'll have to keep on your toes, mate,' he says to Jeremy, then glances back at Margot. 'Can't wait to hear more.'

He reaches over to clap Jeremy on the shoulder.

'Sorry but someone's waiting for me. See you in a couple of weeks.'

He doesn't look back as they watch him winding through the bar, hand raking through the layers.

'Great bloke,' Jeremy says, bumping down onto the banquette next to her. 'Knows absolutely everyone. Involved in several start-ups, apparently. You know, the kind of guy who's always ahead of the wave.'

'Right.'

'He's very ambitious for St Mark's.'

'That's an interesting word.'

He tosses back a palmful of nuts and clinks her glass.

'You two will make a great team.'

Her stomach isn't so convinced.

By the time she's walking back home across the Fields, the sky has lightened to a milky blue, like a toddler tamed out of its tantrum.

There's an empty seat ahead of her, caught in a pool of weak sunshine. She walks over and sits down, glad of the solitude at last.

Jeremy's explained how the elegant five-storey terraces fronting the park are home to Highbury's rarefied gene pool of literati, glitterati and legalati. A century and a half ago, their owners would have been stalwarts of St Mark's, when numbers ran to more than a thousand even on a normal Sunday. Jeremy would be ecstatic now if he managed to pull in a quarter of that at Christmas or Easter. He's already aired his frustration about the fact that many of these houses will happily support the fundraising appeals, but their generosity never translates into bums on seats. That's where you come in, Margot. A new face to bring in a new congregation. You and Fabian, a great team.

She shudders. Somehow she will have to make that one work.

She closes her eyes, wrenching her hair out of its ponytail. Her black clothes are sponging up the heat. She can imagine Clarissa upbraiding her for being such a sap, next time they meet up a drink: *Lame, M, lame. Imposter syndrome, so not 2016.*

Some boys playing a scratch game of cricket nearby; a man is throwing some kind of spongy toy for his dog; people are walking past her on the grass. The honeysuckle bush in the garden behind is rendering the air almost laughably sweet. Just a few more minutes. The agenda for Tuesday's PCC meeting can wait. No rush to get back to the dingy curate's flat, with its smell of wet dog, mushroom-coloured stigmata on the wall behind the TV, and rusty cooker with its please-themselves hotplates. Not forgetting the front-door bell playing *Zadok the Priest,* courtesy of some joker in Church House. After ten days, she's ready to rip the wires from the wall.

She swallows. She knows exactly how fortunate she is. A flat of her own, after four years of hairy-basined communal living at Wilhurst – *Big Brother* for the holy. More to the point, she's lucky to have this job at all. Every other ordinand in her year had posts sewn up by December or January; she was still homeless by mid-April. The central London parishes you'd think would be right-on and liberal might just as well have signed up to Resolutions A and B for all the difference it made. The stained-glass ceiling resolutely in place.

Jeremy was the only one to say yes. The moment they met at the Pets and Owners' Meet and Greet at Wilhurst, she'd looked around everyone else scoping out their prospective new incumbents and knew she was the one who'd struck gold.

It's late afternoon when she stands up to go. There's no evensong tonight, but she has a couple of hours prep, ahead of her first full week as the vicar's number two. Joint number two. She must try not to forget about Roderick. Just because he's still away on whatever kind of break seventy-year-old, single, soon-to-be-retired, male priests treat themselves to doesn't mean he's not a lynchpin at St Mark's.

The back route to the flat is longer, but she takes it to avoid bumping into any of the parishioners on Highbury Grove. The thought of some of those prospective encounters makes her roots prickle. If she'd been free to choose, she'd have lived in a different borough, several miles away preferably.

She pops into the twenty-four-hour shop near the roundabout for some chocolate and a couple of magazines, then crosses over two sets of lights and turns the corner into Mildmay Grove. And stops. Paralysed.

Slivers of blue light are dancing off the parked cars. There's a small crowd standing on the corner, blanketed by an eerie hush. Powerful arc lights are trained on her terrace, even though it's a bright summer afternoon.

She sleepwalks towards the knot of people.

'Sorry, can I just go, excuse me, sorry, I live here, can I just squeeze through?'

No one moves or even turns to look at her. Her hands are clammy. She reaches into her pocket, then grabs a couple of shoulders from behind.

'Can you let me past? I need to get through. Look, I'm a priest.'

One of the men gawps at her, then steps back just enough to let her pass. She pushes forwards as hard as she can and stops dead.

Mildmay Grove looks like a live news feed. There's a jagged tear where most of her house used to be, a cat's cradle of blue and white police tape criss-crossing the street. The air is foggy with dust, reeks of something cloying and metallic. Margot feels like her senses are scrambled.

'Poor sods,' says a large woman next to her, her arms hugging her chest.

'Gas,' announces a man in front. 'Not bloody terrorists, at least.'

'Shit,' the woman answers. 'What a way to go.'

Margot is worried she's about to vomit. The Lloyds' TV blares out from breakfast right through to midnight.

'Yeah, well, no one in at the time, the coppers just said,' a man further back shouts over other people's heads.

'Are you sure?' Margot whispers, her breath shaky.

'Coppers said so, didn't they? Something to do with a dodgy boiler jobby.'

'They was lucky.' An elderly woman to Margot's right wearing a dirty bobble hat leans in close, licking her lips. 'Could've been very nasty, very nasty.' She squints, peering at Margot. 'You was wasting your time, love. No need for last rites, after all.'

Margot can't drag her eyes away. There's something obscenely intimate about it: her small sanctuary of sanity and calm now exposed to a couple of hundred onlookers idling on the street. The building looks like a doll's house vandalised by a wayward child, the front wall almost completely ripped away, ribbons of paper fluttering in the arc lights as though part of some macabre festival of the grotesque.

Something's glinting on the back wall. It takes her a few seconds to realise what it is. The frame of her leavers' photo from Wilhurst, now dangling sideways, the hopeful smiles of 120 ordinands buried beneath a filthy layer of dust.

Her legs break into a jive.

'Mind how you go.' She turns to her right to see the guy from two doors down, the one who's always popping around for a pint of milk and, she suspected, the milk of human kindness, now reaching for her arm, his eyes full with concern.

'Shit, you look like a ghost. You OK?'

She lets him guide her to sit down on the curb.

'You got anything valuable in there?'

She lifts her eyes towards the pulverised mess and shakes her head. Any other Sunday, she would have been home by now. Someone hands her a bottle of water.

'This your place, miss?'

She looks up again, registering the black uniform beneath the high-vis jacket, then the pale face of a skinny young policeman, wispy strands of strawberry blond escaping from under his cap.

He licks his finger and flicks at his pad. Maybe this is also one of his first days on the job? His hand is trembling slightly. She takes another swig of water, noticing herself noticing these details, as though some sort of anchor to prevent her vanishing entirely. Behind the policeman, a couple of people now seem to be capturing this exchange on their mobile phones.

'Was.'

'So I need to take some detai—'

'Oh, sorry, I'm sorry, officer.'

She drags her phone out of her bag and stares at the screen.

'Take it if you need to, miss.'

He taps his phone against his cheek, lower lip slightly out.

'Dad?'

'Don't sound so thrilled.'

She closes her eyes.

'I can't talk now, it's just, I'm not—'

'Don't tell me, they've already got you hosting a leper convention?'

'Please, Dad.'

'Joke, Margot.'

'Now is not a good time. My fla—'

'When is, exactly?'

She can't answer.

'Just call back when you can finally spare some time.'

The screen fades to black.

'Not more bad news, I hope?'

It's the policeman's professional kindness that finally tips her over.

Chapter 3

Middle of August

The bed and breakfast off Essex Road has two things to recommend it: the mates' rates agreed by the owner, because her sister's in the church choir, and the solitude it provides. As Margot staggered out of Mildmay Grove that evening three and a half weeks ago, as someone ushered her into a minicab to be gathered into the vicarage by a shocked Jeremy, more than any of the possessions she'd lost in the rubble that briefly constituted her home, more than the thought of what could have happened if she'd returned half an hour earlier, her overriding terror was for the loss of her freedom, now that the curate's flat had been obliterated.

She perches on the side of the yellowing duvet and bites on her pen. In terms of comfort, it's possibly even a step down from its predecessor. But the rollercoaster mattress, the gap between the window and its casement, the slimy wardrobe door, the brown lampshades, the gloom, all continue to provide her with the anonymity she craves.

That sense of good fortune is spiced with an awareness that, over the past few weeks, she has been the recipient of unadulterated kindness in its truest sense. The caravan of gifts from St Mark's would gladden the heart of the most adamant misanthropist. A drawer full of clothes lent by Sal and Kath, co-leaders of the Kool Gang, to give back whenever. A *We Love You, Margot* scrapbook from the Kool Gang themselves. A pile of well-thumbed *Reader's Digests* from the flower ladies. A giant bottle of primrose bath oil from the two biddies who always nod in unison, three rows back. That bunch of yellow tulips from Tommy the verger, with a card in beautiful copperplate: *Chin up, Reverend.*

And, of course, four bottles of Chilean red from Jeremy, because what else would a vicar provide?

There's been no fanfare, no virtue-signalling hoopla, just the no-nonsense generosity of people who want to do their bit. She knows how very lucky she is to be in this particular parish, amongst these particular people.

She pulls the sheet of paper on the bed towards her, circling the numbers in fluorescent marker.

1. *Collect Jeremy's surplice from the cleaners*

2. *Call the builder about the leak above the sacristy*

3. *Chase English Heritage about the grant application*

She zips the onesie up tighter. Did Kath and Sal somehow foresee the cross-currents in this room?

4. *Circulate the statement of accounts before Prissy Pamela starts complaining*

5. *Email Islington Council about the alcohol licence for weddings*

6. *Research* Paw Patrol *for the primary-school assembly*

Even as she tries to marshal the priorities, new ones jump up, thrusting their hands into the air. Jeremy loves quoting that line saying that life in ministry is working yourself to death, but slowly. She's already seen how each week, each day, is so unstructured and unpredictable; sometimes feels like they're dealing with life, death and everything in between, all in the same afternoon. But that's the grace, the privilege of the mission.

7. *Remind Jeremy to lay mousetraps behind the organ*

8. *Visit Edwina Walker in Homerton Hospital*

She arrows Edwina to the top of the page. Yes, but when? Trying to get on top of all this makes Sisyphus's to-do list seem like a cheese-rolling competition.

9. *Read through the notes on service composition for the next Post Ordination Training session aka POTTY meeting*
10. *Pin down the choirmaster about the hymn selection for the next quarter*
11. *Phone that young mother whose husband has run off with his executive assistant*
12. *Book waxing appointment*

She scores through the last one and drags out another blank sheet.

1. *Book waxing appointment*
2. *Find a yoga class*
3. *Learn German*

She stops and sighs.

4. *Get a life*

Outside the window, profound darkness. It was always going to be a vertical learning curve; any new job would be. 'Keep calm and muddle on,' as Jeremy would say. She should have it printed on a mug for him. But, then, after twenty-five years plus, he's accustomed to the chaos, the infinite straggle of loose ends. Roderick, too, no doubt. She baulks at the thought of the house-for-duty assistant priest. Things aren't progressing so well on that front. Those liver-spotted hands cradling endless cups of tea, the rheumy eyes watching her every move. She needs to work harder to win him over.

She's just reaching down to pick up the first sheet again when there's a loud rap on the door.

She sits back, frozen. Mid evening on a Sunday? Mrs Bartlet, the landlady, has only knocked twice in three weeks, and then just to bring up an electric heater and some post.

The knock comes again, louder this time.

She grabs a cardigan to cover the onesie and heads for the door.

Mrs Bartlet is standing outside in the hall, tea-towel in her hand. So, too, is one of the parishioners, Gwen Taylor. Cradling a lumpy carrier bag, that eager snaggle-toothed smile of hers wide in anticipation.

'I hope it's not too late, Reverend?'

One of the navy blue, all-weather, Crocs is already over the threshold.

Mrs Bartlet nods at them both and shuffles back to her own quarters and the latest must-see Scandi thriller.

Margot stares at Gwen. Is she here to remind her about the silverware cleaning rota?

'I just wanted to deliver some baked goodies for you, Reverend, you being homeless and so on,' she gabbles. 'David told me I shouldn't, it would be OTT, but a little coffee and walnut sponge never hurt anyone. I've popped some strawberry-jam tarts in as well. All you have to do is keep them shut tight in the Tupperware.'

'Oh, well, that's so kind of you, Gwen. But you really shouldn't have.'

'Why ever not?'

Margot tenses. It's such a fine line. She knows she should invite her in, brew up a cup of tea or instant coffee and sit and have a chat. That's why she's here.

They both stand by the door.

'You've made it nice and comfy here, then.'

Margot smiles, glancing over her shoulder at the tiny room.

'Oh, you know, we priests like our cells!'

Gwen frowns. A double beep from the other side of the room breaks the silence. Margot dashes across to her phone.

Get your holy self down to the Spotted Dick on Stoke Newington high street by 8.30. I need a drink.

Clarissa.

'Just a sec, Gwen.'

She types a reply at top speed.

You're telepathic as well psychopathic. Mine's a double G and T.

She turns back to Gwen, still standing by the door, waiting. Margot feels a twinge of guilt.

'I'm so sorry, Gwen, but I have to head out now.'

'Oh no. Must you?' Gwen's eyes hold hers for a second and seem to be watering behind the round frames. Margot swallows.

'Urgent pastoral business.'

'But I was hoping we could have a proper chat,' Gwen says, glancing down at her bags. 'I wanted to talk to you about all kinds of things I thought we could do at St Mark's.'

She rummages in her pocket and pulls out a plastic sandwich bag.

'And I brought some herbal tea bags. I know they're your favourite.'

Margot swipes at her nose. She's starting to feel clammy with conscience.

'I'd love coffee soon, Gwen, but right now I'm afraid I do have to go out.'

Gwen looks down at the carrier bag she's still holding.

'I hope you're not allergic to nuts.'

She places the bag on the floor by the bedside table, does one last swift recce of the room, pulls on her raincoat belt and backs out into the corridor.

'People shouldn't impose on you so much. It's not fair.'

She leans in suddenly, yanking Margot into a vast spongy hug, then turns and shuffles down the corridor, head bobbing as though reassuring herself. Margot watches, relieved yet stinging with shame, and closes the door as soon as it's safe. She pulls a pair of jeans and a sweatshirt out of the cupboard and rushes to get changed, desperate to be out of there.

'Call it an act of charity, M,' says Clarissa at their table in the Spotted Dick, twenty-five minutes later. 'I knew you were bound to be at home squeezing your spots and knocking back the Dettol, so thought I'd better intervene.'

'Pretty good guess.'

Classic Clarissa. She's the one who needs to talk, apparently, but has pivoted things within seconds so that Margot is now in the role of supplicant. That's been the shadow-play of their entire eight-year friendship.

'So, how's the thesis coming along?'

'Nice try, Reverend. We're here to talk about you.'

'When do you have to submit your first draft?' No one procrastinates like Clarissa.

'Real bummer about your flat, M,' says Clarissa, reaching for some crisps. 'But then you were always whingeing on about what a dump it was, so maybe being blown to kingdom come was the best result. An act of God, even?'

Margot feels her shoulders relax for the first time in weeks. She pours the rest of her tonic into her glass.

'Got the PCC eating out of the palm of your hand yet? The names of all the mouth-breathers in the front row off pat?'

'Naturally.'

'I'm a teensy bit envious. Who knows, it could have been me. Maybe I took a wrong turn back there, choosing academia over what should have been my true vocation.'

Margot splutters on her lemon slice.

'What's so funny, M? I'm a deep well of compassion, not to mention moral rectitude. Parishioners would have lapped me up.'

Margot leans back, cradling her fingers.

'So, then, you're up for pastoral visits where you have to force down a slab of three-week-old Battenberg? And where you can't quite make out whether that sour smell you noticed in the corridor is cat's piss or something else?'

'Count me in,' says Clarissa.

'Right. And ever ready with your smiley face on, even at the pharmacy counter in Boots, when you're buying some laxatives or hair remover, just in case someone from the congregation comes over to complain about the lack of chairs with arms?'

'Where do I sign?'

Clarissa opens the second bag of crisps and scatters a handful on the table.

'OK, getting serious now, because it's all good grist to my thesis mill, let's talk about the antis in your panties. Any of the swivel-eyed brigade put dog shit through your letterbox, just because you're a girl? Or written to the bishop yet saying you're defiling their space?'

Margot winces.

'Would you like it if they were?'

'Just asking, M. Your fault, anyway, for choosing to work in the most androcentric institution of them all. Though to be fair, you are taking up the feminist cudgels for us all.'

Margot sighs. How many times have they ping-ponged through this?

'That's your chosen mission, Clariss. I just want to make it through to July alive.'

'You can't let the zombie churches or the pompommed birettas win.'

Margot glances down at her watch. She's on the early shift tomorrow and the gin is brewing a headache. Clarissa puts out her hand.

'Seriously, M, I'm so glad we did this. I've missed you.'

Margot reaches for her drink. She catches sight of a couple of guys by the bar, one of whom is looking over in their direction.

'Me too.' She swirls her ice cubes around. 'Sometimes it's like being a hothouse plant. Good to get out and get some fresh Stokey air.'

She glances back at the bar. The two guys are pulling on their jackets. The one who'd looked at her earlier smiles at her as they leave.

'Talking of which,' says Clarissa, who never misses, 'any hotties in the congregation?'

'You're crazy.'

'Got to have something to get out of bed for.'

'The last time most of this lot had sex, Harold Macmillan was still in Number Ten.'

Apart from Fabian, that is, but the less thought about him, the better. He's been away on some fact-minding mission the past few Sundays and that suits Margot just fine.

'Demographics dictate there must be at least two or three aged under thirty.'

Margot drains her glass.

'You know the rules. Don't cruise the pews—'

'Don't fuck the flock, yeah, yeah. So? What's the answer?'

This has the potential to become another Groundhog Day conversation between them.

'I can't even have friends in the parish other than in the most professional, hands-off sense, let alone some guy waiting to rip my clothes off as soon as the chalices are packed away. The parish curtains would twitch off their rails at the moral abomination.

'Tragic, Margot, tragic. You're two degrees off frigid already.'

The Wilhurst principal's parting maxim that your life is a sermon as much as any of the words that you preach is tattooed on Margot's brain. You either sign up for the role, hook, line and sinker, or you don't. The thought of becoming involved with anyone until she's made it safely past next July at the very earliest is unthinkable. But how to explain that to anyone, even – especially – Clarissa?

She reaches across for the second crisp bag, but Clarissa has emptied that one too, even the crumbs. Not such a good sign, she registers. She takes out her lemon slice and chews on that instead.

'Anyway, I've already got an admirer.'

Clarissa jerks upright.

'M, you dark horse. What's his name?'

'Gwen.'

'What the fuck?'

32

'It's cool. She just happens to be in her late sixties,' she pauses, 'a very active, helpful, member of the congregation.'

'There was me worrying about you being sex-deprived.'

'In fact, she was just visiting when you called.'

'You're kidding?'

'Brought over some hand-baked goodies and the lemon and ginger teabags she knows I like.' Margot swallows. 'Said she felt sorry I was all alone, holed up in my B and B and wanted to do something to help. Very solicitous, but a bit intense, you know? I was kind of glad when you texted.'

'Creeped you out?'

She laughs, glad of the release.

'I guess.'

Clarissa watches her a moment and shrugs.

'Actually, M, you know, maybe she really was just being nice and your job is to suck it up?'

Margot flushes, the shift of tone unbalancing her.

She walks into the vestry the next day, remarking yet again to herself how much the church's — indeed, the Church's — character is reflected in its physical reality. Wilhurst taught her many things as an ordinand: how to decode the mystery of priestly ontology in a Twitter-crazed world or to determine the difference between the 1662 *Book of Common Prayer* and the 2000 revisionist *Common Worship*. But nothing could have prepared her for the clutterfest that is the St Mark's parish office.

Every surface in here is buried under multiple layers of detritus. Hundreds of dusty out-of-date orders of service, yellowing copes of the *Church Times*, bulging lever-arch files, a bottle of sherry still bearing its ragged Christmas bow, plastic bags stuffed full of tinsel and fading crêpe-paper daffodils stashed beneath the desk. Quite what Brown Owl and the tantric yoga teacher think on their way into the church hall each week is anybody's guess.

'Coffee, anyone?'

Roderick glances up and gives her the gimlet glare he seems to have reserved just for her. She smiles back, her determination to build bridges still intact. She knows that he has a long, apparently distinguished, career as a naval chaplain behind him, as well as twenty years' service here at St Mark's. Half the congregation seem to knit him jumpers or offer to darn his socks. Even the young mothers treat him as some sort of dilapidated pet. And maybe that simulacrum of domestic care is the whole point? Perhaps the resentment he seems to feel towards her as the newest, youngest, member of the team is because he has no other life to retire to? In his own way, he's also one of the left behind, just like so many of the millions who have just voted for Brexit.

Jeremy is jotting down yet another of his lists when she walks back in, carrying the tray.

'Hopefully we can palm off some of this lot onto the Care Bears,' he says, winking at her. Or the Ever-Readies, as she can't help thinking of them in private moments. One of them even has a photo of the vicar on her phone as her screen saver.

Roderick steeples his fingers, scowling at no one in particular.

Jeremy takes his mug from the tray, dives in for a chocolate digestive, reconsiders and takes two.

'Plenty here to share out between us. You especially, Margot.'

Roderick's mouth sets into a purple line as Jeremy points at his computer screen.

'The head of Highbury High wants someone to talk to his Year Ten RS group next month. Part of a series of talks by different faith groups from all over Islington. According to the email, you'd be the only female on the list.'

A gravelly growl from opposite her.

'The school doesn't specifically ask for Margot, Roderick,' Jeremy soothes. 'But an occasion like this needs someone young and hip. Correct me if I'm wrong, but that rules out you and me.' The chuckle lasts several seconds. 'Sounds like a perfect chance to reel in a few teens. Stealth marketing. Our chance to show we're cool.'

'Sure, be happy to.'

Addressing a class of GCSE students can't be that much of trial? It'll make a change from the diocesan events she's despatched off to for 'educational purposes', where the C of E's fixation with arcane minutiae is exposed in all its non-ironic glory.

Jeremy taps a reply, crumbs dancing off the keyboard.

'Good thing we've got a girl on the team,' mumbles Roderick, the moment the vicar has stepped outside. Margot looks up, surprised at being spoken to directly.

'Perfect for all our ministry with children, women, the sick, all the fluffy stuff. Just as our Lord God intended.'

As usual, no eye contact. In fact, she's not sure she was meant to hear: she's caught him mumbling to himself a few times and forced herself to put it down to age or corrosive loneliness.

But no. This time, he lifts his chin to face her and sniggers, before returning to his crossword in the *Church Times*.

A dangerous battle for the long haul, she realises wearily, as wheezy exhalations fill the silence between them.

Chapter 4

Late September

The bus is inching down the Archway Road in almost total gridlock. She's arranged to be at the school early for a pre-briefing with the head of religious studies, but her dentist's appointment overran. She's already twenty minutes late and the parish budget doesn't run to taxis.

She wipes a smeary arc into the condensation and looks back down at her speaking notes, her nerves starting to jangle. Maybe the icebreaker joke about *The Great British Bake Off* isn't right? But then what would hit the spot for a group of fifteen-year-olds, forced to listen to the meanderings of a wannabe priest standing in front of them for half an hour?

Is there an Eleventh Commandment she's missed that stipulates the curate of the parish must always be allotted all youth-related activities? Though the vicar was right, she can't imagine Roderick doing this particular gig. He scowls if a baby so much as gurgles in church. But he's almost seventy: it's not his fault if he has all the energy of a Galapagos turtle.

There's a discarded *Metro* on the seat in front of her. She's just reaching for it, hoping for some kind of serendipitous inspiration, when a hand grips her wrist.

'Hello, Margot.' Prissy Pamela, church warden and disapprover-in-chief, as the puffed out powdery cheeks now testify. 'What a coincidence. May I join you?'

Margot disguises the frustration as she shifts over to accommodate the Waitrose bags and the golf umbrella, arranging her face into the requisite smile.

'Bit of luck bumping into you. I've been wanting to quiz you for a while about that ugly scrap of rug that's appeared from nowhere in the Kool Gang's play area. Looks like it's been dragged out of a skip in Hackney. Do you happen to know who—'

A loud shout from the front of the bus makes them both jump. Someone is arguing furiously with the driver.

'As I was saying, a piece of tat like that doesn't give the impression St Mark's really wants to—'

The noise at the front has intensified. The rest of the bus falls silent, the air acquiring a grainy static.

Margot cranes her neck to try and see what's happening. A man is swaying by the doors halfway down; she can see the long straggles of filthy hair, the stained raincoat, the tracksuit bottoms dragging along the ground, a couple of plastic bags by his side.

'For fuck's sake, open the FUCKING doors!'

Several people shift back towards where she and Pamela are sitting, as the man starts hammering on the glass. He swivels round suddenly and Margot gasps as she sees that he's a woman, her features pitted and hard, her eyes unfocused, and probably barely older than Margot herself.

'Let me off the fucking bus!'

They're at a set of lights, but the driver sits looking straight ahead, his shoulders rigid.

Someone turns towards Margot, an expectant look on his face. Then someone else. And another woman again, to her right. The collar. They're expecting her to act. This is your job. The fourth emergency service.

The bus abruptly accelerates hard though the lights, sending the woman lurching onto the floor. Her howls send shivers through Margot, like the unearthly shriek of the foxes on Highbury Fields. The woman curls up into a ball, gulping sobs shaking her gaunt frame.

Pamela turns towards Margot, lips pursed.

'Isn't it dreadful that someone like—'

'Sorry, Pamela, but I need to get through.' She stands and starts to step over the carrier bags.

'Wait – what, Margot, where in God's name are you going?'

Margot ignores her, pushing past into the aisle, with what feels like every pair of eyes in the bus trained on her. As she edges forwards, she can see how very frail the woman is, the tiny wrists, the jut of her collarbone. The acrid smell is now hitting her hard.

'Watch yourself,' an old man whispers.

'I wanna get off. Lemme off. Just lemme off.'

Margot kneels down beside the rocking figure, steadying herself on the back of the seat alongside her.

'Here, hold on to me. We're almost at the next stop.'

The woman's cheeks are scarred. She must be at least six or seven kilos underweight. Margot touches her right shoulder and the woman jumps back as though she's been scalded and glares at Margot. Then she narrows her eyes.

'Fuck, you a priest?'

Maintain eye contact. Keep it neutral. Keep it together.

'Fucking perverts. I hate the lot of yous.'

They stay locked in a rigid embrace for a few seconds, then the doors open with a hiss, the driver slams open the inner cab door and runs down the aisle towards them.

The speed with which the woman staggers to her feet catches Margot off guard. She's still kneeling herself as the woman stumbles out onto the pavement, dragging her bags with her. The driver helps Margot back onto her feet without a word and heads back to the front. Just as the doors are closing, the woman whips round again and leans in. The ball of spittle lands dead centre on Margot's chest.

She's still shaken when she arrives at the school gate a few minutes later, her notes still on the bus, her hair plastered to her face in the drizzle, her black trousers smudged with dirt from kneeling on the floor.

A gaggle of teenage girls, all wearing hijabs, are chatting outside by the buzzer. One of them spots Margot – or, rather, the collar – and turns to the group, which erupts. It's not personal, she knows that. But as she squeezes passes and presses on the entryphone, the temptation to retaliate this time is intense.

The blonde on the reception desk takes one look, glances back down and directs a scarlet fingernail to her right. Margot rushes on, then catches her reflection in the trophy cabinet and stops. There's a women's toilet opposite, but it's locked. She spots a men's toilet two doors down, glances around and takes a chance. Her luck's in: no one at the urinals, at least.

The stain on her black shirt refuses to budge and she rubs at it so hard that it becomes encrusted with paper flecks. She pinches her cheeks to try and get rid of the pallor and is just applying some lipstick when she stops, hand in mid-air. A cubicle door opens behind her and a tall guy in his early thirties steps out, re-looping his belt.

'Oh, sorry,' they both say.

He takes in the picture she presents.

'The ladies was locked.' She pushes her hair back. 'I'm here for the RS talk. You know, St Mark's?'

'Got you.' He tips his head. 'Bit early for a kissogram.'

He moves to the washbasin alongside her and glances at the lipstick in her hand.

'Being an anorak isn't compulsory.'

He holds his hands up in mock submission.

She bites her lip. 'Sorry, that came out wrong.'

She turns away to reach for some paper.

'Forget it.'

The amusement in his voice makes it even worse.

'I'm just so late and, well, you know, a bit all over the place.'

She turns back to look at him.

He hands her another paper towel.

'Here you go.' He smiles. 'Nothing ever runs on time in this place.'

'Really?'

'It's my job to knock us into shape.'

She waits, unsure.

'Felix Porter. Deputy head. Good to meet you.'

She looks down at his hand and then takes it.

'And you are?'

'Oh, I'm sorry. Margot. Margot Goodwin.'

'Wish me luck,' he adds.

She glances back up to meet his smile.

'The RS teacher was still in the staffroom two minutes ago, probably finishing off some urgent business on Paddy Power.'

'I'd better——'

The door behind her slams open.

'Oopsy.'

A teenage boy takes a pantomime step back.

The door bangs closed again behind him. Margot stares at it.

'I'll deal with him later.'

She shoves her make-up bag into her backpack.

'Nice meeting you.'

'You too, Margot. Have fun in the bear pit,' he deadpans.

She keeps her eyes trained on the middle row while she settles on the edge of the desk. So much for the personality she'd tried out in advance: a bit witty, a bit tart, a bit 'I used to be/am one of you'. She hopes they won't notice the bullseye of spit on her chest.

'Hi, everyone. Great to be here. Thank you, Mr Cooke for inviting me.' Six or seven rows of studied indifference. 'I know what you're thinking. What kind of weirdo would want to dress up like this every day?'

A few look up from their phones or picking at their nails.

'Wouldn't I rather be working for Zara or Google or some fintech start-up?' She pauses. 'I mean, not exactly cool and sexy being a priest in 2016, is it?'

A couple more are interested now.

'Because if ever two words go together – like vodka and Coke or Posh 'n' Becks – it's religious and nutter, right?'

One or two of even snigger a little. Her breath is coming easier now. She shifts further back on the desk, pushing some lever-arch folders to the side, black lace-ups dangling a few inches from the floor.

'So I thought I'd just spend the next few minutes telling you what I do and why I do it.' She clears her throat. 'What it means to live well and act wisely and, yes, to really love our neighbour.'

Several pairs of eyes roll upwards like fruit machines. Slow down. Slow down.

'I'm hoping to try and convince you that I'm not a weirdo. Or if I am, not because I'm training to be a priest.'

The RS teacher laughs a touch too heartily.

'Just popping out for a sec, Margot.'

He gives a little wave as he pulls the door shut behind him.

'And then you can shoot some questions at me at the end. So I thought I'd start off by reading something just to set the scene. You may recognise it.'

'"If I speak in the tongues of men or of angels, but do not have love, I am only a resounding gong or a clanging cymbal. If I have the gift of prophecy and can fathom all mysteries and all knowledge, and if I have a faith that can move mountains, but do not have love, I am nothing."'

She knows every word by heart, but can hear the tremor in her voice.

'"If I give all I possess to the poor and give over my body to hardship that I may boast, but do not have love, I gain nothing."'

She takes a swig from her water bottle.

'"Love is patient, love is kind. It does not envy, it does not boast, it is not proud. It does not dishonour others, it is not self-seeking, it is not easily angered, it keeps no record of wrongs. Love does not delight in evil but rejoices with the truth. It always protects, always trusts, always hopes, always perseveres."'

She breathes in and looks up from the sheet of A4.

'It's just all about sex, isn't it?'

It takes a moment to locate her. A girl sitting on the radiator at the back, long dip-dyed brown hair, Facebook skin, black-ringed eyes.

The room stiffens. Margot reaches for the water again. The air in here is chalky and dry.

'What is, exactly?'

The girl smirks, folding her arms tightly.

'OK.' Margot picks at a thread on her jacket. 'Let's think about that a moment. It's an interesting point – sorry, I don't know your name?'

The room ticks in silence.

'Cyd,' a boy shouts from the other side of the room.

'Twat,' Cyd snaps, twisting round.

'Short for Cydney, right, with a C, I'm guessing?'

'OK, well, Cyd, it would be great if you could tell us a bit more about why you think Christianity, the Bible and all the rest of it, is all about sex? Flesh it out for us a bit, you could say.'

Half the room groans. Get a grip. This isn't the Comedy Store. She's in a roomful of toxic teens with ADD, in full Christians-to-the-slaughter mode.

Cyd twists her foot over her knee, and yawns. She winds a strand of hair around her index finger.

Margot waits. She can do this.

'The whole thing's about who you can fuck,' Cyd says at last, 'or, more to the point, who you can't.'

Several of them double up with laughter.

'You, for example.'

More cackles erupt. She's grown used to stares, but this is taut with danger.

Cyd looks like she's enjoying every second.

'Bet you never have, because you're not allowed to, being a nun.'

Laughter is now ricocheting off the walls like sniper fire.

'You reckon?'

Stupid.

'You mean you *are* allowed to have sex? Fuck me.'

The volume cranks up even further then switches abruptly to complete silence. Margot whips around.

'All right, 10 G, dial it down. Some of us have work to do.'

'The vicar was telling us about her sex life, sir,' someone yells.

'Well, I can see that would be riveting.'

He's looking at her, but her head has emptied. A small frown creases his forehead and he turns back to the class.

'OK, well, fun over. If I have to come in again, it'll be detentions all round. Got that?'

She can't look at him as he leaves. The moment he's gone, a couple of the boys start to kick each other and the turbine of noise threatens to start up again, but Margot steps forward and claps her hands as hard as she can. They're taken aback.

'Right, we all heard what he said.' She digs her nails into her palm. 'Let's see if anyone else has any questions before we wrap up.'

A pimpled face ginger by the wall offers her a life raft: a question about the Big Bang. Four, five, minutes later, after she's raced through evolutionary theory, intelligent design and the teleological principle, just to keep talking, the buzzer finally goes off and they're all up and shoving past, leaving her alone like a piece of driftwood.

She sits still for a few moments, eyes closed. Then she hears someone by the door. Cyd. Watching Margot, a look of triumph on her face.

Could this day get any worse? she thinks, as she walks back to St Mark's. The incident on the bus; her own inadequacy in the face of such suffering; the fear and disgust she'd felt towards someone so lost, so clearly on the margins. *Whoever despises his neighbour is a sinner, but blessed is he who is generous to the poor.*

And as for the school. She shudders. Jeremy seemed to think she would turn up as some sort of hip brand manager for the C of E, cooler than a glass of Aperol Spritz. A handful of lippy teenagers and she'd crumpled.

All capped by that full-frontal humiliation in front of the deputy head.

Her phone starts to tremble in her bag.

Jeremy.

She hesitates, then reaches for it.

'I've got a solution for us, Margot.'

'Sorry?'

'Mildmay Grove won't be habitable for at least six months, they tell me, maybe more. Though at least we were up to date with our insurance payments,' – he clears his throat – 'which hasn't always been the case.'

She senses danger.

'Though as St Luke reminds us, *life does not consist in an abundance of possessions.*'

Fat chance of that on a curate's stipend.

'So I've just heard that a family near the church have a spare room they may be looking to rent out for a few months. It'll be free in two or three weeks. That can tide us over for a while. Much cheaper than the B and B, which makes your incumbent happy.'

Margot's mouth falls open.

'Not one of our families, sadly, but Nathan and I go back a long way.' She hasn't heard him sound this excited since someone left a £50 note in the plate a few weeks back.

'He's an architect – private houses, arty, cubey stuff, you know – but things have been a bit choppy recently, one way and another. Between us, I think they could do with some extra cash. There are a couple of kids, twins. It's one of those big rambling places about five minutes' walk from here.'

'Yes, well, we—'

'Great news, isn't?'

She doesn't trust herself to answer.

'Oh, yeah and one other thing. The mother, Elspeth, left a while back. I haven't, you know, asked for all the details. But she's not coming back any time soon. Thought you'd be able to relate to that, given, your own, you know,' – he pauses – 'hinterland.'

She stares at the phone.

'Family life, can't beat it. What better medicine than to walk through the front door of home?'

'It's not my family, Jeremy.'

'They'd be doing us a favour and who knows? Maybe it's mutual?'

House-sharing with one father, two kids and no mother?

Chapter 5

Mid-October

Forty-nine Aberdeen Avenue scowls down at her, hunched and haunted-looking. A rambling gothic monster, complete with weather-distressed exterior, grudge-ridden ivy, the skeleton of a buggy on its side on the mossy basement steps and a sodden stack of takeaway-pizza flyers on a ledge by the front door.

Does anyone even live here? She still holds out the hope that they don't. It looks like a house abandoned by love.

'Get the doorbell, will you, Margot?'

Jeremy is puffing up the steps behind her, balancing a sausage bag and a couple of carrier bags containing the entire sum of everything she managed to salvage from the rubble.

She presses a couple more times and is about to lift the tarnished lion's-head knocker when the door opens.

A tall man in his fifties with thinning blond hair beckons her in and motions to the phone at his ear. The apron around his waist a map of grimy stains.

He finishes his call and turns back to her.

'Sorry about that. You must be, er…'

'Margot.'

The vicar got there first.

'Nathan's worse than me at names.'

Both men laugh.

'Nathan Armstrong. Good to meet you, Margot. Come on into the hovel.'

Margot steps into the dark interior, eyes adjusting to the tidal wash of debris in the hall. The place looks like it's been hit by some natural disaster. Which, she remembers, it has.

The three of them walk down a narrow corridor into the kitchen. She stares through the door at the half-emptied shopping bags disgorging things all over the floor, at the upended saucer of cat food below a hamster cage balanced precariously on a stool, and curling school notices stuck haphazardly all over the fridge. Through the window she can see a patch of muddy scrub and a child's swing, its seat dangling off a broken chain.

She walks further into the room and stops.

Two tangle-haired boys are sitting the table to her right, books, crayons and the remnants of a snack spread out in front of them.

'Are we interrupting your homework, boys?' Jeremy asks, waving.

'Come off it, Jeremy,' says Nathan. 'The boys view homework as a crime against humanity. Right, guys?'

Both heads have swivelled towards Margot. Identical right down to the chocolate smears on their chins.

'Sam on the left, twenty-eight freckles, Josh on the right, twenty-nine,' says Nathan. 'Cuppa, anyone?'

Jeremy's never knowingly turned down that particular invitation.

'So boys,' says Nathan, emptying the teapot into the sink, 'Margot here is going—'

'The girl vicar,' says the one on the right. Just as well she came in civvies.

'Nice to meet you, Sam.'

'Josh.'

They both scowl. She's being evilled by a pair of chocolate-coated basilisks. Then, after a few seconds, they both look away at the same time, the novelty already over.

'We've allocated you the downstairs berth, Margot.'

She catches a quick look between the two boys.

'There's plenty of space down there, plus a shower next door. More private for you as well.'

'Your very own priest's hole,' the vicar chuckles.

'It's bedlam in here sometimes,' Nathan adds.

She's heading out to the hall to pick up her coat and a couple of things from the car, when there's a thumping on the stairs to her left. Margot looks up, surprised. Both twins were still in the kitchen when she left it. She has no time to move aside before someone crashes into her, scattering toiletries and magazines all over the floor.

'Fuck.'

'Are you OK? Here, let me, oh, you're—'

Margot stares in shock. The girl with the dip-dyed hair from Highbury High, now glowering at her with thermal intensity.

Margot pulls her arm back and flattens against the wall, still holding some of the magazines.

'Cyd, the vicar's here,' yells one of the twins, skidding to a halt next to Margot.

Jeremy walks up and glances at Margot.

'We've met,' she explains.

'That's a coincidence.'

'You've taken my room.'

Margot's mouth opens and shuts.

'Dad said she had to, even though Cyd said why do we have to have a nutt—'

'Josh,' snaps Nathan, now standing right next to Margot. 'I hope it's clean down there, Cydney?'

Cyd snatches the magazines out of Margot's hands and charges back up the stairs.

Six months of this? Jeremy's taken leave of his senses.

Later, after the vicar has left and Margot has reluctantly unpacked her belongings – for now – placing aside all the clothes and jewellery and make-up Cyd has yet to collect, Nathan knocks on the door to offer the guided tour.

It doesn't take long. The ground floor with its scruffy living room and musty, chaotic study. The floor above with the mint-green bathroom littered in waterproof toys, Nathan's bedroom, and the boys' rooms, Arsenal posters plastered over one and Spurs posters over the other, and a couple of other bedrooms whose only function seems to house yet more spill-over mess.

'So there you go. Welcome to Chateau Armstrong.' He shrugs.

Margot glances over his shoulder at a narrow wooden staircase leading up to the attic and its mad-as-hell inhabitant.

Nathan follows her glance.

'Don't worry about Cyd, Margot. She'll adjust. It'll be good to have another woman in the house.' He clears his throat. 'You know, a role model, of sorts.'

Margot's cheeks tingle. That little speech prickles with so many thorns, she'll be picking them out of her flesh for days.

'Feel free to snoop around,' Nathan says, heading off into his bedroom.

She looks back up at the attic stairs and turns away, a leaden weight in her chest.

Every object on this landing simmers with intent. The fading print of a Monet landscape in the silver frame above the banister. Had Elspeth chosen it? The dimpled vase full of shrivelled peonies on the bookstand: a forgotten wedding present, maybe? And who do the twins take after? Those freckles, that level stare? And what about Cyd?

She walks slowly back down to the basement, unable to believe she's here in this place. She collapses into the lumpy bed half an hour later, evidence of the room's previous occupant all around her. Old film posters still up on the walls. Fading magazines in the bottom of the wardrobe. The stubborn tang of pina colada body spray. She yanks the curtain closed to block out the orangeade glow from the street lamp outside.

And then, right on cue, as if he's laser-attuned to maximum angst, a text.

You've not forgotten dinner on the 20th? I've booked our usual. Danny can make it for 8. Dad.

Forget? She has to take a running jump at it every year. She pulls the duvet over her head.

Help to understand why I'm here, what the point of all this is. I know how you weave in and out of all our lives, making your presence felt. But this, this, just feels so wrong. Give me the patience – the strength – to cope in this messy, messed-up house as long as I'm here. Help me somehow make it through in one piece.

And please get me through this dinner, she adds, as she pulls the duvet up to her chin, shivering.

This unhappy house is webbed with memories.

Her own.

The train pulls out of Waterloo in an agony of creaks.

'Good evening, ladies and gents. This is the stopping service to Weymouth, stopping at Woking, Winchester, Southampton, Brockenhurst, New Milton, Christchurch and Bournemouth.'

Margot's breath catches at the familiar litany. She watches the tangled trackscape of Clapham Junction slip by, followed rapidly by the stations at Wimbledon, Surbiton, Weybridge; the lights from the houses backing onto the track beckon in the dark, the pitch-perfect domesticity of suburbia, or so it looks to her.

She reaches down for her book.

When did her home ever feel like that? Ever?

These journeys – this day of all days – churn up emotions that threaten to unseat her from her moorings.

She glances back out as the farmland outside Basingstoke hurtles past. And why does he always choose pizzerias? That would never have been her mother's choice. Her tastes – the actress in her – ran far more to bistro louche: monochrome prints of 1950s' film stars on smoke-gloomed walls, *sotto voce* Aznavour, waiters mangling their 'Rs'. Dorset didn't run to too many of those.

At least they always had the sea.

She won't be able to stop by the beach in Highcliffe tonight, though a trip down here without breathing in any sea always feels like a small tragedy. Growing up down here, she loved nothing better than walking all the way along the beach to Mudeford one way and Barton-on-Sea the other, hair slapping against her cheeks, brine on her tongue, the indignant screech of terns circling overhead. Autumn and winter, above all, when the space, the emptiness, the liminal beauty of it, was often hers alone, the shades shifting up and down the palette, the cone of quicksilver light tossed about on the waves, the inexorable pull and push. The sense the sea always gave her of things being renewed, when so much in her world seemed broken beyond repair.

Danny is staring at her in that way he has.

She fingers one of the browning carnations in the jar between them.

'So how's the new job, Danny?'

He shrugs, snapping his breadstick into equal pieces.

Fitness coach, his third fresh start in as many years.

The silence falls thick again. The unholy trinity – Ricky, Danny and Margot Goodwin – hunched over two macho quattro stagionis and a limp vegetable lasagne. The middle-aged couple on the next table can't believe their luck at the promise of drama.

'Doing much fishing, Dad?' Danny asks, swivelling away from Margot.

'Not much time right now, son.'

Those days out on the riverbank were amongst the few happy

times. Margot had forgotten just how much.

Ricky clears his throat and reaches for his glass of Chianti.

'So, well, here we are again. Twelve years on.'

Margot looks down, her breath shortening.

'To Annelie. To your mum.'

Danny turns back to Margot as though he's waiting for the 'May God rest her soul'. She'll never make that mistake again.

'To Mum.'

The woman alongside catches Margot's eye and looks away. Ricky replaces his glass and folds his napkin into a small triangle. Maybe he's also relieved to get it over with?

'What about your job, then, Margot?' Danny asks, refilling his glass to the brim, and tilting his head. 'I was hoping you'd come in uniform.'

'Thought I'd leave that to you.'

The pull of the script is just too strong.

'Ha friggin ha. I came here straight from the gym. Two hours training of my own a day, as well as all the client sessions.' He takes a large swig. 'Practise what you preach. You'd know all about that. Well, the preachy bit, for sure.'

'Pack it in, will you, Danny?' snaps Ricky.

'Just kidding. She knows that, don't you Margot, unless bants are now verboten.'

'I said, leave it.'

'Come off it, Dad, that's a bit rich coming from—'

'Danny,' pleads Margot. The couple next to them have now stopped talking altogether.

'What was that thing you always used to say?' Danny plants his elbows further on the table. 'Oh yeah, that's it, the Church is the Tory Party at prayer.'

Margot's head is thudding, as it does every year. The pebble-dashed past never giving up. It's crossed her mind her father might even have preferred it if she'd found a job with the Tory Party rather than do what she's actually done. Just before she left for

Wilhurst, he even speculated about what her mother would have said as extra ammunition. She rubs her forehead. Who knows what she would have said? For all those comments she used to make about helmet-haired oddballs when *Songs of Praise* came on, wouldn't she have wanted Margot to choose something about which she felt so certain? When she herself had spent most of her own life regretting the dreams she'd lost.

'Listen, you two. I've got an announcement to make.'

Margot looks at her father, curious. Then again, there's only so many years anyone could suffer being in sales management at SmileTime Party Accessories.

'You might think it's a bit of a bolt from the blue.'

'Shit, Dad, don't tell me you've found God too?'

Margot focuses on the garlicky crumbs next to her knife.

'The thing is, well, I've met someone.'

Her head jerks up.

'And we've decided.' He stops, clears this throat again. 'We thought, well, what the hell, we're going to tie the knot.'

Margot's mouth goes dry.

'Her name's Linda. We met at a sales conference in March.'

Danny rocks back in his chair and blows out his cheeks.

'Jesus, Dad, you're a fast worker.'

'Yeah, well, you know. Anyway. There you go. The *News at Ten*.'

'Yeah, shit, well, well done, I guess.'

Danny lifts his glass and clinks it against Ricky's.

'Cheers, son.'

Ricky turns towards Margot in expectation.

If she opens her mouth any time within the next few seconds, they'll all regret it.

The taxi has slowed to a crawl in the mangle of cones and barriers running toward Hinton Admiral. The landscape around her is suffocating, low-rise. The big announcement is running round her head like malware.

Her mother once started to try and explain where it had all gone went wrong, when Margot was about fifteen. But she ran out of words. Margot knew Annelie's career – or loss of it – was part of it. She took on some small parts when Margot herself was young: she can still remember sitting up on the counter, legs kicking in time as her mother walked up and down the lino reciting her lines. That was one of her last roles: *The Merchant of Venice*.

The miserable have no medicine but hope.

By the time Margot was seven or eight it was all over: the intense, dangerous, giddying rush of walking out on stage night after night, of slipping into someone else's skin – gone.

Trying to pinpoint the happy moments of her parents' marriage now is like delving into a lucky dip and coming up with fistfuls of sawdust. Just a few snapshots remain. Her mother's hand on his knee as they all drove off somewhere for a weekend, the two of them belting out *Wonderwall* as she and Danny rolled around in the back seat. The occasional belly laughs in front of *Only Fools and Horses*. All of them charging through the sprinkler on a melting summer's day, Margot's ruched swimsuit turned a dark plum in the spray, Danny aiming a striped beachball at her head.

Eighteen years of marriage and those are pretty much all the good times she can remember as the tumbleweed rolls past.

They hadn't needed anyone else to rent them asunder. They'd achieved that all by themselves. Her father's youthful socialism coarsening into middle-aged rancour; her mother's bitterness at the unravelling of all those dreams.

The miserable have no medicine but hope.

And now he's invited another player to join the cast of the tragedy?

The taxi driver is humming along to Wave FM, loudly but off-key.

'Could you try cutting through here on the right somewhere?'

'You the expert then, love?'

He glances at her in the mirror, then shrugs, pulls across the traffic and turns down a small side road. She braces herself and then, brutally, there it is. It must be eight years, more. New Milton Community Church. Red-brick, squat and bland, caught in a stranglehold of nondescript 1930s housing, that small scrap of grass at the front where the toddlers used to play, the prefab meeting hall at the side.

She turns to watch it fall away behind as they pick up speed towards the station. All these streets pitted with memories, the shadows edged with barbed wire.

The taxi bounces hard against a couple of dips in the road, the chassis groaning.

She'd only started going there by chance. She and Lorraine were slouching home from school, kicking pebbles into tyres outside the mock-Tudor double-fronts on Marine Drive.

'Doing anything fun this weekend, Margie?'

'What, apart from watching Dad and Danny watch non-stop football on the telly, you mean?'

Lorraine popped in another piece of gum.

'Why don't you come with me on Sunday afternoon? You know, to our church?'

'Um.'

'There's plenty of cool stuff. Discos, ping-pong and snooker, weekend camps sometimes.'

Margot hesitated. Things were worse than ever at home. So much so that she sometimes worried the other kids would sense it, as though all the verbal violence clung to her like the smell of chip fat. But church?

'I'll think about it, OK?'

'Stevie S and Kieran sometimes come along,' Lorraine added over her shoulder, eyebrows indicating she knew she had sealed the deal.

Turned out Lorraine's parents were pillars of New Milton Community Church. Her mum ran the worship band and her dad had a regular preaching slot. That first Sunday when they drove by to collect Margot, Lorraine's dad had wanted to come in and say hello to her own parents, but Margot had fobbed him off, ashamed at the thought of either party meeting the other.

Everything shifted when she stepped inside that church. It might have been red-brick ordinary on the outside, but its interior was silvery with light. The only other church she knew was the echoey barn they all trooped into for the school carol services, complete with bum-torture pews and grim stained-glass windows. The openness of this place, its bare simplicity, suddenly made her feel weightless and free.

A woman in her mid twenties came over to Margot and Lorraine as soon as they walked in. She was wearing a turquoise hairband, a gappy smile and a badge declaring *Welcome to the Glory!*

'Hi there, Lorraine. I see you've brought a friend.'

'This is Margot, Gilly,' Lorraine said.

'So happy to have you here in Jesus's home today with us, Margot. Always great to see a new face. You're going to have lots of fun!'

Margot had gone there to escape, that was all. A brief spell of calm before returning to the war zone. But after a few weeks of slipping out of her back door after lunch every Sunday to meet Lorraine, this was the place she most wanted to be. It was like standing at the top of the water slide at the aquapark and just letting yourself go. She was made to feel welcome in a way she'd never felt before by this group of happy, friendly people who told her God was like a rainbow and talked about the Good News and the glory days and how Jesus would take care of her own personal happiness: all she had to do was let Him.

Right, wrong. Heaven, hell. Born again, saved. After the eggshells of home, these were simple certainties to live by. She was dizzy with the pleasure of it, snatched by the shoulders and whirled around six feet off the ground.

Gilly asked them all one Sunday afternoon whether welcoming Our Saviour into their life wasn't the biggest thrill in the world. Margot's arm was the first to be flung in the air. She'd found her compass for life.

The only thing that bothered her was the secrecy. She knew what her father's reaction would be to her joining a gang of God-botherers, as he called them. And there were so many sedimentary layers of secrecy within the Goodwin household by then, what was one more?

One Sunday afternoon, she slipped her key into the back door, hiding the new copy of St John's Gospel she'd just been awarded for regular attendance behind her back. She always came in tentatively, just in case. Sure enough, a crash greeted her as she stepped through the door: the sound of a bottle hitting something hard. She made straight for the stairs without stopping to check. She knew the drill.

'I told you: I'm never going to another of your moronic work dos again. Got that?'

Up on the landing, Margot couldn't make out Ricky's response.

'SmileTime Party Accessories,' her mother screamed, voice blurred. 'All those big ideas of yours, all the big "I am".'

'What, and a few walk-on parts in Birmingham Playhouse makes you Helen Mirren?' Ricky spat, slamming open the kitchen door as Margot ran up to the attic, glad that Danny was out with his friends at least.

By the time she tiptoed downstairs a couple of hours later, the customary phoney peace had descended. The crescendo of verbal violence always followed by a simmering regrouping, while the TV held court at top volume. She reached the bottom step and saw her mother taut-jawed in the kitchen, slamming the iron down on something pale blue. Margot edged forwards. The new skirt she'd planned to wear at the church disco, now with a sooty, long-tailed comet above the hem.

Her mother looked up. She either didn't notice Margot's expression or was too far gone in her own misery to care.

In bed, pillow wedged around her head, Margot always asked for help the only way she knew how. But she was convinced this was one prayer that wouldn't be granted, no matter what Gilly might say.

Chapter 6

Late November

Goldilocks for grown-ups. That's what breakfast in the Armstrong house feels like. In the half-a-dozen times Margot's joined them at Nathan's insistence, it's always been the same. The five of them around the pine table in tinkling silence, chocolate milk splashes enamelling the boys' homework, Nathan only glancing up from the *Daily Telegraph* to offer a coffee refill, Cyd glued to her phone, scraping her spoon across her bowl.

Not everyone can be a morning person. After a few months of red-eye starts, Margot's not even sure she is. But the body language here spells 'archipelago'. Quarter to eight on a Wednesday morning. They could be talking about President Elect Trump's plans for his first day in office. Surely that deserves a mention? Or havoc wreaked by Storm Angus on the south coast last night? Shouldn't the boys be joshing each other about last night's north London derby or something? Or Nathan grilling Cyd on her history coursework? One of them could even ask her, the black-clad cuckoo, what she's up to today. A visit to see her spiritual director in Cambridge, in case anyone's interested.

Maybe they discussed tactics before she moved in last month. Always stay schtum at mealtimes to stop the holy one launching into grace or, even worse, a sermon. Or is there some sort of breakfast vow of silence they observe, Trappism on toast?

But this feels like business as usual. Or is it just since Elspeth left? The empty chair at the table, even when every seat is filled. Cyd and the boys probably see her as interloper. She wouldn't blame them if they did. She's starting to feel like an interloper everywhere. Including her own family. She breathes in.

'So who's been to Paris, recently?'

Four faces look up.

She raises the mug in the air and the boys' heads snap towards Nathan.

'Oh, that.' He shrugs. 'Boys, do I need to give you lunch money?'

Cyd scrapes her chair back hard. Margot waits a beat then gathers her plate and mug and walks to the sink. She catches Cyd's eye and risks a smile. Sorry about your mum. Sorry about your room. Sorry Mother Theresa's moved into your home. Cyd slams the fridge door and charges out of the kitchen.

Margot is fixing her collar studs in the hall mirror a few minutes later when she becomes aware of being watched.

'Not exactly the front cover of *Vogue*, is it?' She tries to keep it light. 'Unfortunately, it sort of comes with the territory.'

She looks back at her reflection, this time through Cyd's eyes. Scrappy haircut. Eye make-up barely there. Studs in her ears so small she needn't have bothered.

'Tragic.'

Margot's head snaps around again, but Cyd is already back up on the landing. She runs her finger inside the collar. She's starting to wonder if she's been sent here as some kind of punishment.

'Must you go, Margot, when we're all so busy getting ready for Advent?' Roderick growls, trumpeting into his old-man's hankie. Her loathing of that scrap of grimy cloth and all it's intended to signify is intensifying by the day, corroding her soul.

'God knows, we all need tea and sympathy and the chance to unload to an understanding ear sometimes, Roderick,' Jeremy says. 'And it's only every couple of months.'

'Nothing wrong with spiritual directors, of course, Vicar. I just don't see why it needs a whole day out. Everything's so touchy-feely these days.'

Jeremy smiles and walked towards the kettle.

'Have fun, Margot. Give my best to Hadley.'

'Probably spend the whole day shopping,' Roderick snarled, just loud enough for Margot to catch as she heads out of the door.

She looks out at the clothes wholesalers on the Commercial Road as the coach heads towards the M11, remembering that parting shot of Roderick's. At first, she attributed his endless moods to arthritis or gout or some other aged-priestly ailment. But she knows the hostility towards her is more complex than that. The loneliness hangs over him like a shroud: the crabbiness, his shell. She must keep reminding herself of that. Even so, the constant sniping is starting to get under her skin, even making her sometimes question her ability in the role. They're supposed to be on the same side, yet she expects someone to shout, 'Behind you!' every time he passes her in the vestry. If he had his way, the Reformation would never have happened. That arthritic finger unable to stem the tide.

She somehow needs to lance the boil.

Half an hour later, the coach pulls out onto the motorway. It's a startlingly blue November day, crisp and even. She offers silent thanks that Hadley became college chaplain at Christ's rather than staying in Stepney. Doddery's right: the window-shopping opportunities are so much better in Cambridge.

The familiar flat Hertfordshire landscape slides past. Even after three years at Trinity Hall and four at Wilhurst, Cambridge still exercises its magic. This, for her, was where the story began.

Her first year in college was the textbook experience that they all mostly had: random parties, essay crises, a couple of brief try-out relationships, dipping in and out of various different versions of herself to try and find the one that fitted her best, the oblivion they all shared to anything outside the eight-week bubble.

What she didn't have – want – was any involvement with the college chapel or any other church of any kind, including the university Christian Union, no matter how hard they tried to pull her in. The previous couple of years had put paid to all of that: she'd had her fill of granite convictions that didn't help when you most needed them. Her faith hadn't just been shaken, it had been obliterated. And, if anything, the monochrome certainties she'd found so appealing as a teenager fuelled her fury.

Then, a term into her second year, something shifted within her. Even now, she can't say exactly why. It was subtle, whispering at first; so quiet she barely noticed. She was studying the metaphysical poets one week and was awestruck by the brilliant showmanship of John Donne, starbursts of language punching holes in the universe. But it was when she discovered George Herbert that the world hushed and something fingertipped her soul. *Heart-work and heaven-work make up his books,* said one of his other contemporaries. She couldn't have agreed more.

That I may run, rise, rest with thee.

She read and reread Herbert's *The Temple* over the next few weeks, aware she was somehow being reeled back to somewhere she had been before. *Dare to be true.* The silky tug of the thread, sinuous and strong.

Later that term, a friend invited her to evensong at King's. As they kicked through the frost-encrusted leaves carpeting Burrell's Walk, the postcard-perfect silhouette rising above them, she realised this would be the first time she'd stepped inside a church in more than five years.

The chapel's interior was lit by flickering candlelight. She sat back, absorbing the extraordinary physical beauty – the

Renaissance rood screen, the chequerboard floor, the griffins and unicorns staring down from the walls, the clarity of the boy sopranos – above all, the warm, maternal hush.

Lighten our darkness, we beseech Thee, O Lord; and by Thy great mercy defend us from all perils and dangers of this night.

As the congregation recited the rest of the Third Collect for Aid Against All Perils, she knew at that moment, she was experiencing an overwhelming sense of the transcendent presence of God.

Over the following weeks and months, that feeling continued to strengthen inside her. She didn't confide in anyone, unsure how much she wanted to open up about this newfound sense of faith or what it even meant. But she felt alive to a feeling of possibility in a way that was completely new. She'd read somewhere about a humble, questioning faith, 'marbled with doubt', a groping towards the light rather than the glare of the halogen bulb, and knew that, this time round, this was who she was. She was being given the space to be less than sure, trusting rather than dissecting God, understanding that there were no handrails to faith and that you have to ask questions to get answers.

It was in this this quietly searching place of faith that she had finally found her own personal spirituality.

The call to serve in ministry, when it came, was unmissable, no matter how much she tried to deny it.

Margot Goodwin, priest?

It was like a voice on a loop inside her head, catching her off guard, as seductive as if someone was whispering in her ear – gentle, persuasive, insistent. It was terrifying.

It must just be the cosmetics, she kept telling herself. She'd been seduced by the hypnotic beauty of the liturgy, the shimmering glamour of the medieval chapels, the soaring Bach or Monteverdi, the allure of the alliterations. History was glad-handing her in its fleecy folds and she'd fallen prey to its charms.

But she was fooling herself. The call she was hearing –

which would never leave her in peace – was visceral, intimate, unanswerable. She was a tuning fork against a table, resonating to her core.

By the time, the following summer, that the chaplain asked her to read 'God's Call to Samuel' one Sunday morning, it was all over. The passage might just as well have been 'God Tells Margot to Get a Move On'.

Doors kept opening, obstacles falling away: green lights on the runway enabling her soar.

'Religious experience comes in many guises, Margot,' the college chaplain said when she went to see him. 'It can be anything from a moment of ecstasy that transforms our faith and our understanding of ourselves, an epiphany if you like, to something far quieter, more dogged, even. It sounds to me like you've got yourself a plan.'

'I'm still not totally sure.'

He poured out two glasses of sherry and handed one across.

'You can try and run away from God, but the outstretched arms are always long enough to pull you back.'

'What if I've misheard?'

'God is in it, trust me. You haven't misheard. God will carry you through and over the obstacles, beside, beyond, within you.' He smiled at her over his glass. 'It can be a bumpy journey, but you're in safe hands.'

He wasn't kidding about the bumpy bit. The application process, the push to get accepted at Wilhurst and the four years that followed were even more excoriating than she'd expected. It made getting into the Royal Marines look easy. She lost count of how many times she felt like giving up as she struggled to acclimatise to an acronym-obsessed universe, which emotionally strip-searched anyone daring to want to venture inside it. All part of their so-called 'deskilling' process, where you were apparently broken and reborn. Nothing was off limits: her hopes, fears, phobias, dreams, the most private emotions she'd never planned to share with anyone. One of the other ordinands described it as benign dictatorship. Margot thought the Stasi must have had gentler methods. Four years of unpicking eschatological arguments, yet they weren't even allowed out to see the dentist without three different permission slips.

From the corner armchair in Hadley's room, Margot can see the diamond of green below, neon bright against the pale sandstone of the chapel. No wonder the whole place registered so high up on the Ricky Goodwin elite-ometer. She watches as a trickle of undergraduates moves back and forth, little clusters forming and then scattering to go their different ways.

Hadley hands across a cappuccino from the Italian coffee maker behind her. There's even chocolate powder sprinkled on the top.

Margot glances at the family photos on the bookcase. Hadley doesn't conform to the norm in any way – if normal even exists in this profession. She was born in the hamlet of Helena, New York State – whose Mohawk name translates as 'the place of the thorn bush', as she loves reciting; she worked for fifteen years as an attorney in Manhattan before hearing her own call and eventually moving her family to the UK. She's talked about the double jeopardy of being a priest who's both black and female, not to mention with an atheist husband and a young family in tow. But she's also told Margot she feels that being a working mother has made her a better priest. What better introduction to unconditional love than mediating between two warring under-tens?

Hadley takes a delicate bite of her ginger snap. Margot wouldn't be surprised if they were home-made.

'So how are things? Keeping all those men in their place?'

They share a smile.

'Always seems ironic to me that, if you're male, being a priest is viewed as a pretty dull thing to do, yet if you're a woman, you're an insurgent.'

Not only did she strike gold with her incumbent, she also hit the jackpot with her spiritual director, Margot reflects yet again.

'I remember how tough it is, that first year in the firing line, because you're never off duty, are you?'

Margot nods, licking cappuccino froth off her finger.

'So anything you want to unload about today to your counsellor in a cassock?' Hadley is dressed today in an impeccably cut skirt-suit: she's probably the only person in the whole of the C of E who could make clerical wear look catwalk-chic.

A young couple are kissing against the courtyard wall below. Margot watches as they finally pull apart and stroll, arms around each other's waists, towards the porters' lodge.

'Margot?

Hadley is watching her.

'All OK so far, I think. Ish'

'How about the grumpy house-for-duty?'

'He's a bit of a work in progress.' She breathes in. 'Not sure he'll ever be convinced of the value of a girl on the team, but I'm working on it.'

'Sorry to hear that. The Church tends to be at least fifty years behind the rest of society and it sounds like your colleague could double that. But keep plugging away and ask him for his advice. Flattery always works, in my experience.'

Hadley's deliciously deep laugh makes it all seem so easy.

An hour later, they're strolling out for lunch across Clare Bridge, having stopped in Petty Cury so that Hadley could admire a pair of leopard-skin wedges.

'This is where it all started for you, isn't it, Margot?'

She nods. Exactly this time of year.

'It's a journey for the long haul. I'm sure you're already looking at your incumbent constantly fighting fires and wondering whether he's spending so much time being a vicar, there's no time left over to be a priest. What happened to the person of prayer?'

Margot laughs. 'Once or twice.'

'The key to it all is balance.'

Hadley holds her arms out as though walking a high wire. Probably another of her talents.

'You're doing a lot of giving right now, Margot. Socially, spiritually, emotionally. We women do a lot of self-sacrificing, one way or another. But don't forget your own needs. Eating and sleeping properly, exercise, all the usual stuff. And most importantly, the F-word.'

Margot looks at her, confused.

'Fun, sister. Let your hair down when you need to. Tend to the allotment of your soul. Good to have your own place as well, even if it's only a cubbyhole.'

Margot sighs.

'Change of plan there. There was a gas explosion, so I'm now living with a family near the church. Jeremy's suggestion. He was really keen.'

Hadley frowns.

'A family?'

'Two young boys and a very angry teenage girl. Oh, and no mother. She cleared off, sadly.'

'Not good.'

Margot's breath shortens.

'OK, well, hmmm. Watch out for yourself, OK? From all you've told me about this priapic fundraiser and the super-keeny parishioner, your hands are pretty full right now.'

Fabian and Gwen. Problems squared. The only saving grace: that he's barely been around the past couple of months, doing deals with oligarchs or whatever it is he claims to do.

'You don't need me to remind you about the I/thou distinction and protecting your boundaries. You know you can only ever be a professional friend to those in your care.'

A punt glides past, its cargo of students huddled under blankets in the sharp November sun. Their laughter hangs in the air long after the punt has moved on.

Again, Hadley is watching her.

'Whatever some people may say, you don't have to be in role every waking minute, Margot. Get yourself some fun, girl. You're twenty-eight, not eighty-two.'

'True.'

'I was lucky. I was already married when I started down this path.'

It hangs in the air between them.

'Just choose your friends, your fun, carefully. No off-your-face photos on Facebook or "semi-naked curate" trending on Twitter, if you get my drift.'

'Chance would be a fine thing.'

'I'm always here, remember.' She touches Margot's elbow. 'Helping you steer that path between Scylla and Charybdis as you make it through to July. We don't want you shipwrecked on this most important of journeys.' She smiles. 'Now would you rather a pub lunch or the café on the Sidgwick site?'

Later that evening, Margot's back in the basement hidey-hole researching her idea for this week's sermon: *The Priest in Literature and Popular Culture*. She could take it from Chaucer to Dibley, drawing endless gags from the gap between aspiration and clay-footed reality.

It came into her head as the coach was pulling out of the station and past the crenelated skyline of Drummer Street. The time spent with Hadley has energised her, just as she knew it would. She could throw in a reference to *Father Ted*, check if there's a vicar in *The Archers*. All references to *The Archers* go down well. She's got a curacy to secure here.

She clicks open Google and runs down the links offered for 'parish life'. Something halfway down catches her eye: *Vic-i-leaks: Scenes from Parish Life, 10 November 2016.*

Intrigued, she clicks again. The screen shows a drawing of a woman in a black shirt and dog collar with a Zorro mask over her face. Margot wonders whether she's chanced upon some esoteric strand of porn, but clicks again.

Hi there! Ever wanted to know what life feels like for a girl in the C of E?? Welcome to my new blog. I'm a curate in shhhhh-who-knows where and I'm going to tell it like it is, warty flower women and all. I was going to call it Her Master's Voice or Hello!Luja! but Vic-i-leaks does the trick! I'm looking forward to sharing my top tips about which colour lipstick works best at the altar, how to fend off randy colleagues and all the goss about the PCC! See you again soon! xxx

Margot stares at the screen. It's as though someone is looking inside her head.

She rereads the page several times.

Just someone letting off steam, she decides, writing in caricature to keep their insanity intact. She knows the feeling. All the POTTY lot like nothing better than a good bitching session when they meet up for their training evening every month. The girls in particular.

She'll look forward to following this blog very much.

Part II

Another Self

Chapter 7

Mid-December

Christmas wouldn't be Christmas without the curate taking on all the elves' activities, with the nativity play the crowning glory of the holly wreath.

Margot knows from masterminding the Harvest Festival production what a big deal these set-piece occasions are for Jeremy. What the vicar wants, the vicar gets.

She flicks on the light in the store cupboard behind the organ. The musty smell in here hits her like a left hook. She needs to track down Mary and Joseph from wherever the verger hid them last January: they're already well behind schedule in embarking on their tour of parish families.

She drags down a large cardboard box from the top shelf and leans back as a cloud of dust billows from the coils of last year's balding tinsel. Yet another spending request for when the vicar's in the right mood. She tries several more boxes but still no luck. She's about to concede defeat when she comes across the happy couple swaddled in a red-and-white-striped towel in a wooden box marked 'spare chalice'. She admires the verger's solicitousness, but if the original shepherds had had this much trouble, the last two millennia might have turned out differently.

She unwraps the wooden figures and holds them up to the bulb. They could do with a refresher coat of paint. She closes the cupboard, excited at the prospect of the children's faces. Despite everything, she still loves every minute of it.

'Success!'

Jeremy and Roderick glance up. Roderick's eyes are bleary. Maybe he's just woken up from one of his power naps.

'Excellent, Margot,' Jeremy says, placing Mary and Joseph on his desk. He points at the advent calendar on the windowsill. 'Do the honours for us, will you?'

She peels back the little window for today to reveal a small toy drum. No chocolate calendar this year, as the vicar's on a pre-season regime.

'The season of giving and Gift Aid.' He chuckles, as happy as a camel approaching an oasis. 'Those cracks in the roof tiles need fixing urgently. A healthy dose of Christmas cash for all those jobs always helps.'

Just sometimes she feels uncomfortable with all this talk they have to have about money. *No man can serve two masters.* But Jeremy loves telling the old joke about the vicar on a plane that hits heavy turbulence: when someone pleads that he 'do something religious', he starts taking the collection. And she knows he's right. No stonking cheque from the Church Commissioners is going to drop onto St Mark's doormat any time soon. The days when the national Church had money sloshing around its vaults went out with Wolsey. Jack of all trades, guarding the purse strings, or curer of souls?

'Four drinks dos next week alone. Hope my liver's up to it,' Jeremy sighs, signing his name one by one in an enormous pile of Christmas cards.

Margot sits down opposite him, and clicks open her mail. Then, on a whim, she clicks again.

Here we are again then, the season of Slade, muddled wine and dry-as-a bone mince pies. My head is exploding at all the jobs I've been given – curate's privilege – but at least this is party season and I might get some nice smellies out of it. Awesome xxxx

She exits the screen and chuckles as she pulls up the treasurer's end-of-year accounts.

The Aldwych is twinklingly festive as Margot heads towards the bar in Covent Garden where she's meeting Clarissa to hear the Big Idea she insists on disclosing in person.

It's a cold evening, the air needle-sharp. A huge spruce covered in white lights stands outside St Clement Danes, like a belle ready for the ball. Most of the window displays she passes, though, seem to bear only a tangential connection to the Divine nativity of the Christ Child. In fact, a visitor from Zog might well assume the celebrations were about the latest Son of Apple: behold, the iSaviour is nigh.

She zips up the saggy padded coat someone donated to her after the explosion. The down inside has sunk to the hem, making her wonder whether she resembles a black hovercraft floating along the street. She looks over the road, where a scene straight out of Breughel is playing on the open-air ice rink at Somerset House. She glances at her watch and makes a quick detour across.

The beauty of it in the bitingly cold air takes her breath away. Scores of people of all ages are skidding, spiralling, spinning across the circle in a chaotic, exhilarating, multicoloured ballet, all to the accompaniment of music and laughter and the hiss of metal on ice. Perhaps it's the ever-present frisson of potential calamity – you're only ever a blade's edge away from disaster – or some magic lent by the strings of fairy lights and the tang of frost, but there's an alchemy here through which everyone seems to gain in grace the moment the glistening circle takes them in.

There's a sermon in here somewhere. There's a sermon in everything, everywhere.

She walks up to the barrier and drops her head on her arms, surrendering to the moment. Right in the centre of the rink, a skinny exhibitionist is throwing a spin, arms hugging his waist, legs corkscrewing into a blur. The other skaters pull back, clapping or jeering at his antics. Most people – couples, arm-linked teenage girls, parents with their arms wrapped around the shoulders of young children, even the larky young guys – just seem happy to go with the flow.

Margot glances up at the pale neoclassical stone around her as Charles Trenet's *La Mer* burbles out over the ice. It's an enchanted space. Her mother would have loved it. She swallows.

'Hey.'

A tall figure has slammed into the barrier right in front of her. She turns to a woman bundled in scarves to her left, but she doesn't react.

'You don't remember, do you?'

His face is half hidden beneath the blue tartan trapper hat. She tenses. So many faces to log, most of them expecting her to have their entire life story on tap.

The hazel eyes are laughing, dragon puffs mingling with her own.

'The circumstances were a bit unorthodox.'

Funeral? Hospice? That blessing Jeremy did in that block of flats constructed over the medieval burial pit?

'Highbury High.'

Margot stares at him.

'You were in the gents.'

The babushka next to Margot turns towards her and tuts.

He bites off a glove.

'Felix.'

His fingers are warm around hers.

'Margot, right?'

She nods, buying herself a little time. Something about his smile unsettles her.

'Your hair's different.'

A couple knock into him as they jack-knife past and Felix snatches hold of the barrier next to her, watching the pair crash onto the ice a few feet further on.

'It's not easy, I can tell you.'

'Fun, though.'

'So how are you, Margot? Oops, hang on.'

He steadies himself. She holds onto the barrier more tightly.

'I'm good, good, thanks. You know, busy time of year for us.'

'Why, what, oh, right.' He laughs. 'Sorry.'

She shrugs.

'Something called Christmas?'

He smiles.

'I'm here with a couple of old friends. Pete was giving it the whole blah blah on the way over, but he now seems to have forgotten how to do the quadruple Salchow or whatever it's called. We're going to grab a drink afterwards,' he pauses, 'if you maybe fancy joining?'

Clarissa.

'I'd have loved to, but I've got to be somewhere.'

'Shame.' He smiles at her. 'Another time.'

He pushes himself off, gives her an uncertain wave and carves an unstable line of Ss back to his friends.

She rests her head on her hands, unable quite to pull herself away.

Your Chardonnay's getting warm.

Two minutes, she stabs back at the keys.

'Fancy a quick bolero?'

He's right back in front of her again, a huge grin on his face.

'Tell you what.'

She gasps as he snatches her arm and pulls her though a narrow gap in the barrier and out onto the ice.

'Stop, stop, no, what are—'

'No skates, no problem.'

She screams as he pulls her against him, then spins her round and round with a flourish. A dozen people must have gathered around them cheering, until man in a fluorescent tabard starts charging down the rink.

'Oops,' whispers Felix, his breath hot against her ear.

All of a sudden, Margot doesn't care what this looks like or who is watching her. The laughter bubbles out of her like uncorked Moët.

'You're looking a bit flustered, M. Vicar kept you late plaiting paper chains?' Clarissa drains her glass. 'Though you're in civvies, I see.'

'I'm so sorry.'

Clarissa waits for more, but Margot busies herself taking off her coat and scarf.

'What can I get you?' asks the waiter, twiddling with his earring.

'Just a toni—'

'Another bottle of this and some more Japanese crackers, sweetie.'

He's spun on his heels before Margot can argue.

'No hair shirt tonight, M. We're celebrating.'

Margot's fighting hard to be present.

'Something about your Ph.D.?' she asks. Clarissa has the focus of a Navy Seal when she chooses.

'Guess again. Something sexier this time.'

Margot looks at her blankly. It's like the knob on the dial keeps slipping again and she's back out there on the ice.

'Your early Christmas present.' Clarissa picks up her rucksack and thumps it onto the table between them.

'Er, some sparkly Louboutins?'

'Nope.'

'Two weeks all by myself on a Caribbean island?'

'Nice try.'

'Bradley Cooper gift-wrapped?'

'Warmer.' Clarissa pulls out her laptop and taps for a couple of moments. 'Ta-dah!'

Margot leans in.

'Your hot-off-the-presses what-man-could resist profile on *Guardian* Soulmates. Soulmates! Loving that name.'

Margot frowns. Did Clarissa really just say that?

'Hello? Ground control to Major M?'

'Where did this come from?'

Clarissa picks up her glass and leans back in her seat.

'Do you know what, Margot? You haven't been a whole load of fun recently. You know, this whole Little-Miss-Sad-Sack-I-live-for-my-job routine.'

Margot opens her mouth then changes her mind. She reaches for her own glass. One of the Care Bears was grilling her yesterday about when she's going to find a nice boy and start a family, because isn't it a shame, a lovely girl like you all by herself and your mother would be so pleased, wouldn't she? An unattached curate's love life: the gift that keeps on giving, from Mr Collins onwards. An unmarried female cleric loose in the parish? Gossip fodder to the power of a million, particularly if she's under thirty and doesn't look like the back of the number 73 bus.

What if someone saw them on the ice, she suddenly thinks, hand rushing to her mouth.

Clarissa is glinting at her above the rim of her glass.

'Margot Goodwin, the Grinch Who Stole Christmas.'

'I'm not trying to spoil your fun.'

'*My* fun? This is about you, M. Stopping you ending up as a desiccated harridan with a houseful of cats.'

'I can't do this, Clariss. But thanks for thinking about it.'

'Stop being so lame, Margot. We won't use your real name. It's just a bit of a laugh.'

She can't tell her. She'll have to.

'I can't get involved with anyone until after the priesting. I can't afford to let anything jeopardise it.'

Clarissa snatches up the bottle and pours a refill.

'You're a curate, not a nun.'

'But I—'

'I know what your job means to you. I've been with you every tortured twist and turn of the way, remember?'

Margot nods.

'There's no rule that says your life has to be put in cold storage while you serve your title, is there?'

She leans in closer.

'You're not going to let your old dad be the only one with a rocking love life?'

'That's not fair.' She knows which buttons to press on the console.

'It'll be hashtag "oldhag", if you're not careful. A hot fling with some oversexed stranger could be just what you need.'

Margot closes her eyes, her cheeks still warm from those crazy few seconds on the ice.

'A bit of secret nooky as light relief from the Godly Goodwin. Where's the harm in that?'

Margot blows out her cheeks. She needs to close this conversation down.

'Look, just read the profiles, OK? You don't have to do anything.'

'OK.'

'You will?'

'Only because I know how desperate you are for any distraction.'

'My supervisor says he's never come across such a powerful reading of the symbolism of menstrual blood in relation to the Church as Mother Incarnate.'

'I'll bet.'

'OK, feast your eyes on this.'

Margot looks down at the screen. It's showing a photo of her wearing that skimpy fuchsia bikini in Fuerteventura at the end of their second year.

'What if anyone sees this?'

'Why would they? And anyway, this is Mary Godfrey, not Margot Goodwin. Her face is obscured by that stupid floppy hat you always insisted on wearing. And who in your congregation is going to be cruising a dating website?'

'I've given you a sense of humour.'

No comment.

'And a selection of fascinating pastimes.'

Margot suggests, 'Ability to administer the last rites? Fastest PCC minute-taker in the western world? Encyclopaedic knowledge of Marks and Spencer twinsets?'

'How is your new best friend, by the way?'

Margot sighs.

'Gerty, was it?'

'Gwen. Ever more intrusive, since you ask. Me and my shadow.'

'So you need a reason to be busy. Let's get to work.'

Even as her nerves are jangling, Margot can't help noticing the irony of how someone obsessed with the suppression of the female in patriarchal religious tradition is happy to serve up her best friend like a piece of sirloin on Sainsbury's meat counter.

'OK, check this out. "Hi, I'm Mary. I'm twenty-eight, smart, sociable, love art, theatre and music all the way from Beyoncé to Bach."' This next bit's genius. '"I'm an old soul and I hope you are too. Let's have some fun."'

Pull the plug on this now. It has disaster written all over it, no matter how kind Clarissa's intentions. Yet she can't quite bring herself to.

The nativity play seemed to hit all the right spots, she's hugely relieved to see. The stress has been at Wilhurst levels the past few days: she woke up yesterday with Post-it notes stuck to her cheek like Day-Glo depilation strips, listing all the props they still needed to find.

Sal and Kath worked miracles with the costumes for the donkey and the oxen, as well as the two genuine shepherd's crooks from a junk shop on the Holloway Road. None of the lambs lost their tail. Mary and Joseph were flawless. She managed to bribe one of the Magi into handing over his iPad just before he walked on. And people even laughed in all the right places. Enough cute quotient for the younger parents, and a fine line on Brexit between Leave and Remain.

The nativity star's dad high-fives her so hard afterwards, she might just as well have delivered Arsenal to the European Champions League.

She's on her hands and knees retrieving some stray balls of lamb fluff as the church empties, when a hand rests on her shoulder.

'Don't get up.'

She scrambles to her feet.

'You missed your vocation, Reverend.'

'This is my vocation, Fabian.'

Fabian doesn't do jokes if someone else is making them.

'This kind of thing is where you come into your own, isn't it?'

She takes a step back and brushes down her surplice, the world's least come-and-get-me garment, you'd have thought.

'Hold on a second.'

He closes the gap between them and reaches down to remove a wisp of straw from her hair, brushing her cheek as he does so.

'You and I must have that team talk sometime.'

She gives a neutral nod.

'We need to liven things up a bit round here. Way too much dead wood, in my book.'

She looks at him, puzzled. He rubs the piece of straw back and forth between his fingers then holds it up and blows it away from him They both watch it spiral to the ground.

'I've been on the road a lot recently, as you'll have noticed, but once I've tied up a couple of deals, you're right at the top of my list.' He leans in towards her, smoke on his breath. 'I haven't forgotten about that thesis.'

Jeremy is striding up the aisle towards them, beaming. Fabian gives them a little wave and heads off to the side.

'Such a great guy,' the vicar says.

Her right cheek is still smarting.

'Great play, Margot. Even some of the die-hards gave it the thumbs-up.'

'Wow.'

He chuckles. 'Can you pop into the office? Gwen just wants a word.'

Margot composes her face into a smile as they walk back down to the vestry.

Gwen is standing by one of the desks, one of her carrier bags in her hand. Her face lights up.

'Just wanted to drop a couple of Christmas goodies off for the team.'

Jeremy looks over at the collection of chocolates and wine bottles already building on the cupboard, in anticipation.

'Happy Christmas, everyone,' Gwen says, laying another box of candied orange onto the desk.

'My favourites, Gwen,' Jeremy says, slightly unconvincingly.

'And I've just got a little something extra for you, Margot, as it's your first Christmas with us and you work so very hard.'

Roderick delivers a phlegmy cough.

'We're so very lucky to have her, aren't we, Vicar?'

Margot stares down at the red rectangle covered in spotty Rudolphs that Gwen has just handed across. Jeremy nudges her.

'That's so incredibly kind, Gwen.' Her voice sounds as though she's inhaled helium. 'You shouldn't have.'

Nobody speaks for a few beats.

'Aren't you going to open it?' Gwen asks.

'It's not Christmas yet, Gwen,' Jeremy says with one of his sympathetic chuckles.

'Five days and twelve hours to go,' rattles off Roderick.

'But I want to see your face when you unwrap it.'

Jeremy is now staring hard at Margot, who flushes. The package might as well be ticking in her hands.

'Please,' says Gwen, dabbing at her hairline with a balled-up tissue.

Margot starts peeling at the paper.

There's an envelope inside. She opens it and gasps.

'Oh, no Gwen, I can't possibly take this.'

'Come on, Margot,' hisses Roderick. 'Don't keep us all in suspense.'

'Well, Gwen's incredibly kindly given me—'

'A half-day at the new spa on Upper Street,' chirrups Gwen. 'The two of us, Margot. Thought it would be a proper treat after all your hard work.'

Hi Margot, Linda's invited you over to ours for Christmas lunch. Danny, too, if he can make it. It'll be a real family do. Dad x

Margot stops on the doorstep outside the house on Aberdeen Avenue, staring down at the text. Does he think she's got a normal nine-to-five job?

Ours.

She's so angry she calls straight back, still standing on the step outside the front door.

'Can't or won't?' So much for the chummy patter.

'Dad, this is Christmas we're talking about. St Mark's has two services on Christmas Day and Midnight Mass the night before.'

'Christmas is a time for families to be together.'

She leans against the wall in disbelief. So many possible ways to answer that.

'There are no trains running. And I don't have a car, remember.'

'Yet another reason to do a different job.'

The front door opens with a bang, throwing a harsh slant of light into her face.

'Oh, hi Cyd, boys,' she says, shrinking away.

'Thought you were carol singers,' says Josh.

'We were going to tell you to fuck off,' adds Cyd.

Margot turns away, holding the phone back up to her ear.

'Sorry, I'll have to call—'

'What am I going to tell Linda?'

'Dad, I'm really sorry. I'll meet her another time soon, I promise.'

The twins have disappeared, but Cyd is still slouching against the doorjamb.

'You staying in our house for Christmas, then?'

Amidst the festive cyclone, she hasn't thought this one through properly. Cold fingers thrum her ribcage. Christmas lunch alone. Those tragic one-person portions of cake from M & S.

'Not sure yet, Cyd.'

She takes a tiny step back to allow Margot to squeeze past, making it clear, yet again, how much of an imposter she is.

Twenty-eight minutes to midnight. The church lit solely by hundreds of candles, casting a gauzy haze across the pews. The hushed anticipation thrills Margot: the profound sense that not just here in Highbury, but right across the world, people are waiting for the magic to begin.

The crib is bathed in pale pink light from the tiny bulb the verger managed to fix ten minutes before people started arriving. Mary and Joseph are installed centre stage, largely unscathed from their three weeks of sleepovers. The air is spiked with aromatic pine and candle wax, and holly branches trail the windowsills, their scarlet berries tiny glinting jewels in the flickering light. Jeremy's tree stands to the right of the altar, its bald patch disguised by several strings of new tinsel and a line of rainbow bulbs. Even the choir is pitch-perfect tonight.

The Angel Gabriel from heaven came
His wings as drifted snow, his eyes as flame

Margot has never seen the church this full, the aisles, the west end and east end all humming. Anyone who's anyone is here, plus what Jeremy calls the post-pub 'one in 365' lot and passers-by who just fancied a little ooh-aah festive flavour. They've had to bring in extra seating from the Kool Gang's club. Tommy had to arm-twist a few loyal regulars, otherwise several important posteriors would have had to squeeze onto plastic chairs designed for five-year-olds.

She watches Jeremy stride to the lectern, Tudor-resplendent in his gold brocade, his face split in a grin.

'Family. That's what Christmas is all about. The Holy Family, of course, as we all picture the arrival of baby Jesus in that humble manger, with his proud new mum and dad gazing on. But also our own families. All of us coming together, arguments and petty differences put aside to drink deep of the miracle of love.'

Margot's suddenly glad she isn't in his sight line on hearing this. She's revisited that conversation with her father in her head repeatedly over the past few days. Part of her arguing that the right – Christian – thing would have been to have somehow trekked over to be with them tomorrow and given him their happy families scenario. The major part of her insisting she should avoid that kind of emotional assault course.

She looks back over at the congregation. Kath catches her eye and smiles. Her invitation to Christmas lunch demonstrating once again the generosity of so many people here. Several other people are also smiling up at her. This is her family, isn't it? The people she sees, talks to, cares for, even disagrees with, week in, week out, with whose lives her own is now woven. Even that woman who never comes to Margot's side of the altar is looking at her warmly. All these people with their messy, complicated, normal lives, just like hers; their dreams and fears, their insecurities, their imperfections, their constant striving to do better next time. She's been privileged over the last few months to be a part, however small, of helping to share God's love with them.

All these people drawn here tonight by something, by some, possibly, indefinable force. All seeking in their own way a sense of celebration, community or peace.

'In the name of God the Father, Son and Holy Spirit. Amen.'

Jeremy walks back from the lectern, giving a tiny nod towards his watch. She glances at her wrist. People in the congregation start nudging each other, a ripple running through the pews.

The pealing begins above them, clear and confident in the star-studded night.

He is here. The Christ Child has come.

Chapter 8

Early January 2017

It feels like icy splinters are filling every corner of the draughty barn on Aberdeen Avenue. Sometimes when she's forcing herself out of bed for early communion, this place makes Mildmay Grove seem like the Elizabeth Taylor Suite at the Savoy.

Still, what the plummeting temperatures and the dull January light – and the fact that they're now back in Ordinary Time after Christmas – tell her is that she's almost halfway through. Just over six months to hold her course steady and retain her sanity.

New Year's Resolution Number One: keep trying with Roderick. He can't help having the sourness of ten-day-old milk. She'll be a priest on the cusp of retirement herself one day. God willing.

Two: avoid that spa outing with Gwen at all costs. Be gracious and grateful but, above all, be unavailable. Maybe she could donate the voucher at Jeremy's next fundraising raffle? Although who's going to buy tickets to spend five hours with Gwen in a swimsuit? She stops, appalled at hearing herself think that.

Kindness. Compassion. The harder it is, the more it's needed.

Three: avoid any Soulmates outings at all costs.

Four: Cyd. She sighs and sketches in a row of question marks.

Five. She walks over to her window and leans her forehead

against the freezing pane. Delete all thoughts of that insanity on the ice rink. The very last thing she needs in her life right now.

She opens her eyes, walks back to the mirror and clips her collar in place.

Six. Don't screw up her first solo baptism on Sunday afternoon.

Normally it'd just be funerals in this first year, but as Jeremy's going away for a couple of days, he seems happy to bend the rules a little. She didn't probe more about his trip because she sensed the cordon. One thing she has noticed: he's reduced his biscuit intake by a third.

'Bit of an emergency baptism,' he says, when they're sitting in the vestry later that day.

'I spent an hour on the phone with the mother a few weeks back explaining that it wasn't possible do a christening on Christmas Day morning, no matter how much she was prepared to contribute to the heating fund.' He wipes his forehead with a rueful smile.

'She wasn't happy. Said the baby had been down for Rugby since the first scan, so how could it be so hard to fit in a little baptism at her local church? I was worried she might get on the phone to Lambeth Palace, but I managed to convince her that the third Sunday after Epiphany would be even better, as it's the season focusing on the revelation of God the Son as a human being in Jesus Christ – and that Eastern celebrations celebrate His baptism in the Jordan River. She seemed to like the exotic twist.'

'So that makes the friends and family the Magi bearing gifts?'

'Coming from all over the shop, apparently. St Mark's might find itself on the pages of *Hello!* yet.'

'It's only a matter of time,' snarls Roderick, eyeballing Margot.

'What's that buzzing sound?' asked Jeremy.

'Oh sorry, mine.' She pulls her phone out of her bag. 'Hi, sorry I'm just—'

'It's raining men, hallelujah!'

'Not now, Clarissa.'

'There's been a Noah's flood of interest. It was my brilliant profile-writing wot did it. Maybe the fact that you're in a "caring profession". Men love to be coddled. Listen to this. "Hi there Mary, from one old soul to another." So we need to draw up a top five.'

'Gotta go, Clariss. Just pick one for me,' Margot whispers, aware of the interest around her.

'Someone doing your shopping for you?' Jeremy asks.

'Kind of.'

Just sometimes, Clarissa makes her feel like a ball of play dough in the hands of a furious child.

She gets home much later usual, because the PCC meeting ran on so long. Amazing how much time fourteen people can spend debating the right volume for clock chimes. Even more amazing that someone would complain in the first place. Yet she knows, of course, that for some of them, these meetings are a date in their diaries to look forward to, a free evening's entertainment. By the time they got to the subcommittee reports and Vicar's Matters, Margot's stomach was performing *Tubular Bells*. She'd started playing PCC bingo, one point for every time started a response with 'yes, but', but stopped when she caught Gwen looking down at the page. The evening was topped off by the fact that she was hassled yet again by that homeless guy outside Boots. Look at her in her collar; she'll be good for at least a fiver.

All she wants is egg on toast and an early night. But when she walks into the kitchen, Nathan is sitting at the table, running his finger around the rim of a whisky tumbler. There's a tangle of football socks and name tags next to him.

'You're late, Margot. Can I tempt you?' he asks pointing at the bottle.

It's a plea rather than an invitation. How can she say no?

'Sure.' She pulls out the stool opposite him.

'Could I ask you a small favour?' He clears his throat. 'It's, well, a little bit unusual.'

Frantic rustling breaks out from the hamsters' cage in the corner. What does he have in mind? Bagging up any possessions Elspeth may have left and taking them to Oxfam? Begging her to return to the bosom of family? Rating his attractiveness in the north London new-divorcé stakes?

She waits. Nathan downs some more whisky.

'It's the boys.'

'Oh?'

'They've got head lice.'

Margot laughs. She can't cure leprosy either.

'Elspeth used to deal with all that. They came home with some alarmist note from school and then I saw Josh's head was crawling. I just thought you might have some idea how to deal with it because, well…'

She's female?

'I can Google it.' He looks sheepish.

'It's just one of those things you realise you know nothing about.'

This is Margot's cue. Her early night recedes into the distance. She reaches for the bottle.

'Jeremy didn't say too much about what happened with Elspeth,' she says carefully.

'I'm pretty thin on detail myself.' He picks up a needle with a stubby thread attached and runs his finger over the point. 'Wife bored/miserable/premenopausal/deranged. Tick as appropriate.'

She waits.

'Whatever. Wife falls for big swinging dick three doors down. Wife and big dick run off into the sunset. Husband and kids cry and mope and then, well, try to rebuild their lives.'

He swipes his hand across his forehead. There's no sign he's going to embroider this brutal summary. The light from the microwave glints green in her glass.

'And, well, do you, the children see much of her?'

'The lawyers are poring over the details. The kids see her

occasionally. That's all she seems to want.' He looks up at her, his eyes red. 'Big dick taking up too much of her time, apparently. Not that I'd ever tell the kids that. We're trying to keep it civilised.' He drains his glass. 'My arse.'

Jeremy said it's been about six months, but, as she knows more than anyone, there's an ineluctable law that says time telescopes in direct relation to pain suffered.

The needle point threatens to draw blood from Nathan's finger. A small vein is flickering at the side of his temple. She's desperate for him not to cry.

'I'm so sorry it's all been so hard, Nathan.'

She reaches across and squeezes his hand.

'Why don't I get us some coffee?' She pushes back the stool. 'You know what. It would be a pleasure to have a crack at those nits. A little light extermination can't be that hard. I'll just imagine they're my least favourite members of the congregation.'

He nods, swallowing hard.

'I can even write a sermon about it.' She pours some coffee into the filter. 'I was worried you were going to ask me to sew on those name tags. My needlework teacher was some kind of psychopath. I can still smell the staircase leading up to the room.'

'There was one other thing.'

She glances back at him.

'Could you keep an eye on Cyd? This whole – you know – has knocked her sideways.'

She nods, her grip tightening on the mugs.

'I can't tell you how worried I am about her.'

'It's a tough age,' she replies, wincing at the cliché.

Nathan smiles up at her.

'I have a feeling you're going to heal this family of ours somehow.'

She hands him his coffee, tongues of apprehension flickering inside her.

She lies in bed later that night, looking at the little altar of Christmas presents still sitting in the same place on the floor by her bed a month on. Baroque earrings from Sal and Kath, scores of scented candles from Kool Gang parents, a tasselled scarf from Jeremy, anticipatory frilly knickers from Clarissa and, of course, nothing from Roderick, even though she was half expecting a cooking apron with *Women's Work* emblazoned on the front.

And hidden right at the bottom, glowing like toxic waste, the envelope from Gwen. She shudders. There's the right thing to do and then there's the impossible.

She pulls her laptop onto the duvet. No one's around for a chat, not even any of the POTTY lot. This is the loneliest time of day. Particularly tonight, after that conversation with Nathan. She turns off the light, then a few minutes later, sits up and flips open her laptop again.

Vic-i-leaks: Scenes from Parish Life, 20 January 2017

You've just staggered through Advent and Christmas and now here's Epiphany to deal with. I don't mind being busy, though. It's the fiery-breathed dragons that do my head in. You just feel like saying, 'Bugger off, Winifred, and give me a bit of peace, will you?' Maybe I'm suffering from Parma-violet poisoning? One old trout gave me a bottle of Charlie she must have been hoarding since the Silver Jubilee. And all these comments on how I look. So what if I like to wear bright purple heels under my surplice? Some people need to bog off and Get a Life.

She clicks again.

Vic-i-leaks: Scenes from Parish Life, 27 January 2017

The Spanish Inquisition were amateurs. I had to spend four hours – FOUR HOURS – next to some whiskery old dragon interrogating me about my sex life. I know most of them haven't had a whiff of action since the Blitz, but if I hear anyone else say 'you'd make a lovely mum' I'll commit geronticide.

It's rapidly turning into her guilty pleasure.

Roderick seems furious, deep chevrons bracketing his mouth. He won't look at her as they're robing up. It's not her fault the vicar asked her instead of him. Maybe Jeremy wanted to reduce the risk of the baby's head bouncing off the altar step.

She's in the porch chatting to the tenor when the baptismal family make their entrance. Jeremy's thumbnail was spot on, she realises. Carmen, stick-thin in expensive neutrals, and a labradoodle – which she refuses to leave outside – under her arm. Slick-haired Hugo, scrolling through his BlackBerry as they run through the order of service. She wonders whether they took her for the office secretary at first, as though everyone on the clergy team wears a dog collar, just like everyone working at Sainsbury's wears orange and purple. It takes some nimble footwork to convince then of the unique symbolism of a woman carrying out a baptism, including referencing the Madonna and Child and the pouring on of the waters of life. There's also an awkward moment when she takes them to the font and Carmen has clearly been expecting fifteenth-century craftsmanship, rather than a battered silver bowl perched on a scruffy wooden table.

Nothing in her eight years of study and training have prepared her for the terror of this. The entire congregation is now watching her trying to juggle baby Oscar into a more comfortable position without dropping him or prompting him to throw up all over her surplice. He's far heavier than she expected: a plump *putto* straight out of Raphael, dressed in what looks like expensive oyster silk. Two hundred pairs of eyes are clocking her every move, gasping every time the baby wriggles. All these cloths and jugs and balms to negotiate with a writhing eight kilos in your arms. She can't even wipe her hand dry on her robes. Oscar's tiny fat fingers are clamped tight around her collar as though even he knows he's got the rookie. This must be how a bomb-disposal expert feels removing their first live pin. Talking of which, Roderick's supposed to be on standby support, but he's stayed way over by the altar rail, arms crossed, a tight smile on his face.

At least Jeremy will be thrilled when he hears how many are here, particularly as Carmen and Hugo have not only paid for the flowers and the service sheets and the post-service canapés, but also donated a healthy cheque for 'sundry expenses'. The vicar loves these cheques most of all.

'In baptism, God calls us out of the darkness into his marvellous light. To follow Christ means dying to sin and rising to new life with him.'

Margot beckons the baptismal party to form a semi-circle in front of her.

'Parents and godparents, the Church receives Oscar with joy. Today, we are trusting God for his growth in faith. Will you pray for him, draw him by your example into the community of faith and walk with him in the way of Christ?'

'With the help of God, we will.'

Their voices ring out pitch-perfect, tutored no doubt by Carmen.

Margot reaches for the jug of baptismal water, her hand on Oscar's head. The symbolism of the moment is intense, the water heightening the touch of the priest's hand on the baby like an electrical connection.

She glances down at the whispering biddies in the second row, probably speculating about how that nice young curate feels to be cradling a baby and wouldn't she secretly like one of her own, it's not natural, is it, everything topsy-turvy. She glances over towards the French family who held their own baptism here last autumn and look like they're comparing notes. At the elderly goateed American next to them who—

She gasps. Fourth row back on the family's side. Denim jacket, pink shirt, tortoiseshell glasses. Head down, reading through the service sheet.

Baby Oscar gets so much water thrown over his head, the

antique silk gown becomes drenched and one of the godfathers has to rush off for a muslin cloth. Margot mouths apologies and stumbles on with the service, mind unspooling.

'Oscar James Wilson, I baptise you in the name of the Father and of the Son and of the Holy Spirit. Amen.'

'Amen,' agrees the congregation.

Oscar arches his back, jerks forward and pokes Margot in the eye, then lets out an enormous howl. Indulgent titters break out below. Roderick stares straight ahead. She runs her hands under the silky folds and plops the baby back into his father's arms. Even as she struggles to compose herself, face flushed, she's aware of small pops of euphoria inside her.

She has just completed her first baptism welcoming another human being into Christ's grace.

And Felix is sitting a few feet from where she's standing at the altar.

'Let us offer one another a sign of peace,' Roderick reedily instructs the congregation.

There's no way she can follow him down the aisle to shake hands with the end seats. He scowls as she backs away from him, but she wheels round towards the table bearing the consecrated bread and wine, to the confusion of Steve, the beanpole acolyte. Time is with her: the sidesmen are taking longer than usual with the collection plates, thanks to the size and generosity of Team Oscar. Margot breathes in and starts to prepare the communion chalices, hands betraying her. She looks down into the ruby reflection at the amount of wine she's just poured in. Steve starts giggling. *This is my blood of the new covenant, which is shed for you and for many for the forgiveness of sins.* There can be no pouring of any extras into the jug or down the plughole after communion. Any dregs will be hers to drain. It looks like she might have to down the equivalent of several glasses of port before the final hymn.

By the time she and Roderick are processing back behind the

crucifer and choir at the end of the service, Margot's head is papier mâché. She trains her eyes on the fire exit.

'Well held, Vicar,' Hugo bellows a few minutes later, grabbing another champagne flute from a passing tray, as the guests mill around the food tables at the back of the church. The orange squash she's just filched from the children's table is churning inside her.

'He's full of beans, isn't he?'

He raises his glass in salute.

'Don't worry about the Bonpoint dress. I always said it was a waste of four hundred quid.'

Her hand flies to her mouth. Hugo laughs.

'Just kidding. Carmen borrowed it from someone. Oh, hey, Felix. You made it? Wasn't sure we'd ever be able to drag you in here.' Hugo turns towards her. 'Sister Margot, meet Felix, an old mate of mine. Lives around here, so he's come for some free booze.'

She rotates slowly to face him.

Felix smiles at her, eyebrows raised.

'He needs cheering up,' says Hugo, in a mock whisper.

'Good to see you again, *Sister* Margot.'

Hugo frowns.

'You two know each other?'

'Reverend Goodwin, can I have a word?' Gwen has hold of Margot's wrist and starts to pull her towards the west end.

'Hang on, Gwen.' Too sharp. Too late.

'I've got a wonderful idea.'

'That's great, Gwen, but right now I need to—'

'A St Mark's book club! Everyone would love it. And you're so educated and well read. We can plan it when we go for our spa—'

'Gwen, I'm sorry but I do need to go back to our visitors.'

Her voice sounds furry inside her head.

'But we don't have a date in our diaries yet.'

'It's top of my list. Honestly.'

Margot swivels round and starts to walk back, glancing over her shoulder to give Gwen a reassuring smile. Gwen doesn't return it.

Felix is standing alone by the table. She can see Hugo with another group over to the right, holding Oscar aloft like a rugby trophy.

'Hey.'

'Hey.'

Her face is burning, her mind blurring at the edges. Several members of the congregation are pressing in on her field of vision, waiting, wanting. She keeps her eyes trained on Felix, acutely aware of the sensation of his arms around her in those few insane moments on the ice.

'So I guess you don't ever come to church?'

'I don't think Hugo does either, to be fair.'

She smiles, before catching sight of a windmill of arms over to her right. One of the coffee ladies is waving her towards the kitchen. The verger is also making frenzied gestures further back.

'You were very impressive up there, Margot.' He reaches for a bowl of crisps and offers it to her. 'Can't have been easy with, well, not quite so little Oscar slithering around. Rather like us on the ice.'

She laughs, possibly a touch too loudly.

'Carmen would not have been happy if you'd dropped him,'

'Today's my first.'

A sideman passes with another tray of drinks. Felix takes two and hands one to her.

'Great. Well, here's to, I guess, a long and happy line of wriggly infants.' He smiles. 'As it were.'

She watches him raising the champagne to his lips, taking in the long fingers, the smatter of freckles by the watch strap.

'You've always been an atheist?' Her voice echoes in her ears. How much communion wine has she downed?

'I'm a historian, I'm afraid. We're all about stuff that actually happened.'

He looks down at his glass.

'Sorry, did that sound rude?'

'Plenty of historian believers out there.'

'Absolutely. No, no, you're right. Sorry, I didn't mean to offend you.'

She waits, amused. Then suddenly takes a step back. Prissy Pamela is barrelling towards them from the other end of the aisle, arms pumping, jaw set in an ominous line.

'Sorry, I'm monopolising you,' he says in a half-whisper, leaning in.

Pamela is now two pillars away.

'Would you like a drink some time?'

'Oh, well, I—'

'I dunno, tonight, maybe?'

The disciple in the stained-glass window above them is glaring down at her. She looks back at Felix.

'Can't, I'm afraid.'

'Sure, no problem.' Her cheeks are on fire.

'My dog's sick.'

'Oh. I'm sorry.' She frowns. 'Should you be here?'

A tiny pulse around his mouth.

'My wife's looking after him.'

Pamela's hand grabs Margot's arm, diamonds digging into her flesh.

'Sorry to interrupt.' She nods briefly at Felix. 'The dishwasher's leaking, Reverend. Did you not see us calling you?'

Margot looks from Felix to Pamela and back to Felix. The San Andreas Fault might just as well have splintered open.

'I'll be there in two ticks, Pamela.'

'*Now* would be better, Margot.'

Pamela lifts her chin and marches back toward the kitchen.

'Almost ex-wife,' adds Felix quietly.

Pamela scowls back over her shoulder.

He takes a tiny step forward.

'It's a bit complicated.' He stops. Margot's head is throbbing.

'We're living in the same house but kind of separately?'

'O-kay,'.

Her poker face is failing her. Over by the kitchen door, Pamela looks like she's guiding a plane onto a runaway.

'I must go.'

He lays a finger on her wrist.

'We'll do that drink some other time soon?'

'Margot!'

She rushes towards the group at the kitchen door without looking back over her shoulder.

Chapter 9

Early February

Married.

It's like a swarm of hornets.

Why now?

Divorced would be bad enough. Still married? Off the radar of 'no'. Apart from being a breach of God's will for the rite of marriage, a boyfriend of any description during this make-or-break year would be challenging. Whatever Clarissa may think. Unless, that is, you're male yourself and can slip him in through the lodger loophole. But a female curate with a still-married guy?

She shudders. This may be 2017, but many people in the Church of England still abhor divorce and adultery. Not to mention the visceral terror of 'knickers and vicars' tabloid disclosures or the idea of 'defrocking', with its soundtrack of saucy-postcard sniggers. A friend at Wilhurst had to go through the faculty trauma with the bishop's advisor, just because her fiancé had been briefly married to someone else. Apparently, there are three categories of rule-breaker: she knows which would apply to hooking up with the not-yet-divorced deputy head of your landlord's daughter's school while you're halfway on the road to priesthood.

There'd be disciplinary proceedings. She'd probably be asked to resign. Or have her licence revoked. Conduct unbecoming to a priest.

She looks at her reflection in the dusk.

And yet, his arm around her waist, whirling with abandon in the freezing air. The weightlessness.

He briefly made her feel normal again.

She shuts her eyes.

The only way she will make it through to July is by focusing totally on her work at St Mark's. Head down, heart closed.

Starting with tomorrow's visit to see Arthur.

Seven months in, she knows that these weekly outings to Highbury's neediest – the infirm, the elderly, the lost – are just as valuable as all the sacramental duties, sometimes even more so. Offering a sympathetic ear, reassuring lonely people that someone still cares about them, making phone calls or writing letters or even grocery shopping for people unable to do so can be more to the point than standing at the lectern on a Sunday.

Nevertheless, she dreads most of them. Casual socialising was always an alien concept to the Goodwin family. And sitting with someone with early-stage dementia sucks away at her emotional reserves, as does royal family chit-chat with a lonely spinster, when she's always shrinking from that moment when you glance up at the clock and face the 'could you just stay a bit longer, love?' plea. The hardest thing – the greatest relief – the click of the door behind her.

But Arthur is different. He may be seventy-seven and as good as imprisoned in his flat, reliant on the sporadic visits of carers, but he's managed to keep both his impish humour and his ramrod dignity intact. Something about him reminds her of her grandfather on her mother's side, the 'mustn't grumble' mindset, the quiet courage. Arthur was never a very regular churchgoer even when he was well, but good 'ordinary' people like him are a lesson to everyone. Clergy more than most.

'What's a young slip of a thing like you want to be doing a job like this for?' he asked her the first time they met. 'I'm happy you are, though, love. Perks an old boy like me up no end.' He laughed as Roderick glowered over at them.

She knows all about the two sons, the five grandchildren, the promotion to the school first eleven, the merit in grade three trumpet, the holidays in Madeira, the £1 million-plus houses. Yet the pride in his voice saddens her. The family's promises to visit, to take him to see a match at Highbury or for a spin in the new Audi never materialise. Maybe the sons have no idea how frail he is. Sometimes, as she retraces their steps down the dingy stairwell, she's considered picking up the phone to put the paragons in the picture. Except that would be stepping into forbidden space.

'How are you, Arthur?' He's in his usual spot by the three-bar fire, the mug of coffee that Margot's just made on the table next to him.

'Bearing up. Leg's a bit dicky this week. But all the better for seeing you, missy. And better still, no Grumpy Guts. What have you have done with him?'

A lightning wink.

'Back trouble.'

Arthur rolls his eyes.

'Can I get you another cushion?'

'Go on then, lovey. You spoil me.'

She bends down and retrieves the crocheted patchwork blanket – handiwork of St Mark's knitting circle, she recognises the colours of the wool – and lays it back across his knees. He's appreciative of anything she does, however small. It makes her feel she's getting the important bits right.

'All those old hens still clucking round the vicar, then? He loves it though, Jeremy, doesn't he? Perk of the job.'

She laughs, thinking about yesterday's Residents' Association coffee morning, when he was surrounded by a dozen shiny-eyed pensioners.

'All the volunteers are incredibly generous with their time, Arthur.'

He catches her eye and starts to laugh.

'Some of them grating on you a bit, are they, ducks?'

He hands across the plate with the Swiss roll he's just chopped in two.

'No.'

'But?'

She sighs.

'Sometimes it can be a bit delicate, sort of turning down some of the help when there's too much of it.'

Stop right there.

'Ah, I get you. One or two of the old birds want to be your best friend, that kind of palaver?'

She bites into the wedge of sponge.

'Be glad it's not old whatshisname.'

Margot's head jerks up.

'Thingamajig. Flowery shirts, long hair, think's he's God's gift.'

His chuckle sounds like a bag of gravel.

'You mean,' – she hesitates – 'Fabian?'

'That's the one.' He taps the side of his nose. 'Got a bit of a trouser problem, so they say. Knew a couple of blokes did some work for him a few times. Randy old bugger. And I wouldn't trust him as far as I could throw him.'

The Swiss roll is soaking up all her saliva.

Arthur pushes his glass back up his nose.

'You watch yourself, lovely.'

She's saved from having to reply by Arthur breaking into a harsh coughing fit. Asbestos. All those pre-regulation loft conversions.

'Lungs like a pair of ruddy black sponges.'

'Can I get you anything?'

'Pop into the kitchen, there's a good girl, and fetch me a glass of water. Oh, and there's a box of Dairy Milk the boys sent for my birthday. We can have a go at it while we plan how to spend this week's Lotto millions.'

The tiny kitchen is warm from the late-afternoon sun. Not a mug out of place, tea towels folded on the side of the sink. A handful of plants basking on the windowsill, freshly watered. She fingers the papery leaves of the busy Lizzie, looking down at the estate backing onto Arthur's, the tiny grill-windowed flats that make her current home seem palatial. She swallows and walks back in.

'Come on, Margot. Don't polish the lot off in there. I know what you vicars are like.'

She doesn't quiz him further. She's heard all she needs to.

She walks out of Arthur's flat checking her watch. Coffee with Doddery at the greasy spoon on Holloway Road: her invitation, despite his resistance, to try and clear the air. She arrives a few minutes late, full of apologies. He doesn't even look up when she sits down.

'Peppermint tea, please,' she calls across to the counter.

Roderick grunts, reaching for his mug of builder's. He got to choose the venue. None of that lefty latte nonsense: dingy white mortuary tiles, tomato-shaped ketchup dispensers, air lardy with pork fat, far more his kind of thing

He's working his way through a doorstep sausage sarnie. She hopes his dentures are up to the job, then digs her nails into her arm. Fresh start.

He chews away in silence for a few moments.

The waitress refills his tea on her way past.

'Absent friends,' he says, lifting his mug in the air.

'Sorry?'

'Naval toast. Old habit.'

You can say that again. Small flecks of Daddies Sauce are scattered across his chin.

'I can't believe that we're already hurtling towards Lent, can you?'

He carries on chewing hard.

'Someone at Wilhurst said, "You make it past one sacred cow

on the Church calendar and there's a whole herd around the corner more waiting to ambush you.'"

The handkerchief comes out, now doubling as a napkin.

'When you've been in this role as long as I have,' he sniffs, 'there's no such thing as ambushing. It's like a naval exercise. We've been assigned our duties. Everyone knows his place. No room for error or incompetence.'

The hankie swipes across his nose and is then spread back across his knees. Margot swallows and spoons some more honey in her tea, watching the golden ribbon run its course.

'I really appreciate all your help, Roderick. When you're a rookie like I am, it's so reassuring to have a more experienced colleague showing you how it's done.'

RADA-worthy: her mother would have been proud. Roderick gives her a gummy smile.

'Twenty eight years in the Senior Service. If that's not going to instil esprit de corps, I don't know what will. '

'I'd love to hear about all that sometime.'

She props her chin on her hands, avoiding her eye in the mirror. He purses his lips.

'You're a *Guardian* reader, I take it?'

'Well—'

'Naval chaplain on war missions, that's where ministry comes alive. Long tours, most of them, months on end. Life or death situations where you alone are friend and advisor to all, across every rank.'

The sudden wistfulness takes her aback.

'You must have some fascinating stories, Roderick.'

Manky hankie back on duty.

'Great times, great times. The camaraderie when there was a big job on. Sailing into Port Stanley, clinging to the railing on the deck of a destroyer with a Force Eight raging around you, a huge swell rolling beneath your feet. And the subs. Nuclear, of course.

Faslane Flotilla. I've done the lot. The spirit of fellowship on those vessels was unbeatable. One hundred and twenty officers and men, nothing but watches, work and exercise drills. Six hours on, six hours off; eat, sleep and operate assigned equipment. The happiest times of my life.'

'I can imagine.'

He narrows his eyes.

'There's nothing else like it. Everything in its place. You know what's what, who reports to whom, where everyone is in the pecking order.'

The watery eyes bore into her.

'Different world today. These days "wimmin" can even go onto the battlefield, for crying out loud.' He shakes his head, a decrepit donkey trying to dislodge a swarm of flies. 'But then what does an old codger like me know?'

'Would you like a piece of cake, Roderick?'

'No place for girls out there. Disruptive for the lads. Unsettles 'em. Why change something that's been working perfectly for centuries?'

The impartiality of her smile is impeccable. He's moved seamlessly from one male bastion to another without passing Go.

'I'm looking forward to the whole build up to Easter and—'

'You know there was another candidate in the running for the curate's job?'

She places her mug back down. Maybe she misheard?

'Very strong contender. Didn't bother with a Ph.D. and all that malarkey. Just wanted to roll up his sleeves and get stuck in. Top man. Knew all about modern media, Twittify and all that business as well.'

'Oh?' She struggles to control the tremor in her voice. 'But St Mark's has to take its curate through the Common Fund and the bishop put me forward as the candidate, so how—'

'SSM, Margot. Self-supporting minister. Independent means.

No need for the Common Fund. He was family, too.' He crumples the hankie in his hand. 'I will have that piece of cake, in fact.'

Margot waits until the waitress has left.

'How do you mean "family", exactly?'

He attacks the slice of fruit cake with his fork.

'I was away visiting my sister in Widecombe, but the PCC decided to go for the PC appointment.' He sniggers. 'No offence.'

'None taken.'

'As I always say, good for the oldies and all those kids to have a female on board. Someone's got to do it, and rather you than me.'

He stuffs a piece of cake in, then gives a smile full of grizzled innocence.

'In what way was this guy family, exactly?'

'Who?'

She waits while he tunes in.

'Oh. He's Fabian Spence's nephew. What was his name again? Gideon or something. No, Oliver. That's it. Pity, really. When I came back it was all a done deal.'

She takes a quivering breath. She got the slot Fabian's nephew wanted. Why hasn't he mentioned it to her? Or Jeremy, come to that? Maybe he's biding his time until she screws up. One foot wrong and he'll be in. She fiddles with the string on her teabag.

'And what happened to Oli— oh, I'm sorry, excuse me a sec.'

Roderick's mouth twists as she pulls out her phone.

'Boyfriend?'

'Dad, sorry, I'm just in a meeting.'

'Don't have much luck, do I?' says Ricky. 'Linda and I are in London for some show soon. You can get to know your new mother. Got a pen?'

Roderick's lips are cross-stitched shut.

'Twenty-eighth March. We'll meet you about six. Ok?'

We. She drops her phone back in her bag rummaging about for a tissue, anything.

'Sorry, Roderick. My Dad. He's——' she swallows, 'getting married.'

The beetle eyebrows shoot upwards

'What about you?'

'Sorry?'

'Your plans to swan up the aisle? After you're done with the job?'

She shakes her head in confusion.

'I mean, mine and Jeremy's is a vocation. Yours is just short-term, I should think.' He smiles at her. 'Nothing wrong with that. More hands to the pump, the better. The vicar has needed a secretary for years.'

Ten, nine, eight, seven. Her father's call has already knocked her off balance. All she needs is Roderick launching into his views on women dating, back to Eve's original sin.

'No plans on that front, Roderick,' she trills.

'Anyway, I've enjoyed our little chat.' He brushes the confetti of crumbs off his chest. 'Better get back to base.'

He scrapes his chair backwards and unhooks the dusty jacket, wincing as he struggles into it. He's vulnerable, frail, old. As alienated by her world as she is by his.

The waitress comes up with the bill and pushes it towards Roderick. Margot pulls it back.

'My treat.'

He inclines his head.

'I'll meet you back at St Marks. Just got a few bits and pieces to do.'

Extended time with Doddery feels like a pastoral visit in its own right. And she needs space to think about his curate hand grenade. Why hasn't Fabian mentioned it? Or, more to the point, Jeremy?

Vic-i-leaks: Scenes from Parish Life, 10 February 2017

Trouble at t'mill. The Vic doesn't think we're raking in enough dosh from the collection plate. He asked me to make an appeal during the sermon. The old trouts weren't happy. One snapped at him, 'This is a church, Vicar, not a street market.' In his defence, he's thinking of that damp patch over by the organ. And, come to think of it, what wouldn't he give for a sniff at the income of the average market stallholder. Beggars can't be snoozers.'

Chapter 10

Late February

The clatter of wood on wood echoes around her as she walks down the diamond-carpeted stairs. The last time she was in one of these places must have been an outing with Gilly's group from New Milton Community Church, a glittering addition to Margot's non-existent social life. She has a clear-edged memory of scoring a strike and earning herself a round of high fives. It was like gulping down helium after the carbon monoxide of home.

This place is a would-be American diner, young staff in quiffs and string ties or miniskirts and retro hair bows crossing the floor in a gingham whirl. How will she even recognise him? Clarissa just said a shaven-headed guy in his forties who'd be wearing a white t-shirt. She can't believe she allowed herself to be talked into this. And yet she owes Clarissa so much.

A trio of teenage boys assesses her as she walks past the jukebox. Twelve minutes late.

She can just walk out. Tell Clarissa she assumed he'd bailed. Go home and watch the *Kardashians* on YouTube.

'Mary, right?'

She takes an instinctive step back. He doesn't look like a serial killer, but they never do. He's wearing a tight white t-shirt, receding hairline slicked back with something pungent.

She switches on her professional smile.

'Lenny.'

'Saw you scanning the room. Maybe hoping for a better offer?'

She waits for the snorting to subside.

'What can I get you?'

'You're joking. No chick's buying me a pint. You grab a seat, Mary. What's your poison?'

She watches him swagger off to the bar and walk back with their drinks, arms chunky as a weightlifter's.

'You done this before then, darling?'

'Online dating?' Did she just say those words?

'Nah, bowling. We've all done the online stuff, right? Tho' this is my first time on Soulmates. A mate said you get a better class of bird.'

She sips on her Bacardi and Coke. 'I haven't done this since I was about fifteen.'

But as she curves the ball behind her and swings it forwards in a fluid arc, it turns out she still remembers how. She can feel Lenny's eyes on her as she bends to pick up another ball.

'Not bad.'

For a girl.

'You're pretty good yourself,' she observes, as he obliterates an entire row of pins yet again.

'Dead-eye Len, the boys in Kandahar called me. Could hit a moving target at fifty yards.'

Margot heaves up a twelve-pounder from the chute, places her thumb and two fingers inside and chucks it forwards with as much violence she can muster. Dante couldn't have devised punishment enough for Clarissa.

An hour later and she wonders how many more squaddie derring-do she can take and thinks what a shame it is that Roderick isn't sitting here in her place to swap notes, when Lenny leans forward and puts his hands on her knees.

'So, hon.'

She drains her glass.

'Tell me about you. Can't remember your profile blurb, to be honest. You're my fourth this month.'

'Tell you what, why don't I grab us a couple of hot dogs first?'

'I like a girl with a healthy appetite.'

She walks towards the food counter. She could be a primary-school teacher or a social worker. Which wouldn't be far off the truth.

A meaty hand grabs her shoulder.

'Didn't want you to get lonely.'

He wraps an arm around her waist, treating her to the full Lynx effect.

'What are you then? A secretary?'

'Not exactly.'

The ketchup dispenser burps in sympathy as she replaces it on the counter.

'Estate agent, right? You're quite posh.'

'Er, no.'

'Go on then, what?'

Absolutely no way.

He pokes her in the ribs.

'You've got me going now. Hey, you're not a lap dancer?'

'I work with people in a sort of pastoral capacity.'

He tips his head, confused.

'Shall we go and sit over—'

'Come on, put me out of my misery,' he grins, a glob of masticated pork glistening on his tongue.

'Well, I visit people in hospital, hospices, even prisons.'

'Shit, anyone would think you were a priest, from that description.'

She's never been any good at lying. He gapes at her.

'Fuck, you've got to be kidding me.'

Lenny staggers backwards. Ketchup stripes his cheek like a dueller's mark.

'Count me out, OK? You're a bit of a looker, but I'm not into any of that kinky shit.'

She watches his dash to the exit with a twinge of sympathy. All he wanted was a no-ties quickie. Instead of which she comes with more strings attached than the London Philharmonic.

She turns away, her eyes starting to smart. What is she doing here in this garish, thunderous hellhole, duping lecherous strangers, when she should be focusing all her physical and spiritual energy on the task ahead?

When what she craves right now is someone to hold her, stroke her cheek, enfold her into him like two halves of walnut in a shell.

Vic-i-leaks: Scenes from Parish Life, 23 February 2017

If one more person – just one – says something about the way I dress, I'm going to punch their lights out. It's a free world, even after you've signed your life away to the C of E. Not everyone thinks M & S and Debenhams are catwalk chic. So what if I sometimes daub on one of Grazia's lipsticks of the week or have turquoise nails? Last time I checked, we're in England, not some mountain village in Afghanistan.

Cyd is curled up on the sofa in the study, curtains drawn, earphones in, when Margot gets home from work a couple of Sundays later.

'Hey, Cyd.'

She doesn't even look up.

'Got much homework?'

The house hisses around them. The twins must be at football practice, judging by the stud-shaped diamonds of mud she saw on the inside mat.

Margot walks across the rug and stands in front of her.

'I thought I'd go for a wander round Camden Market. Fancy

coming along?'

Cyd finally looks up and shrugs.

'OK, no worries. Just wanted to check.'

The front door reopens behind her just as she's stepping onto the pavement.

'Wait.'

Margot forces a smile.

'I'll get my stuff.'

Cool, stay cool. She grinds her heels into the cracked paving stones, tangles of weeds thrusting up between them. No wonder Nathan never brings any clients here. One glimpse of this scrubland and he'd be disbarred from RIBA. *A garden must be looked into and dressed as the body*, as George Herbert wrote.

'Fuck, I've left my wallet in my locker.'

She's halfway down the path, her sole protection against the freezing wind a ratty black hoodie.

'I can lend you some.' Margot hesitates. 'Bring a jacket, maybe?'

Cyd ignores her and turns right onto the pavement. Margot stands still, collecting herself. She could have spent this afternoon on some rare me-time. Gone to the Tate Modern or Oxford Street or just sat in a café and read.

Keep an eye on her for me, Nathan had pleaded. It's like hugging a porcupine.

They rock together side by side on the crowded tube. It's a wall of noise, no one talking.

'So what's up with your Dad?'

Margot stares at her. It's the first thing Cyd has said since they left the house.

'Your voice goes all stiff when you speak to him.'

'Oh, no, I—'

'He thinks it's weird you're a vicar.'

Several people seated below are now gawping up at them, checking out the deviant in their midst.

'He's still sort of getting used to the idea,' mutters Margot.

There's a groaning sound and a creak of brakes. The train grinds to a halt in the tunnel. Total silence and then a crackle as the intercom spits into life.

'Sorry about the delay, people. Train stuck in front of us. No one's telling me anything.'

A high-pitched screech from the intercom and then silence.

Margot blows at her fringe. The carriage smells of sweat and grime.

'Look at it from his point of view,' Cyd says, swinging herself back and forth from the rail. 'Daughter's a religious nutter.'

Margot closes her eyes.

'What about your mum?'

She snaps her eyes open.

'Another time, Cyd, yeah?'

Cyd scowls and shoves in her earphones.

The moment the train finally staggers into the station at Camden Town, Cyd springs into life, shoving her way out of the carriage and up the escalators two at a time. Margot can see her drumming her fingers at the top as she threads her way upwards through a pack of French teenagers.

'Where shall we start?' Margot pants, out on the pavement. 'Stables Market, maybe?'

'Sorry, can't.' Cyd shoves her phone into her jeans. 'Change of plan. I'm meeting some friends.'

What was Margot expecting? A Damascene conversion to niceness?

'Could you lend me twenty quid?'

She's tempted to refuse but instead pulls out her wallet and hands over the note.

'Why don't we grab a coffee first and then you—'

'See you.'

Cyd snatches the cash and dashes off into the crowd. The guy at the neighbouring stall glances over at Margot, smirking.

She turns away, furious, just as her phone buzzes in her bag. She has to reread the text three times.

Margie, this is your new mum!! See you next week! XOXOXO

Margot stomps across the road under the blank gaze of a giant mermaid sculpture, perched above discount shoe shop. Half woman, half beast, welcome to the club. Her father's found someone who makes him happy, he says. She swallows; she needs to man up, welcome this new woman in his life with love. Hadley, the principal, Jeremy, anyone at St Mark's, would expect nothing less.

She wonders around the market aimlessly for half an hour, weaving in and out of the stalls, listless and lost. She finally settles on a café near the canal and is perched on a stool watching the crowd pass by, when she realises with a jolt that Cyd is a few feet away from her at a Thai food stall. Standing right next to her is a heavily inked guy, maybe ten years older than she is, hat tipped back on his head, his arm around her waist. Margot mustn't be seen, yet is unable to look away. A moment later, Cyd glances over laughing and spots her. She lifts her chin, pulls on the guy's arm and they disappear through the food stalls, his hand now in the back pocket of her jeans.

Margot watches them go, in shock, unsure if there's anything she can or should be doing about it.

It's still preying on her mind when she gets home an hour later to find Nathan and the boys in the bathroom surrounded yet again by delousing paraphernalia. The relief of Nathan's face when she walks in is almost comical.

"'Every single egg must be removed if you're to avoid a second infestation in ten days' time. You're looking for tiny white beads that resemble a drop of hairspray,'" he reads as she sits down on the side of the bath and runs the nit comb across Josh's scalp.

There are so many tripwires in this family, she thinks, swallowing the irony. But, nevertheless, it still feels strange never to mention their mother, no matter how much Elspeth has edited herself from their lives. She remembers how she hated the 'stand well back' signs people erected around her and Danny. It always felt like they were for other people's benefit rather than theirs, all those subject skirters who fought shy of any awkwardness, as though grief was contagious.

'When are you next off to Hastings to see your mum, boys?' she ventures, when Nathan is out of the room

Both boys stiffen.

'Easter, maybe?' she asks, already committed too far.

Sam looks up at her in disbelief.

'Nice place to visit. I grew up by the sea and loved it. All those long summers playing on the beach, windy walks right through the winter.'

Neither of the boys answers.

'Does Cyd like it?'

Sam glances at Josh.

'She stays in her room all the time and Mum says, "Why does she bother?"'

'Cyd knows where Eric hides the keys.'

Another look between them, broken by the slamming of the front door.

'Where the hell have you been?' Margot has never heard Nathan this angry. She moves to close the door to the bathroom but stops.

'I told you that you were grounded.'

Margot walks back and picks up the spray again.

'Come on, boys, let's get this killing spree over and done with.'

'The vicar asked me to show her around Camden Market and then she bailed early.'

Sam wheels around to look at Margot.

'Dad'll kill you.'

'Don't lie to me, Cydney.'

Margot's chest tightens.

'Why don't you ask her if you're so bothered?'

Should she go down? Too late. There's a thumping on the stairs all the way up to the attic, and then the crash of the door.

Josh eyes her in the mirror, wielding a nail clipper at the end of his fringe.

'Did you, Maggot?'

She smiles yet again at the nickname.

'Take your fingers out of your mouth, Sam. This stuff is highly toxic.'

All of it.

Cyd doesn't reappear for the rest of the evening. Nor, to her intense relief, does Nathan quiz Margot about what happened. Should she take a tray of food up? Her arrival would be as welcome as a nuclear winter.

She has no idea what's expected of her here. The older boyfriend, the lie about the school friends, the assumption that Margot would cover her back whatever it was she was up to. Should she tell Nathan? He's asked for her help, after all. Cyd could be at risk in all sorts of ways. Yet to open up to him would breach all kinds of boundaries. And in what way would getting Cyd into even further trouble help?

She knows a teenage heart curdled with grief when she sees one. There's no rule book here. She's on her own.

There wasn't one moment when Margot realised that her relationship with her own mother had derailed. It was a slow-motion tearing away, like a house sliding off the side of a cliff after a storm. The loss of the bond they'd had when Margot was younger, intensified, somehow, by the fact they'd been allies for so long. Margot hit fourteen the same year her mother hit forty. The more she attempted to pin down an identity for her teenage self – the Destiny's Child make-up, the Britney gear – the tenser things became. When Margot came back with her first boyfriend in tow, it seemed to flip the switch on all her mother's buried frustrations. Margot understands that now in a way she didn't then. Ricky either didn't know about Annelie's depression or didn't care, so far lost was he down his own rabbit hole of shrivelled hopes.

In the meantime, Margot fell off her mother's radar.

The tension in the house is now ratcheted up so high, she can hardly breathe. She decides to slip out mid evening for a walk, telling Nathan she just needs to clear her head.

She walks fast, her breath smoky in the chill spring air.

And now, at last, the thought that's been tugging away at her for so long just beneath the surface breaks through.

Married.

Out of bounds.

He lives in the parish. Two hundred people saw them together at the baptism. He's deputy head at Cyd's school.

She's insane even entertaining this kind of debate with herself. She's four months away from her priesting. She's endured years of gruelling preparation to get to this point. All those times at Wilhurst when she thought about quitting but something always kept her on track.

Jeopardise all of that? She's lost her mind.

She turns around, crosses the road and walks as fast as she can in the opposite direction. She's helpless. Hopeless. In the three weeks since she saw him, he's colonised her thoughts.

She can't call him.

She can't not.

She's like that kaleidoscope someone gave her as a child. One small change and the world is transfigured.

There are multiple Margots, all of them her.

Her commitment to becoming a priest is total.

Yet how can she not pick up the phone?

Cars spray past her on Aberdeen Avenue. She squeezes her eyes shut. If the next one that passes is blue. She stands under a streetlight, breath suspended. The street is quiet for a few moments, then there's a loud hiss on the tarmac behind her. A navy Golf speeds past, carving a large arc in a puddle.

The sodium flickers over her head.

Motionless, she watches the car drive out of sight. Her fingers reach into her pocket for the scrap of paper she's worried into a nub. Hugo hadn't even bothered to ask why she needed it when she called.

Hey Felix. This is Sister Margot. Wondered if you still fancied that drink?

Chapter 11

Early March

Margot yanks out one outfit after another and throws them onto the bed. Stepmother? Fairy tales were never her thing – despite what her father and Danny might think about her current job – but the very idea of a replacement mother comes with a whole theme park of associations.

Every time she thinks about it, her stomach tightens. Has he given Linda her mother's ring? A random stranger wearing the thin gold band Margot can picture gleaming in the night light as they read *Little Women* together before bed.

If they met at a trade fair, she'll turn up in a boxy suit, spiky heels and lots of bling. Margot stands defeated in her underwear.

He's only known her five minutes. Why the rush? Is she pregnant? Margot stares open-mouthed at her reflection, pale as a communion wafer.

What possessed her to send that text?

The bar in Earl's Court is teeming when she arrives. She's worried she might pass out before she even reaches the bar. Maybe they're not here? But no, she spots them ensconced over in a corner: her father in an unlikely red paisley shirt, wrapped around a brunette not many years older than Margot herself, decked out in velvet harem pants and a plunging lacy blouse, hair stacked up like a palm tree. Margot looks down at her own Sunday-supplement-safe.

Neither stands as she walks over.

'Linda, poppet, meet Margot.'

Patchouli suffocates her as Linda pulls her down towards her, amid the clink-clank of bangles.

'You and I are going to be mates, Margie. Spirituality's my thing too. Female divinity, Gaia, Virgin Queen stuff, you know?'

Margot looks over at Ricky, sleeves pushed up like a mud-wrestling referee.

'Get you two girls a drink? Campari and soda, poppet?'

'Please,' she and Linda both chorus. He's never poppet-ed her in his life. Pet names were for other fathers and daughters.

'Oopsy,' giggles Poppet, stroking Margot's elbow. Love me or else.

Margot watches Ricky head for the bar, panic rising.

'Richard's so psyched about us meeting. Me too, Margie. A real-life priestess.'

'Priest, actually. Or curate, in fact, as—'

'I'm a healer too.'

Margot frowns.

'I thought you worked in the same line of work as Dad?'

Linda leans in so close, she could be counting the flecks on Margot's irises. 'Knew I had special powers from when I cured my Nan's lumbago just by running my hands across her back. A miracle, you'd call it.'

Margot bites down on her lip.

'I think of it as the universal life force coming to me as an intermediary. Like a satellite dish, receiving and transmitting the humongous energy of human love. Right?'

What's taking him so long?

'We all have the light within us but need to learn how to ignite the inner spark.'

Linda delves into her bag and hands over a glittery business card.

Linda Roberts. Come and be healed. Dowsing, colour therapy, hot pebbles. Distance/ Skype consultations available.

'Insomnia, migraines, self-sabotaging patterns of behaviour, I do them all. Impotence is my speciality.'

'Ladies.' Ricky hands over two enormous glasses of something fluorescent red, topped by a paper parasol.

'It's all about spirituality without borders, right?' Linda slurps. 'The ancient handicrafts. Paganism is the UK's fastest growing religion, yeah? What's your spirit guide called, Margie?'

Margot can't afford to torpedo things within half an hour of meeting her. Ricky leans in, glass held high.

'Bottoms up.'

He clinks his glass against Margot's. Is he on Prozac?

'Knew you two would get on.'

'Scorpios are hugely into family,' says Linda, spreading her fingers across his thigh. 'As well as being the most passionate sign.'

Margot stabs her thumb with the parasol.

He's had other girlfriends. Casual things. But this is different. She must have some kind of tantric sexual hold over him. Or a malign form of hypnotism?

Stop. She should be happy for him. Spread the love. Yet something about their in-your-face intimacy is clenching her heart. Did she ever see him show this much affection towards her mother, ever?

This whole fizzingly sensual display is setting her teeth on edge.

'Have you ever done any past-life regression?'

Margo stares at her.

'We're all reincarnated, so that we can express our inner selves and evolve as beings, tapping into the memory of another soul. Just like it says in the Akashic records, right, Richard?'

Linda starts stroking Ricky's cheek.

'The spiritual records of everything that's ever happened,

accessed through astral projection.'

Margot can feel Ricky scrutinising her reaction.

'Some people say it's just memories passed down through our cell structure or DNA and stuff. But that's bullshit. I know I was a poet in seventeenth-century Azerbaijan. I can see myself walking along the mud banks of the river Kur through the Shirvan plains; I can hear the cow bells tinkling behind me, my wife and six kids by my side. I can feel the midges brushing against my face. I don't need any scientist telling me otherwise.'

If she looks at her father now, the game will be up.

'I just need to pop downstairs. Won't be long.'

She takes as long as possible and returns to find Ricky sitting alone.

She drops back down in the chair opposite him.

'So?'

A flashbulb moment, every syllable worth multiples of itself.

'She's nice, Dad.'

He juts out his lip. She looks away, regrouping.

'I didn't think you were into,' – she hesitates – 'all this alternative stuff?'

'Old dog, new tricks.'

Eight years belittling her most profound beliefs, harping on about finding herself a real job, anything rather the superstitious bollocks she'd tied herself to..

Linda skips back, holding a bottle of wine and three glasses.

'I could your aura read some time.'

Margot realises she has no choice but to reply.

'Not really my—'

'Even vicars have an aura.'

'Thanks anyway.'

'Your aura is your energy field, Margot.'

Margot whips round to face him.

'When your emotions are out of balance, that's when you get

sick,' says Ricky. 'Right, Poppet?'

This, from the man who didn't bother to congratulate her when she graduated? Who helped create a home so fractured she and Danny are still unable to stick together the pieces?

Love is patient, love is kind. It keeps no record of wrongs.

'I bet Margie's chakras aren't letting enough light in.'

An hour later, she's leaning back against the tube train window trying to absorb the enormity of it all.

It's 9.30 p.m. An hour's worth of PCC minutes to be written up by tomorrow morning's meeting. She still hasn't booked in that hospital visit to see one of the old ladies from the front row. Roderick is now not even bothering to speak to her when she walks into in the room. Oh, and her father is getting hitched to a reincarnated Azerbaijani poet.

And then Felix.

Felix, who's chosen not to reply to her reckless, irresponsible, stupid text message, because one of them has a moral compass at least.

There's a text message when she gets off the train. Her pulse quickens. It's her personal phone.

Hello Margot, I've booked in our spa day for a week on Saturday. Your diary was clear. Gwen xx

She must speak to Jeremy tomorrow. Gwen is starting to feel like a blob of UHU in human form. She's also on the PCC, two of the sub-committees, the flower rota, the coffee rota, the reading rota, the intercession rota and the clean-up after the service rota. A twenty-two-carat, true blue parishioner.

Jeremy is in one of his brisker moods when she tackles him the next day. Too preoccupied with the unexpected hike on the Q4 heating bill to focus on much else.

'You're not the first member of the clergy to get a love offering, Margot. It should be listed in the job description.' He scratches his head. 'I remember a widow once knitting me an apricot cardigan and I had to wear it to every Wednesday coffee morning for the next five years until she passed away. Lazing around in a spa for a few hours doesn't sound so very hair shirt to me.'

Surely there must be some Church rule about not accepting gifts over a certain value, like MPs having to register freebies in the Members' Register?

'We're talking about kindly old ladies here. Think of taking her gift as an act of giving in itself. Maybe Gwen thought you looked a peaky and wanted to help?'

'I'd really rather not—'

'What exactly is it you're afraid of?'

Margot hesitates.

'She's one of our star performers, to be honest. We could do with a dozen more Gwens. Some retirees do golf, others do God. St Mark's would be on its knees without people like her. If I remember rightly, she used to be a nurse or something, so she likes caring for people.' He eyeballs Margot over his glasses. 'Go on, spoil yourself. You never know, you might even enjoy it.'

Her hypocrisy eats into her as she waits for the kettle to boil, picking at the strip of plastic detaching itself from the cutlery drawer. What's a few hours of her life to make Gwen happy? She breathes in hard. Except that she's installed Margot on such a lofty pedestal, she's starting to suffer vertigo. She can't shift the sense that what Gwen would most like to do is flip open the top of Margot's skull, climb inside and slam down the hatch.

She walks back inside with the tea tray.

'Oh, yes, Margot, while I remember. There was a call for you.'

'Oh?'

Roderick looks up.

'From the deputy head at Highbury High.'

'Really?'

Margot keeps her eyes fixed on the tray, watching the liquid tremble in the mugs.

'I said you'd call him back.'

Did Roderick just snort?

'Probably wants you to go and do an encore, I should think.'

'Maybe Roderick could go this time?'

'Very funny.' Jeremy starts to chuckle, then clears his throat. 'Why don't you try him now? Excellent outreach opportunity for St Mark's.'

'Well, no, it's fine, I'll call him later.' She rifles through some papers so as not to have to look up. 'Just need to sort out a couple of other things first.'

'I'd do it now while the iron's hot. Here, I jotted down the number.'

Her heart is pounding as she picks up the receiver.

'Hi, is that Felix Porter? This is Margot Goodwin.' She glances at the top of Jeremy's head. 'You know, St Mark's.'

'Oh, hey there.' He laughs. 'I hadn't forgotten where you're from.'

Jeremy looks over at her, beaming.

'No, right. I'm sure you hadn't.'

A couple of beats. Roderick's now also interested, for some reason.

'I was actually calling before to say sorry.'

'Sorry?'

'Yeah, I lost my phone – one of the kids probably stole it, but that's another story. I didn't have your number, so I had the brainwave of calling the church.'

Her jaw is aching from the tension.

'Good plan.'

She looks back at her audience. Jeremy raises an eyebrow, inquiringly.

'So we were wondering if you wanted any of us to pay another visit to the RS group?'

The vicar does a thumbs up.

'Well, I hadn't thought about it, but sure, why not?'

'Ok, well, maybe a conversation for slightly further down the line?'

There's another pause. Jeremy and Roderick are both waiting.

'You're not alone, are you?'

'I can send you some course work ideas,' she gabbles.

'Ok, I get it. So, anyway, Reverend, are we still on for that drink?'

She scrapes her chair back and steps towards the window. A fly is crawling up the windowpane.

No, we're not.

'Sure.'

Chapter 12

Mid-March

The entire family is in the kitchen. Nathan has organised a production line with the boys wiping and Cyd piling things on the table, customary scowl in place. Small puddles of foam sit on the tiles like a bubbling riptide.

'Can I give you a hand?' Margot asks, unclipping her collar.

'Time this lot did their bit, right, Cydney?'

'I'll put things in the cupboard,' says Margot.

'Good day at the office?'

'Very busy. We're gearing up for Lent, so it's all hands to the pump. Special services, talks, choosing the choral anthems, that kind of thing.'

'What's Lent?' asks Sam.

'It's when people give up things they like for a few weeks every year,' says Nathan. 'In your case, boys, that would be guzzling Nutella from the jar, hogging the Xbox and staying up late watching brain-rot American junk.'

Identikit scowls.

'Why?' asks Josh.

Cyd wheels round, smirking.

'Over to you, Margot,' says Nathan.

She blows her hair out of her eyes.

'Well, it's not just about giving things up. Or at least it shouldn't be. Lent isn't just some glorified excuse to go on a diet or detox. Jesus went into the wilderness for forty days to fast and prepare himself for what was to come.' She ignores the snorting to her right. 'So we think of Lent as a time to review your life and how you could be doing things better.'

Her shoulders are starting to stiffen.

'Weird,' says Josh.

'So weird', says Cyd.

'I guess it's a bit like half-time in a football match, Josh, you know, when the teams go off to refuel with a drink and a slice of orange—'

'Mars Bar.'

'Mars Bar, and then come back refreshed and ready to win the game.'

'Much as I'm enjoying this, I need to go and finish my history essay for that twat Porter.'

'Cydney!'

'He's a total prick.'

Margot crouches down by the pan rack in shock.

'You used to think he was hot, Cyd,' shouts Sam, flicking a large bowl of suds, which lands on Margot's shoulder, like scum on wet sand. She waits, breathing hard.

'Fuck off, Sam.'

'Cydney, I'm not telling you again.'

'Cyd loves Mr Porter! Cyd loves Mr Porter!'

'Josh, enough. We've all had things about people, haven't we, Margot? Though maybe not, well, if you, er...'

Cyd grabs a can of Coke from the fridge and stomps out, slamming the door hard behind her.

Danger's invading the room like mustard gas.

When Margot first told Clarissa back in January about this

compulsory spa visit, Clarissa was beside herself. All those gags about mortification of the flesh because you couldn't get more mortifying than the flesh on that woman, Venus de Kilo with added cellulite and, really Margot, what's not to like about an afternoon chilling in a spa at someone else's expense, even if that someone is a pension-age stalker with an obesity-cum-personality problem? You can get a manicure or a facial or even better a waxing, *in readiness*.

But not even Clarissa's foray into gothic comedy can match Margot's fear of what the next few hours hold. Her memories of the one and only time she's been to a spa for a friend's twenty-first celebration don't help. White towels wrapped around glistening flesh, giggling intimacy in the sauna, dripping proximity in the steam room, toes colliding in the Jacuzzi ... now superimposed with Gwen's avid smile and those rippling chins. She's spent the past eight months resenting the restrictions of her professional wardrobe and now she's terrified of shedding it.

'Think of the act of giving as an act of giving in itself,' Jeremy had said. She's trying.

Yet even as Gwen walks towards her beaming, Margot's still searching for a last-minute cop-out. The chunky arms are flapping ready for a hug. Compassion. Kindness. It's two or three hours out of her life.

And she could do with some moral credit in her account right now.

The only escape is to dive in at the deep end. Gwen is making her entrance from the changing rooms encased in a red-spotted swimsuit that pushes back the boundaries of engineering ingenuity. There must be rivets, ball bearings, abutments and cantilevered reinforcements: the compression/tension ratio makes the Golden Gate Bridge look modest.

Margot slices through the glassy surface, the chill of the water emptying her lungs. One arm wheeling in front of the other, keep it smooth, don't look back. As she flips over, arms rotating, legs scissoring in rhythm, it strikes her this is the first proper exercise she's had in months. So much for Hadley's insistence on health and well-being. She reaches the side and looks back to where Gwen is now lowering herself into the shallow end. Margot takes a mouthful of oxygen and glides under the surface, revelling in the remembered sensation. Those long summers with friends camped out on the on their favourite spot on the beach, near the café. Abandoning themselves to the swell, the freedom, the briny unpredictability of the waves. Then, afterwards, the toasty-sweet smell of sand and sun cream, her cheese and tomato sandwiches sweating in the foil, the creased copies of teen magazines, inky smears on their hands. She reaches the side of the pool and pushes away under the water again. Something darker: Danny's voice, small and fearful at the fringes of her memory, always scared of something lurking in the depths, after her father's joke that time. Her mother, huddled under a rug on the pebbles at the bottom of the slope, out of her element and alone.

'Coo-eee!'

Margot hauls herself out of the water before turning around. She raises her hand at Gwen in a gesture uncomfortably reminiscent of benediction.

'The vicar mentioned you were a nurse, Gwen.'

Gwen smiles at her from the neighbouring relaxation chair.

'Last place I worked was an old people's home near Archway. Ten years, and just four days off sick.'

'Marvellous.'

'I started the afternoon singing group, the minibus trips to Brent Cross, I helped with the Christmas and Easter parties, the painting classes and all that.'

'How wonderful.'

The manicurist glances up from Margot's feet.

'Matron said I was the best staff member she'd ever had.'

'I can imagine.'

'Then a new one came in and it all went pear-shaped.' Gwen's face darkens. 'She took right against me, said I was getting too familiar with the residents, whatever that means. Just like that staff nurse at the Whittington. And the other one in Hackney.'

Margot absorbs this. Gwens often have a history of fall-outs. Rage-a-holics, someone at Wilhurst called them. Everything rosy until they're thwarted in their eternal mission to help. She pulls her bathrobe tighter.

'But that's all years ago.' Gwen sucks on her straw. 'I've got St Mark's now. I love knowing how much you all need me there. All the things I can do to help you, Margot.'

Margot reaches for her fruit juice. Forty-eight minutes to go.

'You don't have children, do you, Gwen?'

Gwen looks down at her hands. Margot bites her lip.

'We never could.'

'I'm so sorry to hear that.'

Gwen looks back up and shrugs.

'Between you and me, Margot, I'm glad all that, you know,' she lowers her voice, 'that side of things, is well behind me.'

'It's a blessing in disguise. There are so many other ways I can give of myself.' The chubby fingers reach out for Margot's. 'You'd understand.'

'Your husband doesn't come to church, does he?' Maybe there is no husband?

'David prefers his bowls and his computer course and his sudoku.'

The manicurist motions that she's popping outside for something.

Gwen reaches across and pats Margot's leg.

'So lovely to spend girly time together.'

Margot forces herself to stay still.

'So kind of you to arrange all this, Gwen.'

This crumb produces such a glow of gratitude, Margot has to

look away. She searches for another peace offering.

'One or two of the other ladies can be a bit full-on sometimes, can't they?'

Gwen's eyebrows angle like Tower Bridge.

'How do you mean?'

Margot clears her throat. Too late now.

'Oh, you know, just a tiny bit bossy on occasion. A little power-hungry, even.'

Gwen's grinning so hard, her chins are shivering.

'The vicar and I sometimes call them Care Bears.'

Gwen's hand rushes to her mouth.

'Don't tell anyone else, will you, Gwen?' The sticky heat in here is starting to feel oppressive. 'It's just a bit of a joke.'

Gwen smiles slowly at Margot, then reaches in again and squeezes her fingers.

'You can trust me,' she says, cheeks pink with pleasure.

'Our little secret.'

'Our little secret.'

Margot lies back, Hadley's warnings ringing out like a klaxon.

'So anyway, Margot, about the book club.'

The manicurist walks back in, waving a bottle of varnish at Margot.

'Nothing too la-de-dahdy, maybe *The Thornbirds* to start us off. Goodness, Margot, you're not going to wear that, are you?'

'Hey, careful,' snaps the manicurist as Gwen snatches the bottle out of her hand.

'*Vampish Vermilion?*'

'It's foxy,' says the manicurist. 'One of our best sellers.'

'You don't want to send out the wrong signals.'

The manicurist stares at Gwen. Margot looks down at her traitorous toenails.

'It's just a bit of nail varnish, Gwen.'

'They could get all sorts of ideas.' She looks as though someone is holding a freshly lopped durian fruit under her nose. 'When I know St Mark's is safe with you.'

The manicurist smirks and carries on attending to Margot's right foot. This entire exchange will be all over Twitter within the hour.

'By the way, Carla can squeeze in your waxing appointment early if you like,' the manicurist says.

'*Waxing?*'

'It's a,' – she clears her throat – 'sort of medical thing, Gwen.' She bites her lip. 'A bit sensitive.'

Gwen narrows her eyes. 'Don't worry, Margot.' She raises a finger to her lips. 'Your secrets are safe with me.'

Another red line crossed.

Chapter 13

Mid-March

Their feet are in perfect step, his stride a little longer than hers. Every so often, their elbows graze.

The canal path is empty, apart from the occasional cyclist or young couple pushing a buggy. The surface of the water is midnight green, velvet in the soft morning light. The spring warmth has created a canopy of bosky blossom floating above their heads. A group of mallards are snacking on the moss beneath the bridge, heads bobbing with determination. The air is scented with new beginnings. Late March already. Summer will be soon here. She closes her eyes. Be here, for now.

He's watching her, smiling.

'This is where we used to come for our early-morning run a while back.'

She turns her head away.

'You know, just me and Pluto and a handful of other loonies pounding the path at six-thirty a.m.'

'Impressive.' Her muscles relax back into position.

'Even when it was pissing it down.'

'Even more so.'

'You wouldn't say that if you'd seen us. But I loved the stillness, before the craziness of the day kicked off.'

She takes in the crosshatch of lines around his eyes, the small bump on the bridge of his nose, the freckles.

'So, anyway, Margot,' he turns to face her. 'Confession time.'

She holds her breath.

'Three favourite songs on your phone – and no porkies.'

She breathes out.

'No hymns either.'

She laughs, then hesitates.

'OK, how about "Sorry", "Amsterdam" and,' – she pauses – 'I don't know, some Ed Sheeran? Beyoncé?'

'Bit safe, Reverend.'

'And yours are all gangsta rap?'

'Naturally.'

'Oh, and "L-O-V-E" by Nat King Cole and some Aznavour. "For Me Formidable". My mother's favourite.'

'*Desert Island* book? Apart from the Bible. Obviously.'

'Obviously.' She returns the smile. '*Middlesex*.'

'Read it.'

'Tick.'

'Nice choice, Reverend. Always up for some hermaphrodite lit. OK, moving on. Beach-bum loafing or city culture break?'

'Both.'

She watches him skim a stone across the surface: one, two, three, gone. A pair of mallards carve the air overhead, wings trailing silver beads of light.

'Worst habit?'

'Apart from my workwear?'

'And your 'jokes'.'

Their eyes catch. Someone in one of the huge Georgian houses across the canal flings open the French windows to let in the day. A dog barks loudly.

Margot walks on a few paces and turns.

'This is worse than trying to get into theological college.'

'Should I take that as a compliment?'

The tentative first steps, fingers matching in a mirror. Right until the last moment this morning, she wasn't going to come.

'Are your lessons like this?'

He picks up another stone, laughing.

'My worst habit is that I'm a nosy bugger.'

'So, the inquisition's over?'

'Ask away yourself.'

Her breath catches. They walk on in silence for a few moments.

'Guess I'm not that interesting, then?'

It's her turn to laugh.

'Thing is, Margot, you're a riddle within a mystery inside an enigma, all wrapped up in a cassock.' He bats her arm. 'As Churchill would have said if he'd thought of it.'

His smile is like a challenge: come out and live your life.

They stop for lunch at the Moon and Stars in Maida Vale. Time is both racing and in suspension, like trails of incense in a draughty chapel.

'What did your parents think?'

She watches an elderly man cycle slowly past the window. Felix touches her wrist lightly.

'Sorry, tell me to piss off and mind my own business any time. I warned you I was a nosy bugger.'

'You did.'

She continues folding the crisp packet into ever-decreasing squares.

'And, actually, while the priest bit is totally gripping, the thing I'm most interested in is all the other parts.'

She considers this. In fact, when was the last time anyone made the distinction?

'All me, I'm afraid, all mashed together like a lump of multicoloured plasticine that's gone that yucky trench-colour green.'

The couple next to them have spent the past twenty minutes feeding peanuts to their Border terrier, which probably explains its wind problem. One of the nuts now rolls across the carpet and the dog begins a forensic examination of Felix's jeans.

'Sorry, mate,' says the man, pulling the dog back. 'Caesar's gone a bit crazy. You and the missus got a dog at home?'

'Yup,' says Felix, before wheeling back round to look at her, appalled.

'Where were we?' she asks brightly.

He smiles with relief.

'Well, I guess, I'd love to hear, you know, how – or, rather, why – someone like you ends up in the Church as a priest.'

'Where did it all go wrong, you mean?'

He doesn't laugh this time.

'If you don't mind telling.'

So she does. Guardedly at first, but then, as they're back on the canal walking past the houseboats with the pocket allotments, decks gleaming in the sunlight, warm tarmac smelling of recent rain, she allows the story to take hold.

She can't remember the last time she spoke to someone outside of the safety cordon of the Church like this. She feels like a piece of Sylko unspooling, springing out in exuberant figures of eight.

The gallery is airy, white and minimalist. You could be in an evangelical church, except that it's quiet. They've just stumbled on it at the back of Paddington Basin, all part of the day's hoard of surprises.

The large twisting sculpture in front of them appears to be made of recycled mudguards.

'Is it a yes from you?' asks Felix.

She waves her thumb up, down and up again.

'I basically spend half my life with Bach, Milton and Cranmer. Something like this is like sucking on sorbet after a serving of hollandaise sauce.'

'I get that.'

'It's funny.' She tips her head. You think you have a handhold on what the artist is trying to do, then the meaning seems to suddenly shift and you have to do a three-point turn.'

'Looks like a pile of rusty bike parts to me.'

She elbows him lightly in the ribs.

'But then I'm just a heathen.'

She's aware it was meant to be feather-light, but the words acquired a gravity in transit. He coughs.

'I think I saw a café in here somewhere?'

'Who – what – do you think of when you think of God?'

Thirty minutes of normal banter and yet, inevitably, they're right back here. She hesitates. Every time she gets this question, and she hears it often, she feels the need to try and coin the answer anew.

'OK,' she says slowly. 'Well, I guess God is a person I feel drawn towards.' She tips some sugar granules into her cup. 'And when I think of Him, Her, It, even, I think of compassion and love, endless love.'

'Uh-huh.'

'What I don't think of is some guy in a white robe with a Hollywood beard.'

Felix runs his finger over the bowl of his teaspoon.

'I have to tell you, Margot, and I guess this won't come as a big fat surprise, I just can't believe in the things you do.'

'I've changed one of my top three music choices from Coldplay to Mumford and Sons.'

He reaches across for her hand. 'Does it matter?'

The implications of that question are unanswerable.

His fingers interlace with hers. She has an impulse to pull away, but he holds her hand steady.

'Don't panic, Felix, I'm not on a flirt-to-convert operation.'

'Is that a thing?'

Their laughter releases the tension slightly.

'I know how important it is to you.' He rolls his eyes at himself. 'I mean, obviously.'

There's an artwork on the shelf next to her constructed out of bubble wrap and paper clips. The halogen lights overhead have turned the tiny transparent spheres into phosphorescent baubles, glow-worms blinking out an indecipherable message.

'We haven't talked about you and your wife.'

He looks down.

'Do you really want to?'

Five hours together. It's been all around them like a cloud of asbestos spores. She knows about the quiet but contented childhood in County Durham; the older, married, GP sister in Coventry; the brief disastrous stint as a cub reporter on the *Consett Gazette*; the buttock-clenching fear of flying; the passion for cooking and early-period Rolling Stones.

But not one word about this.

It's tempting to grab a handful of the tiny plastic bubbles and crush them in the ball of her fist.

'It's totally over, Margot.'

She waits.

'But, you know, civilised, thank God.' He clears his throat. 'And just until all the legal stuff is sorted, we're both in the same house. That's it, to be honest.'

'How long?'

He looks down.

'Five and a half years.'

'Any children?'

'What, you think I wouldn't have mentioned them?'

She leans back from the table.

'Sorry,' he says, 'I'm really sorry, Margot. I just know how all this looks. And you know, it's not how it looks.'

She should never have come.

'Do you still love her?'

He breathes out slowly.

'Do you ever stop loving someone if you've once really loved them?' He looks up. 'Isn't that what love's all about?'

She focuses on the tiny balls of light.

'We were both just going through the motions by the end. No heirloom smashing or revenge attacks on Facebook or any of that.' His voice sounds tight. 'And no one else either.'

'Oh God, I'm so sorry.'

Felix stares at her.

Clarissa.

She swipes to answer by mistake.

'Hey, M, what are you up to?'

'Can I call you back a bit later?'

Felix motions asking if he should leave. She shakes her head.

'You're going to be so made up about the next guy. His name's—'

'Can't talk now. I'll call you.'

Margot throws her phone into her bag.

'I'm so sorry.'

'Duty calling?' There's a catch in his voice.

She shakes her head. Clarissa won't be happy. She'll call her later, say it was an emergency. Clarissa likes to be chief choreographer at all times.

There's still a faint line on Felix's ring finger where the band used to be.

'Sure you don't want to call back?'

'It'll keep. What we were saying?'

He laughs lightly.

'I think I was asking for absolution.'

'To err is human, to forgive, Divine.'

'Right'

'No one's perfect.'

'Even priests?' he smiles.

'If only you knew.'

'"Thou art all fair, there is no spot in thee."'

She laughs, weightless again.

'*Song of Solomon?*'

'Full marks.'

'How do you know that?'

'How is a barbarian like me able to quote from the Bible?' he asks. 'You ain't heard nothing. "The Lord delights in those who fear Him, who put their faith in His unfailing love."'

'Wow.'

'So here's my dirty secret. My mum was a regular at the local Congregational Church in Consett. Still is, in fact. Not my dad, mind. We had framed samplers up on the mantelpiece, passed down from my great-grandmother.'

'You're kidding.'

'The church was a community of miners' families and the preacher was one of those real fire-and-brimstone types. During the strikes, I remember the church rolling up its sleeves and getting stuck in, organising food banks, that kind of thing. That was very cool.'

They're walking back towards the canal, the sky now a bruised mulberry.

'Not all bad, then?'

'Don't get me wrong, I'm not some anti-religion nutter.'

'Could have fooled me.'

She giggles at the look on his face.

'No, no, don't get me wrong. I love the music, the art and architecture, the spectacle, all that sort of high-end stuff.'

'The pretty bits, in other words.'

He smiles.

'Not just that. Also the Church's total lack of squeamishness in helping those people most of us would cross the road to avoid.'

'I've had someone spit at me on the bus.'

'Christ.'

'They used to roast priests on the spit. I got off lucky.'

He lays his arm around her shoulder. She doesn't pull away.

'So you're not quite the hopeless case you make out?'

He sighs.

'I'm no fan of celebrity God-bashers. I guess I just feel that science has taken care of most of the hardest questions for us. The fundamental questions as to who we are, why we're here and all the rest of it.'

'The two can co-exist.'

'Somehow, I just can't see that we need to have a God, any God, lighting the blue touchpaper.'

He lifts his arm and turns to face her.

'I just haven't heard what you've heard, Margot.'

She nods and walks ahead in silence, competing narratives shadow-boxing inside her head.

We're not responsible for another's soul. Unless you're a curate, in which case isn't that the whole point?

God wants you to be happy and fulfilled, to lead a life of joy.

He's still married.

Why is she here?

'Does that make me untouchable?' Felix asks, quietly.

She carries on walking a few steps, then stops and retraces them.

His face is a question mark.

She closes her eyes, then guides his face down until his lips are touching hers.

Everything's subtly different. The darkened shops by Highbury Corner, the flashing street signs, the rubbish bins stuffed full of polystyrene cartons, the chewing-gum mosaic on the pavement; everything has acquired a sheen of possibility. The street sweeper who catches her eye and smiles. The huddle of shaven-heads just turfed out of the pub. That woman in the striped tracksuit emerging from the twenty-four-hour store, plastic bag swinging on her arm. They all feel it too.

The smell of his aftershave, coriander and lime, clings to her in confirmation.

She feels burnished with happiness.

The house is sunk in darkness when she turns up on the doorstep, even though it's not that late. She closes the door with a quiet click behind her. Happiness must be radiating off her. The last thing she needs, on any level, is Cyd slouched against the wall, taking notes.

She's halfway to her room when she remembers that she's run out of toothpaste. Nathan's bound to have some in the cabinet upstairs. She's reached the landing when she stops. There's a low whimpering sound coming from Sam's room. She pulls the door ajar and waits until her eyes have adjusted to the low glow of the night light. He's on his knees next to the bed, hands together, his head bent, his shoulders shaking.

Sam suddenly realises she's there and jumps back under the covers.

'Sammy? Are you OK?'

His face is shut. She pulls him towards her, his small body shuddering against hers.

'What's happened, Sam?' She wipes the damp hair from his forehead.

'Were you praying just now?'

He turns his head away.

'You don't have to tell me.'

She strokes his back with the flat of her hand.

'Doesn't work,' he says, swiping his fingers under his nose, leaving a glistening slick across his cheek.

'Well, it still might, you know.'

He starts crying harder.

'Were you praying about your mum, Sammy?'

The pillow is wet where he's been lying.

'Praying's stupid.'

She pulls him closer against her, stroking his hair.

'The thing is, Sammy, it's not like a vending machine. You don't just pop a coin in and out pops your bag of Maltesers. Sometimes our prayers aren't answered in the way we want or expect them to be. It's a bit more complicated than that. But that doesn't mean no one's listening or that they won't be answered, ever.'

He's wearing the Spurs pyjamas he got for his birthday.

'It's like when you're doing one of your jigsaws. You hold up one or two pieces and you have no idea how the whole thing will fit together. Then everything starts to slot in place and, yay, it's done, one complete team photo.'

He finally looks at her.

'Praying can change our lives, Sammy. Believe me, I know, I've seen it happen. Everything will be healed one day.'

'Mum's not coming back, is she?'

Margot buries her face in his freshly washed hair.

'I don't know,' she mutters.

'See?'

'God knows that we get angry and frustrated at what happens to us sometimes, but He is with us, on our team, nevertheless, Sam. Tell you what, how about you and I pray together that everything will work out in the end?'

There's a sudden sound by the door. But it's not Cyd leaning against the doorpost.

'What's up, Sam-Sam?'

Nathan flicks on the light by the bookcase and rubs his eyes. He's wearing a baggy t-shirt and shorts. Margot gives Sam a squeeze and tucks the duvet in around him.

'Just having a bit of trouble getting to sleep,' she says. 'Ready to drop off now, I think, aren't you, Sam?'

He wouldn't want her to say anything. She remembers those

pockets of secrecy, your own personal hope bank.

Nathan touches her elbow as she slips out onto the landing.

'Thanks, Margot.'

She smiles and walks down the stairs, catching the ghost of her reflection. Thought you could escape yourself? Yet, today, somehow, she has. The light pressure of his lips, his fingers running through her hair, cupping her chin. Leaning into him under the lamplight.

She falls backwards onto her bed, singing inside.

No one must know. She pulls herself back upright.

God knows.

Almighty God, to whom all hearts are open, all desires known and from whom no secrets are hidden. Cleanse the thoughts of our hearts, by the inspiration of Your Holy Spirit, that we may perfectly love you and worthily magnify Your Holy name.

She feels a shiver of uncertainty. What exactly has she started here?

She likes back down and closes her eyes.

Part III

Unravelling Threads

Chapter 14

Late March

Surely three months' supply of Kool Gang refreshments can't add up to such a hefty hit to the St Mark's current account? Tommy the verger doesn't know either, and holds the statement up to the window as though that will shed some light.

'Maybe we should drop the chocolate biscuits and just serve plain ones, Margot?' he asks.

It's exactly this kind of detail that Felix loves. The daily nap and weave of her job, just as much as the life or death issues they're all dealing with. Storing up these tiny nuggets to pass on to him all adds to the sense of plenty she's had these past few weeks. Loneliness has been lifted from her life like a veil.

They've only been able to see each other a few times: a couple of snatched meals a few bus stops away, a covert trip over to the cinema at the other end of the Victoria line. Yet, already, even on those few showings, it somehow feels like this is someone who has reached in and found the heart of her. The speed of it winds her sometimes. Stops her in her tracks, But then she reminds herself that the situation they're in inevitably ramps up the intensity.

'I think there'd be a riot if we did that, Tommy.'

The vestry door slams open, making them both jump. Jeremy

ignores them as he walks past straight through into the hall. Tommy's eyebrows shoot up.

Margot's stomach knots. She's started carrying a notebook to stay on top of it all, but still forgot to put in that call a few days ago to the bishop's office about the date for the confirmation ceremony. Maybe someone's complained?

Or perhaps the vicar's being pestered again by some parent clamouring for him to green-light their child into the Church school? Back in January this was happening at the rate of five requests a week.

Maybe she forgot to turn off the immersion heater after lunch yesterday? It has to be something she's done.

By mid morning, she can't stand it any longer.

She pushes open the door to the small back office.

'Jeremy? Is everything OK?'

He looks up at her and pushes his glasses up his forehead.

'I'm sorry about that oversight with the Bishop's office.'

'Sanctimonious bastard.'

'Sorry?'

'Always was an uptight bugger.'

She stares at him.

'Martin Kennedy,' Jeremy says. 'Priest in charge at St Stephen's, Finsbury. He's been there over thirty years. Lifetime member of the smells and bells brigade.'

He nibbles at a hangnail.

'The whole place is so high, it makes you wonder, is the Pope really a Catholic?'

She knows better than to smile.

'You must know all about the theology of taint, Margot?'

She sinks back against the filing cabinet, dislodging a pile of old service sheets destined for the reincarnation bin.

'Of course,' she whispers, shivering. A.k.a shunning or disfellowshipping. Practised by people – men mostly, but not always – who avoid all contact with women priests and any bishop transgressive enough to ordain one. Spiritual contamination is how they see it: all other sacramental acts poisoned by the bishop's willingness to sanctify the unclean.

'I was by the post office on Highbury Corner and he sprinted across three lanes of fast-moving traffic to avoid me. Saw me, looked away, looked back and scuttled over Holloway Road between a taxi and a number thirty-eight bus as fast as his scrawny legs could carry him. Can you believe it? I shouted over to give him the benefit of the doubt, but there was no doubt, spiritual or otherwise. It was a bloody blackballing.'

Her head drops.

'Because of me.'

He gives a weary shrug, the battle fatigue of someone who understands how steep the gradient is.

She's grateful on a daily basis for the risk he's taken on her. But the idea of him being cold-shouldered on Highbury Corner at 10 a.m. on a Wednesday by a fellow man of God? This is N5 in 2017, not the climactic scene in a Russian classic.

Unease bears down on her like a soggy tarpaulin as she heads out later on some parish errands. Her situation would be marked 'fragile, handle with great care', even if she were the perfect curate. Two and half months off her priesting, she still makes so many mistakes. And now, exploding into her life like a forbidden firework, Felix.

She glances up at the flamboyant performance of the magnolia tree above her head and offers a silent prayer for help.

Halfway back to St Mark's, she decides to take a detour. She needs to see for herself.

Stepping out of the sunshine into the glutinous gloom feels like crossing into enemy territory. She pulls off her collar quickly and throws her cardigan over her shoulders.

St Stephen's is empty apart from a pair of elderly women sitting in the front row. She stands waiting for her eyes to adjust to the dark interior. Italianate statues dressed in copes. Roman missals stacked up by the front door. Pinned-up photos of the parish priests in lace and red pompommed birettas, Latin chasubles over their cottas during last year's solemn procession of the Blessed Sacrament, rose petals scattered in their path. Which one is Kennedy, she wonders, inspecting the pictures closely.

She moves forwards towards the altar. Most non-Church people walking in here would assume it was Roman Catholic, rather than huddled at the very highest Anglo-Catholic end of the Church of England's capacious tent. As she inhales the traces of incense, Margot wonders whether she's in fact misunderstood the whole issue. Maybe the group most under attack isn't so much the women wanting to become priests, but this throwback world trying to buttress itself against the insistent tide of modernity? The blustering baroque interior in here, a final curlicued stand against the horror of that tide of oestrogen.

She sits down at the end of the nearest pew and looks up at the light filtering in from the windows at the top. Nevertheless, there's a sense of peace in here you can almost taste. She closes her eyes for a moment, then stands and walks back towards the front door. There's a large laminated notice propped up on a chair that she hadn't noticed earlier.

St Stephen's is proud to be part of the Forward in Faith movement.

She scans down the page.

Worldwide association of Anglicans unable in conscience to accept the ordination of women as priests or bishops ... practice contrary to the scriptures ... a schismatic act ... we are bound to repudiate ... wilfully placed a new and serious obstacle ... it's often said we must be sexists and misogynists.

'Hi there.'

A young priest comes over, head slightly dipped. Early twenties, prominent cheekbones, moppy black curls; a choirboy in man's clothing. Wilhurst was full of them, primed to soak up the attention of female congregants of all ages and probably some of the male ones as well. Just flirtatious enough to keep all persuasions guessing.

'Can I help with anything?' he asks. She recognises the professional smile.

She points to the notice next to her.

'Pretty punchy stuff.'

His smile stays in place.

'It all seems a bit hostile speaking as a – you know – woman.'

The smile wobbles slightly. He crosses his arms across the lacy cotta.

'Well.' He clears his throat, Adam's apple bobbing. She wonders whether he's got – has ever had – a girlfriend, then recoils from her own hypocrisy.

'It's very uncompromising.'

'We're not setting out to offend anyone,' he answers, voice rising. 'It's a matter of biblical teaching. You know, there in black and white.' He smiles, not quite apologetically.

'Offence is in the eye of the beholder, I guess,' she answers, then coughs. She doesn't want to blow her cover.

A delicate flush stains his cheeks. It's like kicking a puppy.

'We're following two thousand years of precedent.' He bites his bottom lip. 'But of course women play a huge within our church in all kinds of different ways.'

'Well, that's a blessing.'

He holds out his hand.

'Reverend Spence. I'm the curate here. Nice to meet you.'

'Oh.'

She scans his face. Yes, it's there.

'Everything ok?'

'Yeah, yeah, sorry, I just, oh it's already half twelve. I need to dash.'

She nods at him and steps outside.

Fabian's nephew. Serving his title in one of the most hardline churches in the diocese. And still waiting, no doubt, to pounce on the job at St Mark's.

His name's Mitchell, M. Chartered Accountant but we won't hold that against him. You're meeting in swanky bar in St Pancras. Perfect 4 Eurostar if mad with lust and need 2 head 2 Paris.

Clarissa is approaching this whole Soulmates pantomime with the focus of an oligarch trying to buy a premiership team. She wouldn't be surprised if she's taken out a bet with Paddy Power that she can get Margot hitched up by Easter. Margot swallows. Who knows how her time with Felix might play out? Yet spending an evening with another Soulmate would be like eating in a greasy spoon after experiencing a Michelin star.

The dishonesty of all this is cancerous. Margot knows that Clarissa is concerned for her emotional well-being. Yet she can't tell her about Felix, not yet. The risks she's taking are acute enough already. Clarissa and discretion do not exactly go together.

As for opening to Felix about Soulmates. Tell him she has a live profile up there as Mary, designed to snare as many men into her orbit as possible? After she's been so insistent on secrecy every time she's seen him?

Somehow, she must unravel all this.

Can't wait until Friday, Gogo. How do you fancy meeting up with a couple of my mates first for a drink? Incognito, naturally. F xxx
Let's keep it to the two of us. I'm too selfish to share you just yet ... M xoxoxo
Love it when you get possessive ;-) F xxx

The inevitable few are still milling around after the family service, drawing deep on St Mark's hospitality, though she knows that for most of this group of stragglers, there's no one waiting for them at home. Jeremy's 'no chucking out' rule is inviolable.

'Margot, I need to speak to you.'

She glances up at Fabian, braced. His hair has been lopped a couple of inches, a making him look gaunter, shorter-fused. Even more like his nephew. A cloud passes over the sun through the clerestory glass.

'In private, if you don't mind.'

She nods down at the pile of papers she's cradling.

'I'm just going to the office.'

'Somewhere else.'

He checks over his shoulder. There's something uncharacteristically coiled about him.

She leads the way through to the hall, past the robes cupboard and the boxes storing all the dusty donations for the nursery. The Kool Gang finished over an hour ago, but the scent of cherry bubblegum still lingers. Discarded shards of coloured paper carpet the floor. One of the Care Bears out there flirting with the vicar will come in here later and snatch up the dustpan, muttering. Margot needs to get to it first.

She places her papers down on one of the glue-streaked tables and sits down.

'This is for the Lenten talks,' she says, gesturing at the pile. 'We had eight last Thursday which, given there was an Arsenal home game and some cliffhanger on *Coronation Street*, wasn't bad.'

Why does Fabian always have this Tourette's effect on her? She'd hate to be a junior assistant in one of his departments. That's probably how he sees her: Margot, the office temp.

He pulls a chair up close and leans in.

'This whole kitchen thing is exploding.'

She frowns.

'Pamela wants to put in some crappy budget solution which, I can tell you, is totally out of the question.'

The aftershave is rich and musky. A patch of grey chest hair is visible below the satin collar.

'She's already been out to some retail park near Harlow.' A

muscle in his cheek flickers. 'It's got to be stopped.'

Margot can't fathom this anger.

'You're an intelligent girl, Margot.' He stops, reconsidering. 'You and I are on the same page, anyway. Why chuck money away on some trashy chipboard we'll have to replace in two years? We need to think much bigger and better. Much more upmarket. This is an opportunity for St Mark's to—'

The door at the far end of the hall bangs open and one of the mothers rushes forwards, dragging her toddler.

'Hurry up, Connor. I told you to tell me as soon as you needed to wee.'

'Hopeless,' snarls Fabian. 'We can't talk tactics here.'

They're not planning an M & A deal between two FTSE 100 giants. Watery sunlight falls on the paint-encrusted aprons on the pegs opposite. Why does he care so much about all this? Surely it's small change to a businessman of his reach?

'You and I should meet for a drink one evening,' he says. ' In the meantime, I'll have a quiet word with Jeremy and tell him not to agree any purchasing decisions. He'll not go against me.'

He's right on that.

'Evenings are a bit difficult for me, Fabian,' Margot says.

'Oh?' He leans back, interested.

'I mean,' Margot hesitates, 'You know, all the PCC and other meetings and the Lent talks and everything.'

'Hmmm.' He nods, eyeing her carefully. 'I know you'll find a time. I'm relying on your support.' He reaches out his hand and she takes it reluctantly.

'I think we understand each other, no?'

She gives a neutral smile.

'You're looking very well, by the way. Glowing in fact. Ministry agrees with you.'

There's a bang and Connor hurtles back through the hall, scattering chairs like a one-child destruction squad. Fabian stands, rests his eyes on her a second too long, and walks back towards the vestry.

She shudders. She's not the first woman to have to deal with a workplace letch. But Fabian is the Lionel Messi of St Mark's, the two grand-a-week star striker who must be kept sweet at all costs. That's how Jeremy sees him. A razor-sharp operator amidst a sea of geriatric good intentions.

But, then, a heavy hand with the Aramis and a display of greying chest hair do not a case of sexual harassment make. Even that time when his fingers brushed slowly against hers when she handed him the chalice. Not everyone wants to sleep with her. She flushes and buries the thought.

Then she remembers Arthur's warning.

She's lying in bed a few days later, reliving the previous evening with Felix – their slow meander past the bars and boutiques of Soho, the glasses of fino sitting on stools in the tiny tapas place, just another young couple absorbed in each other's account of their day – when there's a knock on her door.

'Sorry to disturb you, Margot.' Nathan looks sheepish. 'You weren't praying, were you?'

One day, she must ask him why he always assumes she's doing – or has just been doing – something religious.

'I just wanted to let you know that we'll be away next weekend, from Friday until Sunday night.'

Her breath quickens.

'Disneyland Paris. A couple of the boys' friends went at half term and you know how that goes. Where one wallet leads, we all must follow. So much for my booze-free Lent. I'll need plenty of their house rouge to get me through it.'

'All of you?'

She almost shouts it, her heart one peg away from taking flight.

'Cyd wasn't ecstatic at the prospect, you won't be surprised to hear, so she's staying over with one of her school friends for the weekend. Gives you a bit of peace and quiet for a change.'

She waits until he's safely closed the door behind him before she leaps off the bed, whirling around the tiny room in excitement.

Two night and two days. She isn't even on the rota for either of the morning services, for the first time in months.

Hey guess what? xxxxx

Chapter 15

Early April

'Hey there, Margot, just checking in again. Call me when you have a moment, OK? Would be good to catch up with you.'

The fifth missed call from Hadley.

Margot has deleted all the messages one by one. She'll call her back soon. Very soon. Fill her in on all of it.

She stares down at the text. What was it Hadley said? *We don't want you shipwrecked on this most important of journeys.* Some days, there are so many rocks spiking the path ahead, the horizon is littered with them like dragons' teeth.

Her finger hesitates above Hadley's number. It's late afternoon. She'll be tied up with college chaplaincy duties, or possibly just setting off to evensong right at this moment.

She'll leave a message.

And after next weekend, she'll make that call.

Vic-i-leaks: Scenes from Parish Life, 10 April 2017

The Vic's mad for me to do some more evening talks in the run up to Ascension. Says he doesn't want my brain turning to porridge. A bit late for that, sadly. When I get home in the evenings, all I'm good for is a pot of Ben & Jerry's and a copy of Heat. *The Vicar says he'll even throw in a couple of bottles of his best sherry to get people through the door. But as I said, why waste it on people whose taste buds are so dodgy, they wouldn't know La Gitana Manzanilla from bat's piss? We're in Norf London, not Belgravia.*

Margot stares at the screen for so long her eyes start to water.

The joke's over.

'This way, Madame.'

The accent sounds fake. The fleur-de-lys interior definitely is. *And you're the fakest thing of all*, she thinks, catching her reflection in the ceiling.

That must be him, over in the corner. Turning the menu over in his hands, probably wondering why they're meeting somewhere where the cocktails cost the price of a main course in Pizza Express. He doesn't know Clarissa, though.

He looks like a poster boy for normal with his plain blue shirt and jeans and slicked-back hair. He doesn't look much like an accountant, whatever they look like. What does a priest look like?

She moves forwards, stomach tensing.

Mitchell waits until the cocktail waiter has left.

'I always think it's best to get the formal stuff over with first.'

What is he? Some sort of Soulmates frequent flyer?

'Jobs, education, that kind of thing.'

Straight to the jugular.

'Your profile was a bit of a tease, Mary.'

All of a sudden she's lost the will to dissemble, even for the sake of her friendship with Clarissa. She glances at her watch. She's got food shopping to do for the weekend.

Mitchell scoops up a handful of knobbly green crackers.

'So what is it you do, exactly, Mary?'

'Why don't we talk about something else? Britain cutting itself off from the rest of Europe, for example?'

She at least owes it to Clarissa to stay half an hour.

He gives her an odd smile.

'Know what, you don't have to tell me if you don't want to.'

She's taken aback by the change of gear. He finishes his crackers and reaches over for some more.

'I googled you.'

'You did what?

'Cut and pasted your photo and up popped some graduation shot.'

'How enterprising.'

'Girl priest. Now that is a turn-on.'

She's back through the fleur-de-lys and onto on the pavement in seconds, praying so hard that he won't post anything on Twitter, she can barely breathe.

'And?'

Clarissa is very the last person Margot wants to speak to right now. She shoves her trolley past the chilled cabinets, picking up one juice carton after another in a haze of indecision.

'Not my type.'

'He looked really promising.'

'He turned out to be a creep with a thing about women priests.'

'So what was the problem?'

'It could have been really bad for me. You know that.'

She feels nauseous even now at the thought.

'Relax. He'll just cruise on to the next prospect. It's all a game, this online stuff.'

'For you.'

'I take it you do want to meet a man at some point?'

Margot takes the expensive muesli out of her trolley and reaches instead for a couple of jars of French jam.

'And on that note, ciao, for now.'

She drops her phone into her bag and shoves the trolley onwards. Whenever she does tell her, it's going to be ugly.

She stops by the shower gels.

'Mmm, those jams look tasty, Margot.' She whips round. Gwen is scrutinising her basket. 'Bit pricey though, aren't they?'

'Do you usually shop here?' Margot asks, straining to keep her voice level as she hurries towards the till. She chose this place because it was so far off the St Mark's radar.

'Of course not.' Gwen smiles. 'I saw you through the window when I was crossing the road. Several of the ladies have been asking about the book club. I was thinking you and I could sit down next Saturday afternoon when David's out at a bowls match in Golders Green.'

'Bag?' asks the guy behind the counter, pouching gum inside his cheek.

'No,' Margot snaps to Gwen.

'Suit yourself,' the assistant shrugs. 'It's only five pence, love.'

'No, sorry, I mean, yes, please.' She breathes in and turns back to Gwen. 'I'm sorry, I can't do that Saturday, Gwen.'

'Oh, but I've told the ladies and you had nothing pencilled in your diary in the office so I assumed——'

'Would you mind actually not doing that?'

The assistant looks up at her, blowing out his cheeks.

'Doing what?' he asks.

Gwen is frowning.

'The previous curate was very happy for me to help organise his schedule.' She watches Margot unloading the items in her basket. 'I thought we should get on with it. Easter's almost here.'

'Tariq, can you come and take this tag off for us?' The assistant holds up the bottle Margot had tried to hide beneath the leeks and napkins.

Gwen's mouth falls open.

'Ok, so we'll check the diary,' scrambles Margot.

'I'll talk to you about it at St Mark's.' She sniffs. 'You seem a bit preoccupied.'

'Wait, Gwen, I'll take a look now,' she calls, but Gwen has

already waddled through the automatic doors, head rigid, carrier bags banging into her side.

Gravity is suspended, the normal business of life and all its baggage. She pushes all thoughts of St Mark's to the fringes of her mind, as they stroll around Sir John Soane's Museum and its eclectic displays, everything propelling them towards tonight.

It's late evening by the time they reach Highbury Corner. Margot glances around her, as they leave the tube. It's dark enough to be safe, but her throat is still constricted, every sense alert.

Felix glances at her, and slips his arm around her like a protective band.

She's aware she should savour each second of this walk across the Fields in the fragrant, still warm air. She's aware of every inch of her skin, his fingers warm in hers.

They're crossing over Aberdeen Avenue, a couple of blocks from home, when something smashes into her consciousness. Shouts, screams, an aggressive thumping bass. A scrum of teenagers is crowding the pavement and into the road further ahead of them, forcing cars to slalom left and right. She gasps, as she and Felix move closer. The Armstrong house. Her house. Every window flung open, electronic beats ripping gashes into the night.

'Gogo?'

A pulse is drumming in her temple.

'What's up?'

She's barely aware of him next to her.

'What's up? Why have we stopped?'

There are even more of them spilling out onto the pavement now.

'What, not that lot?' He snorts. 'Just a load of kids messing around. Don't worry, we'll walk straight on past them.' He threads his arm through hers. 'Half of them are probably from Highbury High, God help me.'

Blood is rushing from her head.

Felix starts to guide her forwards but she resists.

'We can't. Not now.'

He's very still next to her.

'I don't understand what's going on.'

'I'm so sorry.'

'Come on, let's just keep walking. It's not far now, right?'

'No,' she snaps.

He drops his hands and takes a step back.

'So are you going to tell me, or what?'

She covers her face with her hands.

'I live there.'

'What do you mean?'

'That's where I'm lodging. It's,' she hesitates again, 'it's the Armstrongs' house.'

'Sorry, I have no idea what you're talking about.'

'Cyd Armstrong's family.' Her eyes are stinging.

He blows out hard.

'Shit, wow. You kept that one quiet.'

'I'm sorry.' Her voice starts to break.

He turns her around to face him, cups her chin in his hand.

'But you're still entitled to a private life.'

A straggle of teenagers starts to walk down the pavement towards them.

'You need to go, Felix. Now. Quickly.'

She pushes his shoulder hard.

'Hey, hey, slow down.' He rubs his hand across his forehead. 'I don't get why you didn't tell me any of this before. I mean, wouldn't that have been easier? But, look, if you'd rather, come back to my place instead. I think we can make that work.'

'Hurry up. *Please*, Felix.'

Something smashes on the pavement up ahead, followed by barks of laughter.

'No, wait, Margot, surely we can sort this? And I can't just dump you here.' He reaches for her, but she sidesteps him and races up the pavement towards the house. She throws one quick glance back when she gets to the gate, but he's gone.

None of them takes the slightest notice as she walks through the open front door. The hallway reeks of alcohol, cheap perfume, cigarettes and weed. Even in this darkness, she can make out a solid mass of bodies all around her. Virtually every girl seems to have masses of dark hair down her back. Every single one could be Cyd.

There must be sixty or seventy of them. Who knows how many upstairs? A couple of boys are lolling against the wall next to the coat rack. She recognises them from that day in the classroom. The one on the right looks as though he's about to pass out.

'Where's Cyd?'

They squint at her.

She pushes further into the crowd.

'Know where I can find Cyd?'

The boy and girl next to her eventually pull away from each other and stare at her.

Margot shoulders her way along the corridor towards the kitchen. Every inch of space looks trashed. One of the curtains in the study is hanging off its rail. Stubs litter the floor. A half-moon of pizza crust dangles from the crook of a table lamp. There's a sticky patch of congealed vomit outside the cloakroom. She finally gets into the kitchen where half-a-dozen empty bottles are floating in the sink like discarded battleships. There's a slick of something across the tiles that could be anything. A couple of girls to her right are attempting to make a smoothie in the coffee machine. Josh's Superman drawing on the fridge now has a penis added to it.

Cyd isn't in here.

She shoves her way back out into the hall, chucking rubbish into a black bag. The frame of one of Nathan's pictures is smashed.

There seems to be even more of them out here than a moment

ago. Then, all of a sudden, she's aware of a change in atmosphere. Two voices have risen above the welter of noise, one male, the other a woman's, shrill but authoritative. The bodies in the corridor start peeling away on either side and she gasps as she sees a pair of police officers striding towards her.

The man spots Margot and comes up to her. She's briefly distracted by the ruddy cheeks and auburn sideburns, trying to place where she's seen him before.

'You in charge here, madam?'

'Not really.'

At least she's not in her collar. He glances at the rubber gloves and the bin bag.

'You live here?'

She nods.

'You are, then. We've had eight complaints in the last half an hour. I've just hauled about forty in from the pavement.'

'Is this alcohol?' asks the vole of a policewoman by his side, holding up a large bottle of vodka.

'I've only just got here myself.' A howl is welling up inside her.

'You are aware that serious criminal damage may well have been committed on other residents' property. They were like a pack of wild dogs out there.'

'Her father's away,' replies Margot, hearing her own sullenness. 'I'm the lodger.'

'We're not concerned with the domestic arrangements, madam. Send them all packing now or there'll be trouble.'

She watches them moving back up the corridor, heads shaking at the debauchery.

Halfway up the stairs, she runs into Cyd. She's two steps higher than Margot. the boyfriend at her side. He takes a long drag from his joint, eyeing Margot coolly.

'I thought you were staying over at your friend's place?'

It's the first thing that comes into her head.

'Well, I'm not.'

'OK, so you need to tell your friends to head off now. The police said that if—'

'Maybe you're the one who needs to head off.'

The boyfriend takes a step down towards Margot.

There's a sudden hush around them.

'We don't want the police to come back, do we?' she says.

'Do we?' mimics Cyd.

'Cyd, seriously, everyone's got to leave now.'

'You're just the lodger.'

'What about your dad?'

'What about him?'

Sniggers break out around them.

The boyfriend traces a finger down Cyd's neck.

The intimacy of that gesture sends Margot over the edge.

'Everyone needs to get the hell out of here right NOW.'

Her cheeks are burning. She turns away and closes her eyes to steady herself, but when she opens them again, an ant-trickle has started to move towards the front door.

'There's a lot of food in the fridge for one frigid curate,' Cyd says, pushing past, the boyfriend cackling as he wraps himself around her.

It's almost 3 a.m. before she finally falls into bed. Four hours spent rubbing wine stains from the sofa, vacuuming up crisps and ash, picking out crumbs from Nathan's speakers, trudging out bags to the bins.

She turns over to the face the wall, lead in her veins. The worst thing entering the house tonight wasn't the drugs or the suction-packed bodies or the lipstick-scrawled message on her mirror, *No Sex Please, I'm Holy.*

The worst thing was seeing the abject loss of control. She was six years old, back in the lavender bedroom, fingering the blanket and staring at the hunched figure beneath the blankets refusing to get up and be normal like everyone else's mum. A Polaroid that refuses to fade: the curtains closed against the late-morning light, yesterday's clothes abandoned on the floor, the air stale. She was wearing her favourite dress, candy pink with the white Peter Pan collar, as though dressing up in something pretty would force them to be on their best behaviour. She knew, even then, that other homes, were not like theirs.

She stares up at the parade of shadows on the ceiling. Their first night together sabotaged, almost as if by design. She turns over yet again at the thought.

Finally, an hour or so later, just as a paler light is filtering through the curtains, she reaches for her phone and starts tapping.

I'm so sorry. It's all so complicated. Can we try again? xxx

A few seconds later, her screen flashes.

Sure you want to?

She types rapidly.

Totally. You were right. About everything. Xxx

Chapter 16

Early April

'Looking forward to your sermon today, Reverend.'

Betty. Or is it Betsy, or even Barbara? She still hasn't quite nailed them all. One of the coffee rota, for sure. She has a wide smile on her face. Margot returns it with 100 per cent interest. All allies welcome.

'It's not me this morning, actually. Roderick's turn.

'Oh.'

Margot tries not to gloat.

One of the young mothers is trying to squeeze a double buggy past. Margot steps back to give her space.

Betty or Betsy leans in and pats Margot's arm.

'Don't worry, that'll be you one day.'

Even a throwaway remark feels like a torch shone in her face.

Sal pulls a face behind her. Gwen also heard, judging by the way she's beaming over at Margot from the Kool Gang refreshments table. There's always an agenda spinning round behind those eyes. But at least Margot's somehow back in favour after that testy moment in the supermarket. Friends close, frenemies closer.

'Pity it's not you today, though,' Betty or Betsy mutters, wandering off towards her seat.

Roderick's been grumbling for ages about being relegated to the C list, Jeremy told her a couple of days ago. That'll be C for curmudgeon, crotchety and Conservative, small and large C. She'd thought about passing on some notes to him about the Hockney exhibition at the Tate, in case he maybe wanted to do anything about God as artist of the universe. But she didn't in the end. What was the point? Roderick would rather eat his own surplice than accept help from Margot.

The church is full to the brim this morning, as sometimes happens for no apparent reason. Care Bears all present and correct, the full cohort of young families, even a sprinkling of new faces to keep the vicar happy.

Jeremy is walking towards her now, looking far from pleased.

'Someone just told me the Church Mole is in today.'

She understands immediately why he looks pale. She glances up the side aisle. Roderick is already in place behind the choir, ready to process in. Should someone warn him? A negative write-up on the Pray Be Seated website can send a church's reputation into a tailspin amongst those who know and care about these things. The readership is small but vociferous.

'It'll be OK, Jeremy,' she says, unconvinced. 'We'll score well on the music and the M and S shortbread.'

There's an audible tremble in his normally jaunty baritone as he stands at the front welcoming everyone. Roderick, now next to her in the choir stalls, is serene. No point in telling him. *Que sera.* She scans the pews. It takes three seconds, tops. Mata Hari has planted herself right under the flower arrangement and is gaping around like a pigeon outside a Chinese takeaway: the Beast of Broadway in a grey-checked twinset.

Margot keeps her eyes on her all through the first hymn, the prayers of preparation and penitence, the Gloria, the Collect and the readings from the Old and New Testaments. There's a little smile each time she bites on her biro, waiting for the killer phrase.

Jeremy walks down behind the servers and takes his place for the Gospel reading. He glances back over his shoulder as Roderick shuffles to the lectern, nodding to his front-row fan club as he goes. The vicar kisses the Bible with an extra flourish at the end of the reading and replaces it on the lectern. The congregation snuffles and coughs as everyone settles back into their seats. Margot holds her breath. She can see Jeremy doing the same.

Roderick adjust the microphone towards him, then turns and gives Margot a quick, surprising smile.

'May the words of my lips and the meditations of our hearts be acceptable in your sight, our Lord and Redeemer, Amen.'

'Amen,' whispers Margot, fingers crossed beneath her robes.

'I'd like to ask you all a question,' begins Roderick. 'What's the most important job in the world? Prime minister? President of the USA? Captain of the England football team? In my opinion, none of these. Because is there really any more important job on earth than being a mother?'

Grey heads shake like a bank of birches rustling in the breeze.

Margot wonders if he knows Mothering Sunday was already weeks ago.

'As Our Lord gave us life, so we cannot give enough praise and thanks for the women who brought us into this world, who succour and nurture us, whose shoulders are always there for us to cry on, who take pride in all our achievements, no matter how small. *When I find myself in times of trouble, Mother Mary comes to me.* Paul McCartney wrote that, not me.' He looks up and catches someone's eye and actually winks. 'What greater satisfaction can there be than to give life to another human being and steer them towards their future as a happy, successful adult. You ladies have been given the greatest gift on God's earth.'

A wheezy pause, while the hankie comes out to do its business.

Margot looks out at the congregation. He's hitting the spot in spades. The biddies are putty, as are the young mums, many of whom look as though there's no one in the world they'd more like to mother right now than this cantankerous old grump with his missed-the-bus demeanour. Even Sal seems to have a tear in her eye. Traitor.

'I don't speak as a father, as most of you know. The Lord didn't choose me for that role.' He clears his throat. 'But I know that if I was female, I would glory in this precious gift you all have been given.' He smiles down as a newcomer in the third row struggles to control a trio of under-fives. 'There can be no purer way of serving God.'

On and on it goes, this encomium to the wonder of the womb. The sleepless nights, the home-baked cakes, the pushing of the little boats out on the pond until the wind catches and they sail off on a path of their own.

'My own mother, Enid Morgan, God rest her soul,' he stops, swiping his eyes with the back of his hand. 'It's been thirty-eight years since she passed on, but I've yet to find anyone who could match her toad-in-the-hole.'

Gone, the impenetrable thickets of multi-clausal prose. Gone, the cul-de-sac non sequiturs. Everyone is lapping up this touchy-feely stuff like ambrosia. What's he up to? The principal once asked them to compose a sermon without once using the letter 'I' anywhere. Roderick has done the opposite. Me, me, me.

'Motherhood, the most worthwhile and fulfilling career of them all.'

Then, all of a sudden, he's wheeled round to face her, a hundred people looking on approvingly.

'Isn't that right, Margot?'

What can she do but nod? Why stop there? Why not go the whole hog and wave a gnarled finger, quoting Thomas Aquinas, 'woman is defective and misbegotten'.

It wasn't me, me, me, after all. It was her, her, her.

One last tear-jerker about his old mum not making it to see

his ordination and then he's gathering up his spidery notes and billowing past her, surplice catching the breeze like a spinnaker.

The Mole has to give that five stars: it was a tour de force in sugar-coated venom. She long ago gave up on any hope of an entente cordiale, but this feels like a shift into very dangerous territory. After this past twenty minutes, it's just a question of when and how full-on hostilities begin.

She wouldn't have had the Armstrongs down as a Sunday-roast family, she thinks, sitting in the middle of them all later that day. Maybe it's Nathan attempting some therapeutic family bonding over the sage and onion stuffing? She wouldn't blame him for trying. She glances over at Cyd's plate, barely touched. She often finds herself sneaking a look at the inside of her forearms.

'We're watching a movie this evening, Margot,' Nathan says. 'Fancy joining us?'

Cyd's knife scrapes through her gravy. But Margot hasn't told Nathan, as Cyd knows very well. This house is fractured enough already, she decided. Yet that decision to hold her peace has put Cyd in Margot's debt and she's furious about that fact. She did it to save Cyd's skin. But that's not the only reason, a voice in Margot's head taunts insistently. Cyd saw the cache of breakfast goodies in the fridge. The champagne. Something was exchanged between them in that moment, a shift in the burden of guilt.

'What's it called again, boys? *Nanny MacDonald?*

'*McPhee,*' they both yell.

'*Returns,*' clarifies Josh.'

'What do you reckon, Margot?' asks Nathan again.

She and Felix were hoping to snatch a drink tonight. But there's a look on Nathan's face. And, in a different way, on Cyd's.

'We're going to stuff ourselves with popcorn and Cadbury's Roses.'

'Now you're talking.'

Squeezed on the sofa between the twins, with Nathan sprawling in the armchair by the fireplace and Cyd knotted into herself on the floor, Margot reflects on the mille-feuille layers of meaning within this room. A motherless family and motherless lodger watch a movie in which a stand-in mother waves her wand to make it all alright in the end. The perfect family movie, insists the box. Does the perfect family even exist?

'Sam, if you stuff in any more popcorn, you'll go pop.' She nudges him in the ribs. He rolls his eyes and reaches for another fistful. There's been a tacit bond between them since that night. She smiles to herself. The end of her first day with Felix.

Emma Thompson is peeling away another layer of prosthetic make-up after Lesson Number Four, when the phone in the kitchen rings.

'I'll go,' says Margot, standing. 'I'll make more coffee.'

'Hello?' The voice is guarded, suspicious, when she picks up.

'Hi, can I help?'

'Who is this?'

The hostility takes Margot aback.

'Margot, Margot Goodwin. Would you like—'

'You my replacement?'

Margot stares at the receiver. There's a flash of purple nail varnish and Cyd is already out of the door, phone to her ear.

Margot should walk straight back into the living room and leave them to it. Yet she stands, watching through the rain-stained window as Cyd paces up and down by the swing, head bowed under whatever weight her mother is placing there. Her heart squeezes at the sight.

An hour or so later, Cyd still hasn't reappeared, long after the boys have gone to bed and Nathan has buried himself in the Sunday supplements. Margot walks back into the kitchen and looks out. The swing resembles a gallows in the dark.

She turns and wonders what she should do. She sighs and slowly climbs the stairs to the first-floor landing. She glances back down. It's like entering a minefield without a map. She carries on climbing and stops outside the attic door, heart thumping.

'Cyd?'

There's a pale strip of light beneath the door. Margot knocks again, louder, and starts to twist the handle.

Cyd is standing by the skylight, her back to Margot. Something about her posture tells Margot she's been crying.

'Are you OK?'

She whips rounds so fast, Margot steps back in shock, knocking over something propped by the chest of drawers. It's a pair of artist's canvases. She reaches down to pick them up, but Cyd rushes forwards and snatches them out of her hand.

'Sorry, I didn't mean to—'

'Mind your own fucking business.'

Her eyelids are swollen, cheeks blotchy.

'I just wondered if you wanted to, you know, talk about anything, because you were gone so long?' She stops. 'But if you'd rather not—'

'You're like some stalker.'

Margot anchors herself by the wardrobe.

'I don't want to upset you, Cyd.'

'Or have you come here to tell me to save myself for Jesus?'

Cyd holds her eye. The threat of the moment empties Margot's lungs.

'I was just worried about you, that's all.'

'I think you're enjoying this.'

'*What?*'

Cyd takes a step closer, heat in her eyes.

'What exactly is the point of you?'

Margot digs her nails into her palms. She can't be intimidated by a fifteen-year-old.

'I just wanted to say…' She draws in more breath. 'I think I understand what you're going through right now, you know, with your mum.'

Cyd's face stills.

Laughter explodes into the room from the garden next door. Cyd pulls a scrappy tissue from her pocket and turns away.

'Just fuck off.'

Margot starts to back away towards the door.

'We've got more in common than you think, Cyd.'

'You've got to be joking.' Cyd spins round again to face her, her face contorted. 'What, your bitch of a mother ran off with the neighbour too? Yours also started a new life like you'd never even existed?'

She elbows Margot so hard as she shoves past that she falls sideways onto the bed. She listens to the footsteps clattering down and the crash of the bathroom door and covers her face with her hands. She was this close to telling her about her own mother.

She starts walking slowly back down the stairs. Jeremy has to find her somewhere else to live. She didn't sign up to being a human shield.

Nathan's switching off the lights in the hall as she approaches. He looks up, surprised.

'Everything OK?'

Bruise-coloured bags sag below his eyes.

'Totally. Just heading off to bed with my Horlicks and the *Collected Sermons of John Wesley*.'

She gives a little wave and walks on into the kitchen, his confused chuckle dying behind her.

So much pain and hurt and she is completely failing to help.

Luck has nothing to do with it. This was meant to happen. That's why it feels so good to be with you, even if our timing's crap, but hey xxxx

She keeps pressing the button so that the ghostly glow illuminates her pillow. He makes her feel like her every nerve cell has become its own LED display.

Sure you're not free til Thursday?? I'm not sure I can wait…

She swallows.

Thursday. Their real first night. Finally.

The hours between have balls and chains attached. But, equally, she doesn't want time to charge on, throwing up balls of dust. It's already April. Three months until Petertide. She doesn't feel ready to be priested. And yet she's never wanted it more.

She's not home and dry until she's kneeling at that altar with the hishop's hand resting on her head.

Lord, help me to get to the end of this year and be ready to enter Your service. I want nothing more than to serve my title intact. But I have to deserve it, don't I? You don't get there just because you've put in the hours, like some kind of reward for good attendance. Help me, please help me make it through.

Chapter 17

Mid-April

This is how burglars must feel. Chest compressed, skin scorched, ears pricked for the slightest sound, the click of a lock, the flicker of an alarm sensor.

It's like stepping into someone else's skin.

Her first time in his flat.

It feels profoundly, viscerally wrong.

Felix hasn't lied to her. It's just that she'd assumed – willed herself into thinking, she realises – that he lived down in a basement like she herself does, that there would be a physical separation from the rest of the house. Her psychological cop-out. There isn't. What there is in this neat two-storey terraced house at the back of Holloway Road is a make-do sofa bed in the living room, a downstairs shower and a rigid set of dos and don'ts to enable this delicate temporary arrangement of hands-off cohabitation to work.

Pattie is away seeing her new guy for a few days, he said. Does that make it worse, knowing her name?

She couldn't face asking for more details. She's entangled deep enough within this web, its sticky fibres clinging to her soul.

'I tidied up a bit,' Felix says, wiping a hand on his apron and passing over a glass of wine.

Tidying, a.k.a. hiding the evidence. But Margot's professional habit of reading clues whenever she walks into a parishioner's home is one step ahead of him. The half-empty bottle of perfume on the mantelpiece. The box of apple and cinnamon sugar-free granola beside the wine bottles. The shopping list in cursive female hand on the fridge, cotton wool balls right at the top.

Traces everywhere.

The room looks semi-abandoned, contingent, with its half-packed cartons of books and framed posters leaning blind into the wall. The bones of a marriage, the his 'n' hers division of the spoils.

She sits rigid on the sofa, watching him destalk the coriander and dice the ginger for his signature dish, humming to himself. He can't be really so oblivious?

'You're very quiet,' he says, looking up.

She looks away.

The room is ghostly with flickering shadows. Five, possibly six, glasses of wine on an almost completely empty stomach. Her eyelashes seem to be glued together, her mouth is sandpaper-dry.

She can still smell the burnt stir-fry left cremated on their plates after Felix spent an hour talking her out of bailing out. It reeks in here from what must have been two packets of cigarettes. That jagged conversation where everything either of them said seemed to miss its target.

It was half-past four by the time they'd finally collapsed onto the sofa bed, fully clothed and defeated. Margot had fallen into a troubled half-sleep, a tight embryo aware of Felix's elbow digging into her as she tossed and turned.

She turns her head cautiously. He's still asleep. The greyish dawn light heightens his vulnerability. Her eyes well up remembering the crack in his voice as he'd tried to reassure her – and her furious, indignant, response. The enormous sense of jeopardy she'd felt was her baggage, not his. She's the one with the 24/7 conscience. Why should canon law be on his radar?

She's wrecked everything.

'Hey, hey, Gogo, stop. Come on. Don't.'

Felix pulls himself up onto his elbow and wipes the tear from her cheek.

'I'm so sorry.'

He reaches for her hand and she lies back down next to him. Margot feels the rise and fall of his chest next to her, as they listen to the birdsong tuning up outside. She needs to get home before they're all wake. Yet how can she leave? Cocooned here in his warmth, her mind finally still. In the most precarious of circumstances, she's somehow safe.

'How about I make us some coffee?'

'No, stay,' she touches his arm. 'Stay. Just for a minute.'

She runs her finger down his forehead, over the childhood bump on his nose, over its tip and down onto his lips. He kisses her finger, smiling, his eyes closed.

She pushes away the blanket he must have thrown over them during the night, breathes in. Feathery touches at first and then with the urgency of all these endless weeks of tension and fear. He gasps as she slips her hand inside his shirt, her lips locked with his.

'Gogo?'

She places her finger on her lips.

In the wrongest of places, at the wrongest of times, this is the choice she has made.

Neither of them speaks again for a while.

'Reverend Dark Horse,' he whispers, kissing the small swallow on her shoulder blade. 'Where d'you get this?'

'Thailand. I was volunteering before Cambridge.' She pokes his stomach. 'No need to sound so shocked.'

He runs his fingers through her hair. 'One more reason why I'm not ideal vicar's wife material.'

The abruptness of it punches the air from her lungs, shocking her out of her state of dizzy denial.

'Aren't you being a bit hasty?' She struggles to keep her voice light.

He checks off his fingertips one by one.

'I can't do flower arranging. I don't bake Victoria sponges or make jam. I wouldn't know one end of a whist game from the other. Jumble sales bring me out in hives. I'd rather stick pins in my eyes than run a raffle. And most nights I'm filthy-tempered and foul-mouthed.'

'Thanks for the warning.'

'And I haven't even mentioned my thrash metal phase. Or the alcohol. The drugs. The stint as a stripper.'

Margot sits up, reaches for her watch and jumps onto the rug. 'It's six already.'

She rushes around the room, throwing things into her bag.

'Breakfast first? Coffee at least?'

'Felix, I'm dead if I don't make it back before the house is up.'

'But you just—'

The look she gives him as she turns is enough of an answer.

When she gets back from work a few days later, there's something's different about the house in Aberdeen Avenue. She senses it immediately, upending the hairs on her neck.

Rasping laughter is coming from the living room. She puts her head round the half-open door and gasps. Ricky is sitting on the sofa, arm slung back against the cushions. Facing him in the armchair is Cyd, feet curled up beneath her, cat that got the cream.

Margot takes a deep breath and walks inside.

A solitary chocolate finger sits on the plate between them.

'Speak of the devil,' says her father.

She drags herself over for the peck on the cheek, her brain rioting at the incongruity. A powerful wave of new aftershave hits her full on. Linda's calling card, even if she's not here in person.

'Had a meeting in Archway, Margot. Looked you up on the A to Z and thought I'd surprise you.'

'Mission accomplished, Dad.'

No one laughs. Cyd is leaning forward, keen not to miss a moment.

'I'm back earlier than normal,' Margot says.

'Fate, then, or something.' He laughs. 'In any case, this young lady has been doing a fantastic job of looking after me.'

Cyd sweeps her hair out of her eyes and giggles.

'You never told me about any of this,' her father says, sweeping an arc to indicate Armstrong World. The cosy universe from which he has been so unaccountably excluded.

'Ricky's been telling me all about when you were young.' Cyd has her own poker face.

'Your step mum sounds *really* cool.'

Margot swivels round, cheeks hot.

'How is Linda?'

'Busy, busy, just like you. She's got a load of new clients through the local veggie café. And of course she's up to her eyeballs in all the preparations for the handfasting.'

'What is that, exactly?' asks Cyd sweetly, beating Margot to it.

'Our wedding ceremony. You girls love all that stuff, don't you?'

Ricky chuckles. Cyd giggles. Margot feels like gagging. Linda in some wood sprite-goth confection, those bangles jangling victoriously on her wrist.

'We mustn't keep you from your schoolwork, Cyd.'

'It's fine. It's just history.'

Cyd inspects a split end. Margot holds her breath. Cyd looks like she's weighing up her options but finally gives a theatrical sigh and jack-knifes her legs out from under her.

'Great to meet you. Margot never stops talking about you. And bring Linda next time you come.' She throws a final smirk. 'I love all that New Age stuff.'

Ricky laughs and reaches for the last biscuit.

Margot counts to the end of 'hallowed be Thy name' as Cyd climbs the stairs.

'Nice kid.' He pats the cushion next to him. 'Come and sit down, love.'

Everything about this feels wrong.

'So, how's it going, all your,' – he pauses – 'stuff?'

She stares at him.

'Not bad, thanks,' she says finally. 'Just a few weeks left until my ordination, all being well. You don't want anything to derail you at the last minute, you know, knock you off course.'

It echoes in her head as she says it.

'Really? I thought it was all a dead cert. The Church doesn't exactly have people hammering on the door wanting to be vicars.'

She opens her mouth to answer and finds she can't.

'I wanted to ask you something, actually, love.' He coughs.'Linda and I would like you to do our wedding. June the twenty-first, the summer solstice.'

He leans back, grinning like a fourth member of the Magi who's just deposited a gift of peerless price at her feet.

'Linda's idea, of course. She really wants you to feel involved.'

Where are the twins? Nathan? Even Cyd, at this point?

'Is that date good for you?'

She clears her throat.

'Dad, I'm really sorry. I can't.'

'We could probably shift the date by a few days.'

'I can't. I'm sorry.'

He leans back into the sofa, brushing some crumbs from his lap.

'I thought you wanted to be a vicar so you could stand at the front and do weddings and all the rest of it, just like the blokes.'

He reaches over for her collar off the chair and starts spinning it round on his index finger. She fights to restrain herself.

'I'm not allowed to do weddings. Just funerals and the odd baptism. No marriages until,' – she brakes – 'if I'm fully ordained.'

Watch him at close quarters slipping her mother's ring onto Linda's finger?

'Surely you can make an exception for your own father?'

'I'm sorry.'

She looks down at her hands. He's still spinning the collar at the edge of her vision.

'You always were a line-toe-er, Margot.'

'I'm not doing it deliberately, Dad.'

'Really?'

He stands up and reaches for his backpack.

'It's not as if it's a bog-standard church do. Linda wants something close to Mother Nature, she said, so all your usual churchy rules don't apply.'

Margot doesn't look up.

'I really want you to do this for me, for Linda. Make it a family affair.'

She shakes her head.

'Impossible.'

'You people are such hypocrites.'

Cyd walks back into the room grinning.

'Don't let me down, Margot,' Ricky says from the door.

There's a second of silence before the front door slams.

Cyd gives a small laugh and runs back upstairs.

The South Bank dances in the early evening light. Garlands of white bulbs are threaded between the lamp posts, their reflection flirting with the lights from the tourist boats gliding past below.

'This is nice,' Felix says, hooking his finger under the strap of her new sundress. He tucks a stray hair behind her ear, leaving a trail of heat.

They look down at the treacle-black water below, pushing and pulling to find its way home. A family is mud-larking on the shore, buckets and spades in hand.

'You've got your deep-dive face on,' he says.

She keeps her eyes on the eddying swirls, pink-tinged and restless.

'Something at work, Gogo?'

She shakes her head.

'I was thinking about my dad.'

'Yeah?'

'The whole marriage thing.'

'Uh-huh. Well, did you talk to your brother about it?'

The sob comes from nowhere.

'Hey, come here.'

She swipes at her eyes. Clarissa always used to warn that if you open up too soon about the family cracks and cranks, it'll be adieu, Mr Perfect. She flinches at thought of Clarissa. How long is it since they last spoke properly?

'I was thinking we could maybe go away somewhere one weekend. Forty-eight hours all to ourselves. Imagine.'

He nuzzles her neck above the strap of her dress.

'Sound good?'

It takes a huge effort of will.

'I can't right now.' She looks back down at the children crouching of the sand. 'But sometime soon. I promise.'

She reaches for his hand, because she hasn't got the energy to explain yet again.

Eight o'clock on Maundy Thursday, she gets a call from Jeremy.

'Can you stand in for me at the Chrism Mass, Margot?' She waits for the burst of phlegmy coughs to stop. 'Roderick's not available, apparently.'

She's already behind with preparing all the children's activities for the Easter. She's got a dozen rolls of crêpe paper to buy for the bonnet-making session and three simnel cakes to bake. But she's delighted to attend one of the biggest get-togethers in the clerical calendar, attended by hundreds of priests from all over the capital, the episcopal blessing of the oils proving the perfect occasion for insider gossip.

Most of the clergy have already finished vesting in the Chapter House at St Paul's by the time Margot rushes in. It must be a good half a minute before she spots another female face.

'Here we all are once again at this sacred ceremony dating back to the apostolic tradition of Hippolytus on AD 215,' says the bishop, his voice redolent with tones acquired at one of the country's oldest public schools followed by one of its most ancient universities.

She looks up at the mosaics on the concentric circles on the dome far above her head. At the Whispering Gallery, the organ that Mendelssohn played, the chessboard tiles over which the funeral cortèges of Nelson and Churchill moved on their final journeys. Her neck prickles. Assuming her place within this ancient chain of service and praise.

She slips out her phone and texts under her service sheet.

Wish you were here!! You would so love this. Xxx

She catches the eye of her neighbour, who offers the kind of look the principal had down to a tee.

She's walking out behind them all an hour later, discussing the address with the vicar of St Mary and All Angels, Bradford, when she stops sharp. Roderick. To the left of a pillar, in animated conversation with Fabian's nephew. A third, older man talking with them, his biretta nodding in time. Martin Kennedy, presumably. She feels dizzy at the sight of them.

'Someone you know?' asks the Bradford vicar. They never miss a thing.

'Easy mistake when there are fifteen hundred of us all dressed the same,' she smiles.

There are small clusters of clergy all the way down the front steps and she needs to weave her way through them fast.

A few steps down, she runs into a handful of women clergy chatting together. One nods companionably at Margot.

'All very nineteen-fifties, this, isn't it?'

'Too right,' says her neighbour, a tiny woman in her late sixties. 'I marched down Whitehall twenty-five years ago and yet finding a woman at Chrism Mass remains harder than squeezing that camel through the needle.'

'Can't say we weren't warned,' offers a Hadley type with an expensive haircut and discreet diamanté studs. 'When I left the Bar, my colleagues – and this is the Bar, let me remind you – told me I was out of my mind to be signing up to such an old boys' club.'

'You new to all this?' the first one laughs amidst the laughter.

'That obvious?'

'Fancy joining us for a glass of wine?'

Margot glances over her shoulder. The St Stephen's two are now standing on the top step, Roderick alongside them. She bids farewell to the group and dashes off through Paternoster Square, trying to decode what she's just seen.

It's Easter morning, so the weather knows its role. Shafts of sunshine are pouring in through the stained glass, creating multicoloured lozenges of light on the floor of both aisles. Hundreds of fluffy yellow chicks are perched on every available surface, courtesy of Sal and Kath. Huge white lilies spread their skirts like cancan dancers from their vantage point on the pillars either side of the aisle. The entire church is gleaming after yesterday's ministrations by Gwen's rubber-gloved band of helpers.

'Alpha and Omega, all time belongs to him and all ages

To him be glory and power, through every age and forever.'

'Did you know the celebration of the Resurrection is older than the word Easter?'

Jeremy beams down at the congregation. He adores these big festive days.

'Easter can fall anywhere from the start of March to the third week of April, because it's so closely tied to the Jewish holiday calendar, based on the solar and lunar cycle.'

Linda would love that bit. Margot bites her lip.

'Alleluia! Christ is risen!'

'He is risen indeed! Alleluia, alleluia, alleluia!'

The gusto of the congregation's response raises the hairs on her neck. She still finds it magical that an event that happened almost 2,000 years ago can induce such joy in these people today.

She glances towards the back of the church. There's a cluster of newcomers – or once-a-year pop-ins – mumbling, stopping, fumbling some more. The vicar will have registered them too.

Gwen is in the front row, trying to catch her eye. Margot's still hasn't pinned down any dates for the book club. She looks away quickly, towards the side aisle where a latecomer is being ushered to his seat.

Her hand flies to her mouth.

Tungsten determination stops her looking over in his direction all the way through communion, the post-communion hymn, the presentation of the children's Easter craftwork and the blessing. He might as well be standing on the dias next to her, his arm grazing hers, for all the difference it makes.

It's only as she's processing back with Jeremy behind the choir at the end of the service that she allows herself a sideways glance. The church is full but they managed to find him a seat between that angular, irritable Welsh woman and a couple of the rowdy Lithuanian children. His head is lowered. He can't be praying, obviously. But there's an air of stillness about him. She wants to reach out and touch his neck. She focuses on the back of the vicar's head.

People swarm around her as usual after the service, the children barging past in a frenzied search for the hidden Mini Eggs. Half an hour in, Margot finds herself hostage to a twice-yearly drop-in, an earnest woman in her fifties who wants the curate's views on the precise, the literal, the absolute historical veracity of what happened that day in the tomb. Margot's desperate to get away, although she can hardly tell her it's neither the time nor the place for this discussion: it's manifestly both. Yet her focus is elsewhere, hypnotised by the view in the Easter garden at the back of the church, where Felix is nursing a cup of coffee, leaning down to inspect the pipe-cleaner figures she made with the Kool Gang on Good Friday afternoon. He's clearly his biding his time until she's free. What does he think this is – a cocktail party?

Several minutes of exegesis of the Gospels later, Margot is finally rid of her inquisitor. She looks back towards the garden and her stomach flips. Gwen is now there, facing Felix, gesticulating energetically, her hands close to his face.

'Yummy simnel cake,' Tommy says, coming alongside her and wiping the crumbs away with a paper napkin covered in Easter bunnies. 'Jeremy's had four pieces. I thought we should share things round a bit.'

She smiles as he moves away with the plate, then swivels right back round. Felix is handing his mug across to Gwen, who takes it with a coquettish pat of her curls. There's a sliver of a second where he turns and looks straight at Margot. She prays he won't wave. He doesn't. Instead, he turns and says something to Gwen and then leaves. Margot watches Gwen watching him go out through the porch and down the front steps. It's only when he's completely out of sight that Gwen turns back, delight all over her face, Felix's mug clasped close like a medieval reliquary, a saintly toenail wrapped in a muslin cloth. She catches Margot looking at her, holds her gaze a moment and walks away towards the refreshment table with her prize.

'And that little performance was what, exactly?'

She crushes a piece of purple-and-gold foil left over from one of the boys' eggs into a tiny jagged ball in her fist.

'I came to see you in your natural habitat.'

'You've already seen me in it.' She holds the phone away and gulps down some water to try and calm herself. 'It was such a dangerous thing to do.'

'Why, though? No one knows anything.'

'In my world, everyone knows everything.'

'You were very good, by the way.'

She starts tapping a knife against the side of the table.

'Felix, do you have any idea how critical this all is right now? I'm just a couple of months away.'

'So you keep saying.' Felix clears his throat.

'Shit, sorry, you know I didn't mean that. The whole thing was totally off the cuff. And,' he pauses, 'you know, I kind of thought you'd be pleased.'

'What, "Easter Surprise, everyone!"? Here's the curate's boyfriend, our very own bunny out of the hat.'

He waits a couple of beats. She closes her eyes.

'You're being a bit unfair.'

'Am I?'

She squeezes her fingers into her palms.

'Do you know what?' he says slowly. 'I felt really proud to see you up there this morning.'

'Uh-huh.'

'I'm trying so hard to understand all this— you, or rather your world.' He swallows. 'And you know what? I'm also going through my own stuff right now, sorting everything out with Pattie. Just to put that out there.'

She draws a long breath, watching the jerky progress of the second hand on the kitchen clock.

'So,' he takes a long breath sighs, 'I had a chat to that rather big woman by the garden thingy. The one you keep mentioning, right?'

Margot's hands feel clammy.

'She thinks you walk on water.'

Margot hugs her arm across her chest. Too many wires starting to tangle.

'Look, sorry, Felix, but I've got to go. I'll have talk to you later, OK?'

She watches her phone skid across the counter top.

This was the warning she needs.

It's early evening when her phone rings.

She's been lying here for hours. She won't answer right now if it's Felix. Or Clarissa. And, especially, not if it's her father.

'Sorry to bother you like this on Easter Sunday, Margot. I'm sure you're in the middle of something fun.'

She pulls the duvet tighter under her chin.

'It's fine, Jeremy. Everything OK?'

A small silence on the other end.

'Well, if you're not doing anything important, I wondered if we could catch a quick drink?'

She stares at her face in the mirror, pale and scared.

'Sure. Now?'

'Half an hour from now in the Heron?'

Something's very wrong.

Chapter 18

Same day, mid-April

The barman is sitting on a stool reading the paper. She drops into a window seat to wait for Jeremy.

Someone's left a Sunday supplement on the table next to her. The whole magazine is devoted to next month's general election: a country increasingly divided, the times completely out of kilter. She pushes it away from her.

Perhaps the reason she's here is something to do with the Chrism Mass? Roderick spotted her there and fabricated some complaint? Unlikely, though, under the circumstances. Maybe Pamela has been whingeing again about the state of the Kool Gang's corner. She wouldn't put it past her. But no, it won't be that either. A hole in the annual accounts?

The other possibility is too appalling to even entertain.

She turns round all of a sudden to see Jeremy staring down at her. The brown eyes are huge behind the yellow frames.

He sits down next to her, then immediately jumps up again and offers to get some drinks. Forty minutes later and they're still pushing around bits of inconsequential conversation like tiddlywinks counters.

She's at a loss. Maybe he was just lonely and fancied some company after all that family-centric activity this morning?

Jeremy reaches for another handful of peanuts and gathers himself.

'Margot.' She waits, still as in a sepulchre. 'I need to talk to you about something.'

She watches him brushing the peanut crumbs off his lap.

'It's sort of sensitive.'

Her heart starts to beat harder.

'Someone sent me an email this afternoon.'

The air thickens, swarming with possibilities, none of them benign.'Something about a website.'

She breathes out.

'Oh, the Church Mole?'

Jeremy bites his lip.

'No, not the Church Mole, though Roderick's sermon got top marks, since you ask.'

His weak smile fades like breath from a mirror.

'Another website. Vic-o-leaks or something.'

She realises she's been braced for this for months.

'Vic-i-leaks, that's it. Written anonymously by a female curate.' He squashes a fragment of nut beneath his little finger. 'In north London.'

Why has she never mentioned it to him? That someone is having a bit of harmless fun pillorying the worst aspects of daily Church life?

Jeremy pulls a crumpled plastic bag onto his lap and takes out the vestry laptop. He places it on the table between them and starts tapping one-fingered on the keys.

'Look, here we go. "Vic-i-leaks: Her Master's Voice". See?'

The familiar figure in the collar and Zorro mask.

'There are all kinds of handy tips. What colour lipstick to wear at the altar. The best hairstyle for when you're doing a wedding or baptism. How to fend off randy older priests. It's all here,' he coughs, 'should you need it.'

She drains the rest of her drink, ice cubes clinking against the glass like tumbrel wheels.

She could stop him any time, but her tongue won't move. The pub is silent around them, other than some low-volume pop; even the elderly regulars at the bar are not talking.

'And,' – she heaves another breath – 'you think it all sounds like St Mark's?'

Jeremy pulls at a thread on his jacket.

'That's what the email I got today said.'

She closes her eyes. Please make it so that any second I wake up from this with pins and needles in my arm.

'Someone thinks it's me dishing the dirt on the parish.' It's a statement of fact rather than a suggestion.

Jeremy pulls a crumpled tissue out of his pocket. She's tempted to pat his shoulder in support.

'I wouldn't go that far.'

She looks down, the bridge of her nose stinging.

'You're the horse that I backed, that I still very much back. But I have to say, this is very odd. Right down to the sherry hidden in the vestments cupboard.'

She looks back up.

'Who was the email from?'

He hesitates.

'I have absolutely no idea. Came from an address like SimpleSaint@hotmail.com or something. As you know, half our congregation don't even own a PC.'

Her head echoes. Someone wants to do her real harm. She's been dangling by her fingernails since July and now someone out there is stamping on her fingers, one by one.

'Of course, I haven't spoken to anyone else about this. But I can't keep a lid on it forever. Nothing spreads faster than scandal, and that would damage us all.'

He looks totally exhausted.

'Jeremy, please believe me. This is nothing to do with me.'

'You've never seen it before?'

She hesitates. 'Well, no, but I—'

'I see.'

'I swear.' She lowers her head. 'At least let me try and find out who's behind it.'

Now he averts his eyes.

'Please?'

He sighs.

'Margot, if you're doing this as some kind of escape valve, it would be much better if you just admitted it now. Believe me, I know this year as a curate is really tough. You wouldn't be the first to swerve off the rails.'

She shakes her head, incredulous.

Vic-i-leaks: Scenes from Parish Life, 2 April 2017

Just under three months until P-Day and then everyone will have to stop treating me like I'm wearing L-plates. Most jobs, you do a bit of training and then you're an old hand. Round here you have to pass Go a billion times before they'll even let you do a baptism by yourself. Women got the vote a century ago, people. When I'm boss, it's all going to change. Proper champagne rather than that own-brand sugary fizz at all the receptions for starters. Plus introducing an upper age limit on all parishioners. Anyone over 65 or without their own teeth will have to find a new home, I'm afraid. LOL, just kidding!!!

Vic-i-leaks: Scenes from Parish Life, 6 April 2017

Blah fucking blah. These PCC big mouths could bore for Britain. Should have been an Olympic sport last year. This lot can spend an hour arguing over whether the Sunday school should serve Ribena or orange squash. What planet are they on? And who gives a monkey's about the colour of the new kitchen tiles? We're supposed to be saving souls here, not starring in Location, Location.

Vic-i-leaks: Scenes from Parish Life, 15 April 2017

If I'd wanted to spend every waking hour with the under-8s, I'd have become a teacher. No offence, but this wasn't exactly why I did all those years of training. Babysitting toddlers and giving primary-school assemblies pitched at Pingu or WonderPets level. Give me a break. And the parents. Like a fleet of Apache helicopters winging into view every Sunday morning.

Margot slams the lid of her laptop. Why didn't she keep a closer eye on this? Why didn't she say something earlier? It's like side-slipping into a parallel universe. As if someone has crept under her skin. That's the worst thing. She's just read twenty-two posts and, while there's no definitive smoking gun, there's a huge amount here that could be St Mark's. Her body aches with the effort of not lying on the floor and giving up.

Simplesaint@hotmail.com. It was barely worth even bothering to type it in, before the message from Mailer Daemon bounced back.

Get a grip. Female curates are two-a-penny now, half the annual intake. You're not the only one with frustrations.

Someone's clearly out to get you, Margot, and they're doing a pretty thorough job of it. These are your words, your thoughts. You didn't actually write them, but you might just as well have done, and no one is going to believe otherwise. You're toast.

She can see the *Daily Mail* headline now. *Girl Vicar Dishes the Dirt!* Worse, *Girl Vicar Dishing the Dirt is Having Affair with Married Parishioner!!!*

Who would have the skills? Who hates her enough?

Oliver, Fabian's nephew. Jeremy said he was a Twitter fanatic. His revenge for not getting the post.

Margot turns over on the lumpy mattress. Or Gwen? The ultimate insider, in and out of that vestry at least three times a week.

Cyd? Margot winces. Does she really feel that hostile to her?

Roderick? He can barely turn on the office laptop. But where's an ill will, there's a way. He certainly loathes her enough.

That Welsh evangelical woman who never comes to Margot's

side of the altar rail. She's some kind of writer, isn't she?

Even Clarissa. Margot shakes her head vigorously. She'd never do anything to harm Margot, no matter how furious she is.

'Who could hate you that much?' Felix asks, in the tiny bar they've found up some forgotten side street at the far end of Crouch End. 'That's insane.'

'Where do you want me to start?'

He reaches for her hand and squeezes it.

'What, you're telling me someone would go to the trouble of setting up a website supposedly written by you to screw up your entire career?' He shakes his head. 'You've been watching too many Scandinavian thrillers.'

It's already a week since Jeremy told her. The walls of St Mark's have sprouted eyes like a dystopic Dali. It's as though everyone is waiting for her to put her head into the noose. Everyone except Jeremy.

But she's no closer to finding out the architect of Vic-i-leaks and even the vicar's heroic patience must have limits.

'This really could be the end for me, Felix. I know it sounds like I'm totally paranoid, but everyone, or most people, think it's me.'

'Seriously?' His expression changes.

'Tell you what, let me speak to a techie friend of mine.'

She pulls at a thread unravelling on her blouse.

'It'll be OK, Gogo. Your vicar seems a reasonable guy. It's most likely all some bizarre coincidence. One of your sisterhood putting the boot in to the Church because she needs to let off steam. Just like you do, right?'

It could be. But it won't.

'Nice skirt, by the way,' he says, leaning over to kiss her hair.

She leans away.

He picks up his pint.

'Pretty crappy day at school today.' He takes a couple of swigs from his drink. 'Some of the girls driving me mental. Snapchatting each other all the way through class. Had to threaten to send half a dozen to the head. Again.'

Margot tenses. Cyd. Taboo between them.

'There Must Be an Angel' rings out from the table between them. Felix's little joke. He snatches it up before she can stop him.

'Reverend Goodwin's office?'

She grabs it back in terror.

'Hello?'

'Is this Margot?'

A stranger on this number?

'This is Brian. Marshall.'

She struggles to remember.

'The guy you were supposed to be meeting at the Odeon last night.'

'Oh, God, I'm so sorry.'

Doubly so, because he's in Clarissa's research team at the university. Hand-picked.

Felix watches her quizzically, dabbing up some nut shards

'Clarissa said you were really keen to meet,' says Brian.

Of course she did.

'I'm sorry, Brian.' Her mind is racing. 'I wasn't feeling well and totally forgot to message you.'

There's a long pause.

'So you want to meet up another time or what?'

'Can I give you a call in a day or two?'

He gives a hard laugh.

'If you can spare the time. Sounds like you're busy.'

She stares at the phone. Clarissa will not forgive this one.

'Anything you want to tell me?' Felix leans back against the bench.

'It's nothing.'

'Right.'

'Just helping out a friend.' She can feel herself reddening. 'It's a bit complicated.'

'But complicated nothing?'

He has every right to challenge her. But where to start? She's demanded such extreme measures of secrecy from him. And yet has been arm-twisted into seeing a random stream of strangers from a dating site. She drops her head. Right now, she has no choice but not to tell him.

'Everything in your life seems complicated, Margot,' says Felix, draining his pint.

Later this evening, she'll have to slip back into Aberdeen Avenue, tense from the risk of sliding her key in the lock, desperately hoping she won't run into Nathan asking her if she's back from a very late prayer group, or Cyd materialising in the corridor, saying nothing, saying everything with her eyes.

She'd like nothing more right now than to be cradled his arms.

How long before he turns round and says she's not worth the effort?

Danny, can I come up and see you sometime soon? I want to talk to out about Dad and this whole marriage thing. Margot xx

We already did that, Margot. Time to deal with it now? Danny

It's not the marriage, Danny, it's the fact that Dad wants me to take the service. I can't. I'm not allowed to. xx

Why don't you just do it as their wedding present? Here endeth the lesson. D

After her mother died, the Goodwins simply imploded, fragments of family and memory scattered like grapeshot.

Dan's hostility baffles Margot, shames her. He seems to be nursing some profound sense of injustice, a wound still festering long after they've both left that challenging childhood behind. What exactly is he blaming her for? Leaving him alone with her father when she left home for university? Because he had no one with whom he could share the pain? Or did she do something when they were both very young that caused this lifelong grudge? So many concentric circles of hurt.

Does he still sometimes do that same honking laugh, a sound so infectious she once found herself rolling around on the rug next to him, unable to speak for at least five minutes? Does he still mix apricot and strawberry jam together on his toast? Is he happy? Will she ever be able to reach him again?

'Morning, everyone.'

Her head is packed with steel wool as she walks into the vestry two weeks later.

Tommy looks up with a smile; Roderick ignores her.

She loops her coat above his greasy rain jacket and takes her seat. Someone has left a coffee ring on her St James's Bible, her leaving gift from the principal. No prizes for guessing who.

'Bad news, I'm afraid.'

She holds her breath.

'The hospital called. Arthur Davies is not doing so well, sadly. He had a fall a couple of days ago and has picked up some chest infection. They said he's going downhill fast.'

Arthur's her talisman and friend.

'You might want to call in, if you have time?'

She flushes. She hasn't been to see Arthur in over three weeks.

'I'll come too.'

'No need, Roderick.'

'Grave times call for seniority,' he croaks, looking over at Jeremy, who's studiously folding the tea towel back into squares.

'I think we're best leaving Margot to handle this one, Roderick.'

There's a rattle on the doorknob. They all look over expectantly to see Fabian stride in. He nods at Jeremy and Roderick.

'Hello all. On my way to a board meeting, but I wanted a quick word with you, vicar, if I may.' He purses his lips. 'In private.'

Several glances criss-cross the room.

The door clicks shut behind Jeremy and his golden-boy fundraiser.

It's mid evening by the time she gets back home. It's still very light, yet another reminder of the summer fast approaching, unstoppable.

Five weeks to get through.

She comes to a stop on the front doorstep. Through the open windows, she can hear Nathan and Cyd having a furious row upstairs.

She slips inside and takes off her shoes. They're on the landing, right outside the boys' rooms.

'Stop stalking me.'

'Stalking? Don't you dare talk to me like that.'

'You're always in my fucking space.'

Margot's shoulders slump. What exactly is her role here? Mediation? Distraction? Or just leave them to it and protect her boundaries at all costs?'

'Christ, Cyd, you're fifteen. The boys are more mature than you. Do you not understand how serious this all is? What the hell were you playing at?'

'That place is like a prison.'

'You'd rather be stacking shelves in bloody Asda?'

'Maybe I would.'

'One of these days, Cydney, you won't know what's hit you. My parents would have gone ballistic if I'd skived off school for one day, let alone eighteen. *Eighteen*!'

Margot goes cold.

'Whatever.'

'I've had it up to here with your stupid— oh God, sorry, Margot, I didn't see you there.'

Cyd seizes her chance, racing up the stairs to the attic.

'I can see why Mum ran off with Eric,' she shouts down, before the door slams shut.

'WHAT DID YOU SAY?'

Margot charges up to the landing, but he's already at the top, hammering on the door.

She hears a rustling behind her and turns to see the boys cowering, chalk-faced, just inside the bathroom. She races over and gathers them into her arms.

'Hey, you two,' she whispers into their huddle, 'how about a quick story down in my room? I may even have some Smarties left.'

She is able to do this at least. The three of them head downstairs, attached at the waist like crabs.

Much later, there's a quiet knock on her door. She glances behind her, where the twins are both fast asleep, sprawled across the duvet.

Nathan looks as though he's forgotten how to stand vertical.

'I'm so sorry about that, Margot.'

'Families,' she shrugs.

He beckons her into the hall.

'Christ.'

He rubs his forehead.

'The school called. As you probably gathered. Cyd's been bunking on and off for months apparently.'

Her pulse quickens. It's coming closer.

'They've issued a formal warning. One more strike and she's out.'

She should have seen it. It's not as though there weren't any clues.

'Was it the head who called?'

Nathan looks at her a moment.

'I don't remember, to be honest. All I know is that we're pretty much screwed unless she starts pulling it together. He was furious, whoever it was.'

Margot glances over her shoulder at the boys, curled up together like prawns.

'He didn't pull any punches about how serious it all is.'

She looks down at her feet.

'I'm so sorry.'

He slumps back against the wall, looking like he's on the point of tears.

'That's not all.' He gives a shaky sigh. 'Cyd just told me, though I don't know why she didn't say so before – her mother's pregnant.'

It's Margot's turn to steady herself.

'Can you believe it? I haven't got the slightest idea how I'm going to break it to the boys. And Cyd seems to be hurtling off the rails so fast, I won't be able to stop her.'

Hugging is out of bounds. But it's the only possible response.

Chapter 19

Mid-May

The hospice where they've moved Arthur is on the far side of Stoke Newington. She's dreading it, because she knows exactly what to expect. She's already visited a handful of other people here. There's only so much of a shell you can form.

It's not the smells. Or the tired smiles of the staff. It's the sense of overwhelming helplessness. Plus, this time it's personal. Arthur has been her steadying anchor with his constant affectionate teasing, all those anecdotes from his youth about the dodgy on-street betting cartel run by Humperty-Back Jim and the scrapes with the rozzers, his pitch-perfect Roderick impersonations.

She dreads seeing him reduced.

'Got a miracle for me in that handbag of yours, vicar?'

The nurse glances up from refilling the water jug.

He is propped against three large pillows in a small, light room right at the far end of the corridor. A lattice of watery sunlight patterns the lino. Someone's left a large unopened box of Maltesers on the bedside table.

'Oi, hands off,' he laughs, 'Matron gave me them. She's a poppet, just like you.'

'How are you, Arthur?' She pulls a chair alongside the bed.

'Could be worse, ducks.'

His voice has the texture of baking paper. There's a pale gleam to his cheeks, the skin stretched taut. He must have lost a stone since she last saw him.

'Grub's a bit runny.'

The small wink squeezes her heart. Does he know how ill he is?

'You're looking a little bit peaky, missy. That vicar being a slave driver is he? Or you been out on the razz too much?'

'Well, I—'

'Just kidding, lovey,' he chuckles, 'take no notice of me. You just look after yourself. You're special, you are.'

His hand is canary-light in hers. His fingers return a tiny pulse of pressure.

'Come here a tick, will you?'

He leans in.

'I'd like you to do it.' Coughing convulses him and Margot waits while he wipes his mouth. 'If you don't mind?'

She takes in the small, sterile space around them. Is he asking her to perform the last rites, when the time comes?

'I told the boys already and they're fine with it, you know, with you being a girl and all that. They said it would make a nice change if that's what I wanted.'

'Oh, yes' she says. 'Of course, Arthur.'

No tears. She owes him that.

'I know you'll do me proud.' He pats her hand. His touch flutters like a small child's. 'Only sorry I won't be there to see you in action.' He pokes her arm gently.

She waits for the wheezing to subside.

'Would you like us to pray a little, Arthur?'

'Nah, don't worry, sweetie. Why spoil things?'

They sit, quiet, still, holding hands. Somewhere along the corridor, a nurse is issuing instructions, accompanied by a bass line of syncopated beeps.

'How about I read to you for a bit,' she suggests, glancing over at the pile of magazines on the windowsill.

'You're all right, darling. I like it nice and peaceful just like this.'

He gives her a smile and closes his eyes. She watches the gentle rise and fall of his chest beneath the baggy checked pyjamas.

The Arthurs are the reason she does this job, she thinks, as she strokes his fingers.

She can't go straight back to the vestry afterwards. The I/thou red line only takes you so far. This may be her job, but it's so much more than that. Anyone who tries to tell you otherwise hasn't committed to it heart and soul.

It's not just Arthur weighing her down. It's Cyd and the rest of the Armstrongs and what they all must be suffering after hearing about the mother's pregnancy. Their pain eats away at the back of her mind like paint-stripper. A new baby. A tiny cuckoo in the nest.

She hesitates, then pulls out her phone.

Can you slip out in an hour or so for a quick coffee? I'd really like to chat xxxxx

'OK, so what's up?'

Margot is so shocked, she sloshes coffee all over Jeremy's diocesan quinquennial vicarage inspection report. The brusqueness of the question has also stemmed the chatter of the group squashed in next to her.

'Oh, hi! How—'

'I've left thousands of messages.'

She looks dreadful. Concave contours, yellowish skin, stains all over her black jumper.

A vice is pressing down on Margot's temples. She doesn't need to check the clock to sense the danger.

'I'm so sorry, Clariss. I've been drowning in work.' She waves the quinquennial report feebly. 'What with Easter and Holy Week and then Whitsun coming up and—'

'I'm familiar with the clerical calendar, thanks.'

Margot's head feels light.

'Brian sends his love.'

Margot drags her papers together.

'Clariss, do you mind if we—'

He's there in two strides before she can stop him. Pushing past the queue at the counter and bending to kiss her.

'God, I've missed you, Gogo.'

'For nothing is secret than shall not be made manifest, neither anything hid that shall not be known and come to light.'

Felix gapes at Clarissa.

'You two haven't met.' Margot steadies herself. 'Felix, this is my oldest friend, Clarissa. Clariss, this is—'

Clarissa pushes Jeremy's report off the bench and thumps down next to Margot. Felix hesitates, then lowers himself down on Clarissa's left.

'So. Felix.' Clarissa angles towards him in a furious curve. 'Tell me about yourself. You know what Margot – sorry, "Gogo" – is like. Plays those cards so very close to her chest.'

Felix and Margot walk back along Holloway Road in silence.

'She's really one of your oldest friends?' he asks finally.

She can't even look at him.

Short of quizzing them about their favourite positions, Clarissa displayed all the tact and sensitive of a rack operator. Felix repeatedly glanced over at Margot for some kind of lifeline, but she was seasick with shock.

'You don't know her.'

He turns to face her.

'I'd be careful if I were you.'

Vic-i-leaks: Scenes from Parish Life, 20 May 2017

Brexit Schmexit. I've got enough politics to deal with here in the vestry without listening to May and Corbyn pontificating about what's going to happen two years down the line. I mean, surely whether we buy the clergy biscuits in Lidl or Tesco is of more real significance, guys? Although some people should keep an eye on their waistline. Just saying.

She can't stop checking. And the postings are becoming increasingly frequent. It's like watching her career hit the barriers in slow motion.

Vic-i-leaks: Scenes from Parish Life, 20 May 2017

Hell's friggin bells. Some of this lot are enough to turn you atheist. Pack 'em off to a nursing home pronto, I say. I've had enough of hearing about surgical stockings and the failings of the NHS. I need fun, fun, fun. Their idea of which is snuggling down with a bumper issue of the Radio Times *and a vat of Ovaltine. What I need is a hot guy to take my mind off things…*

Margot feels like retching, the sensation of being spied on is so intense.

Clarissa. It has to be. No, impossible. She's her oldest friend. They've been through too much together over the years. She may be short-fused and controlling and possibly going through some tough stuff right now, but she's never do anything as vicious and damaging as this.

Margot flushes at even entertaining the possibility.

There are three texts waiting for her when she gets out of the shower the next day.

The worst thing is that you didn't even look sorry. Nine years of friendship and then to be humiliated like that?

Margot's slumps on the bed. She's right. What kind of friend behaves like that? What kind of hypocrite?

The second is Ricky.

Linda's really upset about the handfasting. Surely you can bend the rules for once in your life, Margot?

Hypocrite and prig.

Margot, please call me as soon as you get this, J.

Complete lost cause.

'You don't have to, Margot. Really, it's completely your call.' His kindness stiffens her resolve. 'I could ask Roderick.'

That would have clinched it.

'I'll be OK, Jeremy, But thanks for checking.' She sighs. 'Anyway, I promised.'

'Sure?'

She won't crack. She owes it to Arthur. Also, to Jeremy and everyone else to at least get something right.

People always assume funerals will be the hardest. But she knows from watching Jeremy how much weddings can come freighted with enormous expectations, the church packed full of non-church people, the services complicated by all the additional choreography, the musicians unsure where to play or the guests where to sit, the clench-jawed happy couple praying the whole day will be worth two years' savings.

She's taken three funerals so far: all of them were emotionally and physically draining but still also amongst the most rewarding things she's done in the role. Supply the dignity and compassion, Cranmer's beautiful liturgy will do the rest.

'No one cares about you or your mistakes,' the principal assured them when one of the ordinands worried about pressing the wrong button at the wrong time and turning a sad day into a farce. 'Nor is it your opportunity to start trying to convert a captive audience. Every life is precious to God and a funeral gives us the space for our own individual memories, our own very personal feelings of love, sorrow and respect.'

Arthur. A truly good man. One less ally in her world.

The sons sit staring at her in the vestry, unsure what to say or do. Their pained bewilderment takes her by surprise. They hadn't seen this coming, either of them. Paul, the elder of the two, some big shot in property, pale blue eyes and aquiline nose like his father; Tony, the time-is-money-trader, jittery in his seat, probably not used to having to confront his emotions in this way. Margot offers some suggestions about hymns, a reading or two, who might sit where, as they both listen, nodding, stunned at this sudden twist in the script of their lives.

'I was going to come up and see him next week,' Paul says, after they've finished with the formalities.

'Yeah, he never said anything about how ill he was,' adds Tony, a small tremor in his voice. 'We only found that out when the hospital got in touch last week.'

'I see,' Margot replies. She could have contacted them. Why hadn't she?

'We were going to take him to Paris for his seventy-fifth,' says Paul. 'He's always wanted to go. We'd talked about it, hadn't we, Tone? Up the Eiffel Tower, ride on a bateau mouche, all that. Swapped a couple of emails a while back about the whole thing.'

His palms are raised in supplication.

'I understand. And I know your dad would have done too.'

Simple, shortish, nothing too preachy, they'd said. A sending-off fit for an ordinary, extraordinary man.

As the final verse of 'Abide with Me' draws to a close, Margot worries her voice might betray her. But it holds steady for Arthur, for all the fun and laughter they shared.

It's only afterwards, when the guests have filed out into the sunshine and the wreaths have been taken away and she's left alone to lock up the chapel, it's only then that her tears come. It will take her time to process it. That image of the two sons, inconsolable in their remorse, has hooked under her skin. All those things that should have been said and done before it was suddenly too late.

Grief, the price of love.

She came home from New Milton Community Church afire that day.

'Jesus wants to welcome all those you love into His arms, just as He has with you,' Gilly had told them that afternoon. 'If there's anyone special you can think of – a friend, someone in your own family – whom you haven't yet told about God's love moving in your life, put their picture in your head right now and take a snapshot of it. Click! Hold that image tight, go home and talk to them, tell them about what the Lord has done for you. Be one of Our Lord's disciples in your own small, yet ginormous way. Can you imagine anything more wonderful? I know I can't. OK, so who's thinking of someone they'd like to share God's love with? Margot, why don't you start us off?'

Margot had been plaiting the ends of her hair and looked up, shocked by the sudden attention. She shook her head. Gilly paused, then asked Roger to speak to them all instead. She wasn't going to say it out loud, but Margot had made up her mind. She would go home and tell her mother her big secret at last, all about her other life at the Community Church and everything she'd felt over the past two years. How God's love had taken hold of her and shaken her by the scruff of the neck – that's how Gilly said to describe it – and how it would do the same for her mother too. Free her from the pain and make her happy at last.

The house is tickingly silent as she walks in, just after four o'clock. Why wasn't *The Big Match* on? Maybe they've all gone to the corner shop for an ice cream? But when was the last time they'd done something as normal as that? She stands at the bottom of the stairs, everything alert and echoey around her. She breathes in hard. The smell of her father's cigarettes still hangs in the air.

Unnerved by the whispering hush, Margot starts to waver in

her plan to reveal God's love right here, right now. Her mother might well not be in the mood. She glances over at the stack of unopened mail, the clutter of shoes, the smudgy watercolour of Venice, eternal reminder of yet another of Ricky's unfilled promises. No, her mother definitely might not be in the mood. Proclaiming the Good News can wait until another day. Gilly will understand.

Will she, though? Delay is the devil's work. Now is definitely the time. As soon as her mother gets back, Margot will speak to her.

The clicking of the gas meter in the hall cupboard is making Margot uncomfortable. She'll go up to her room, listen to some music until they all come home. She takes a couple of biscuits from the tin on the counter, and runs up the stairs, avoiding the seventh step, as she always does.

At the top of the landing, she sees her parents' door slightly ajar. She hesitates then walks over and gives it a shove, just in case.

That's all it takes.

Her mother is lying face down on the bed, dozens of photos scattered around her on the blanket.

Margot's head empties as she takes a couple of tiny step forwards.

The pillowcase is patterned with sprigs of blue on faded pink, her mother's favourite. The radio is on low. The picture clasped in her left hand was taken when she was in her early twenties, Portia in the leavers' production, 1975, Bristol Old Vic.

Did she tell her she loved her enough?

Afterwards is a smudge of voices and images and silences.

The legalese, the unforgiving detail of the coroner's report, the bossiness of the policewoman asking Margot repeatedly to run through her account, as though some vital aspect might change if Margot were only to think about it hard enough.

The depression never came up. Aneurism, they said. An abnormal ballooning of a portion of a blood vessel, from the Greek *aneurysma* meaning 'a widening'. She looked it up in the *Encyclopaedia*

Britannica because no one tried to explain it to them and Danny kept asking her what it meant.

A widening. A rupture. A small family blown to smithereens.

Her father planned the cremation service as low-key and private, *Just like your mum would have wanted.* There was a clutch of her old theatre friends, a couple of mothers from the school, a brother and his family who lived up in Glasgow, Lorraine and her parents. A small audience for someone who had missed the limelight so much.

Her memories of it now come cloaked in colour. The crematorium gardens bursting with roses of peach and vermilion. The sky cobalt blue, huge and cloudless like an invitation over their heads. One of the actress friends wearing a vivid emerald scarf. Light pouring into the chapel of rest, so intense that she had to shade her eyes in order to be able to read the hymns.

She and Danny read a poem together, 'Piano' by D.H. Lawrence. Her mother had won a recital competition at school with the same piece.

Softly in the dusk, a woman is singing to me;
Taking me back down the vista of years, till I see
A child sitting under a piano, in the boom of tingling strings
And pressing the small, poised feet of a mother who smiles as she sings.

Margot's voice started to unstitch. It was Danny who held firm, his twelve-year-old's tones childish, yet determined in the tiny chapel.

The glamour
Of childish days is upon me, my manhood is cast
Down in the flood of remembrance, I weep like a child for the past.

She still has that photo of her mother as Portia. It's tucked inside an envelope, at the bottom of a shoebox full of letters, handwritten notes and cards. One of the few things that survived the Mildmay Grove blast. Even now, twelve years on, it's hard to take it out.

Chapter 20

Early June

Unlike her father, Fabian was never going to choose a pizza chain. El Inferno is definitely more his style.

He's installed in the far corner below a huge photo of Picasso in his bare-chested prime. As she walks towards him, she sees he's wielding a toothpick, a plate of olive stones in front of him, the black satin shirt undone two buttons too far. Her heart sinks even further.

'Margarita, Margot? Caju Amigo? Hairy Virgin?'

Felix had warned her not to come. She doesn't have that luxury.

'I'll stay soft for now, thanks.'

'As the bishop didn't say to the actress.'

How many has he had?

At least for now, she doesn't have to talk. She makes it past the guacamole dip, the chicken chimichanga and refried rice, right through to the baked banana in cinnamon pods, barely uttering a word, while Fabian holds court on his burgeoning business empire, the myriad ways he's outsmarted the competition, his merger plans, the approaches from venture capitalists, all the fingers in all the pies.

He finally licks the last traces of pineapple syrup from his spoon, sucks his fingertips clean and pushes his plate away.

'All sounds fascinating,' says Margot, almost surprised to hear the sound of her own voice after so long.

'The problem with you priests is you've never lived in the real world. I mean, take Jeremy. Lovely guy, no question, but I don't think he'd know a P and L account if it grabbed him by the throat.'

Margot instinctively recoils from the disloyalty, picturing the teetering stack of bills and bank statements in the vestry.

'Actually, Fabian, I don't think he has time to think of anything else.'

He narrows his eyes, taking another swig of his cocktail. Then his hand shoots out for hers.

'You and I are two of a kind. We know how the real world works. That's why I wanted to get you by yourself.'

His rings are digging into her fingers. She pushes her napkin off her lap and leans away as far as she can.

'St Mark's has the potential to make a big fat juicy income. You do know that, don't you? Great location, a roomy space, a solidly middle-class local demographic. But it needs drive and business nous, plus,' – he leans in towards her – 'a purge of all the blue rinses. Know what I mean?'

Her cheeks betray her.

'Exactly,' he smirks. 'I've done the sums and worked out how much we could rake in – and I'm talking major spondulicks – if we market ourselves as a professional events venue.'

'I don't understand.'

What's in it for him?

'I'm not talking crappy church-hall plastic glasses stuff,' he snaps. 'Or even just weddings and christenings and all that religious business. This is about corporate entertainment, Margot: business lunches, sponsorship launches, private parties dripping in coke, top-end stuff, right? A church by Great Portland Street tube has transformed itself into a premier gig. Wait.' He pulls a glossy brochure out of his briefcase and slaps it down in front of her. 'All the sexy brands in fashion, media, the arts – they'd lap up holding big events in a place like St Mark's. Glamorous, exclusive, quirky, a little bit cutting edge, a little bit trad, all very postmodern. We just need to tart the place up, put in some funky new lights, glossy paint, cover over all the depressing stuff.'

Her mouth slowly opens.

'All those war memorials and plaques commemorating some old codger who snuffed it a couple of centuries ago, I mean, really, who cares, right? Places like St Mark's can rent themselves out for several grand a night. I've already got a few key contacts lined up to come and take a look.'

That's part of what's in it for him, she suspects.

'All it'll need is imagination and designer savvy.' His fingers tighten on hers. 'I know you're the girl for the job.'

She removes her hand and opens the brochure. It smells of expensive laminate.

'But Fabian, this is a deconsecrated church. St Mark's is very much alive and kicking.'

'Debatable.'

'It's a totally different context.'

He shrugs.

'What does the vicar say about all this?'

For the first time this evening, he hesitates.

'He hasn't heard the whole idea in depth as yet.' He takes another swig of his drink. 'Thought I'd crystallise a few things first. He's a busy man. But he'll be all over it like a rash. I mean, it'll be serious dosh in his coffers. No more begging for an extra few pennies in the collection plate every Sunday morning. It'll put a rocket under the church's finances for years.'

His cack-handedness is breathtaking. Yet even as she thinks that, she detects a kernel of truth in what he says. The church is always short of funds, and 150-year-old buildings don't mend themselves. He leans forward, his breath pungent.

'Some of the old bags are bound to be a bit queasy about it

because of the whole religious thing. That's where you come in again, darling.' He drops his voice. 'We'll have to lose the pews to make way for stacking chairs and that's bound to get the pensioners' backs up. But this is 2017. They need to get with the programme. One of my suppliers has already signed up to take them off our hands and recycle them as retro chic.'

He waves over the waiter.

'So where are we going on to?'

'Sorry, I can't, Fabian.'

'You're kidding?'

'Thanks for a great evening.'

He rattles his car keys close to her face.

'All work and no play makes Margot a very dull girl.'

She holds her poker face steady.

'It's been fun. Another time, definitely.'

'I'll hold you to that. And in the meantime, I'll give you a lift home.'

She starts to protest, but he raises his hand. The conversation's over.

The inevitable black BMW reeks of Italian leather and emetic aftershave.

'Lonely life,' he says, roaring out of the Design Centre car park. He puts his hands together in mock prayer. She holds her breath until they rejoin the steering wheel.

'Ten-thirty on a balmy June evening and our glamorous curate's going home to don her bedsocks.'

They screech to a halt at a set of lights at the top of Upper Street. Fabian leans his arm across the back of her seat, fingers grazing her neck.

'There are three hundred and fifty people in the congregation to look after, so not much time for being – you know – lonely.' She tries to keep it light, pulling away as his hand leaves her to change gear.

'The shepherdess and her flock.' 'Shepherdess' with added *shhhhh*.

Please God, no snarl-ups at Highbury Corner.

'You don't fool me, Margot.' His voice has thickened. 'Young girl like you. Must be so, you know, frustrating.' He sucks his teeth.

'May I?' She reaches forward quickly and flicks on the sound system.

Springsteen. Her father's favourite. She considers twisting the dial, but Fabian's fingers seem to be performing some kind of foreplay on the steering wheel.

'Woo-hoo I'm on fire,' Fabian howls.

Central locking, she realises.

'Thing is with you, it's all about the virgin whiteness, isn't it?'

A car has stopped on the inside lane up ahead, its hazard lights blurry bursts of orange in the windscreen. She's reliving the image of Jeremy's hand clapped on Fabian's shoulder right back on her first day last July.

'Many men would find the idea of a woman at the altar ball-breaking,' he continues. The gears change with a crunch, before the car bolts across Upper Street and takes an illegal right. His eyes are conducting, at most, a cursory relationship with the road. 'I'm not most men.'

'If you go straight ahead here, and take a left turn, we're almost there.'

Two minutes later, they screech to a halt a few doors away from her house.

She starts to pull at the door as soon as they're stationary.

'Hey, what's the hurry?' He tucks the keys into his breast pocket and swivels to face her, arm draped back on her headrest.

'Thanks for the lift, Fabian, but I really need to—'

'You're hot, you know that, Margot? Uptight, but hot.'

He leans closer, garlicky breath in her face.

'I've seen the way you look at me.' She fumbles at the door. 'It's always the quiet ones.'

'No, sorry, you—'

He drags her face round and with one move his tongue is deep inside her mouth, lashing from side to side, bathed in boozy saliva.

She pushes him back as hard as she can and manages to snatch the keys out of his breast pocket.

He leans across the passenger seat as she stumbles out onto the pavement.

'Hard-to-get is always best,' he slurs. 'Little Miss Virginal, I don't—'

'What the hell do you think you're doing?'

Margot hauls herself upright, her whole body trembling. Felix has his hand clamped around Fabian's arm.

'Who the fuck are you?' shouts Fabian, wrenching himself away and moving across to try to open the driver's door. Felix gets there first and pushes him back inside.

'A passing Samaritan, you tosser.'

Loud barking breaks out right behind Margot. A Dalmatian tied to the fence.

'Time you buggered off, mate,' Felix warns, through the driver's window. 'Mind you don't get pulled over on the way home, know what I mean?'

Margot is shaking so violently, she has to hold onto the railings next to her.

'You'll pay for this, you bitch.'

Felix holds up his phone. 'Photographic evidence. And, like I said, Islington is crawling with police cars.'

Fabian spits out of the window and slams his foot on the accelerator. Felix stands watching him from the middle of the road.

'What are you doing here?' she whispers.

'Didn't take a genius.'

The future rears up in tabloid block headlines. She starts to sob. Felix takes off his jumper and wraps it around her. Cyd or

Nathan could walk out of the house at any moment.

'Come here, it's over now.'

'You can't come in.'

'Obviously.' He strokes her hair. 'Come on, let's get you a drink. What a prick.'

She allows him to lead her back towards the Fields, sanctuary and peril all wrapped up in one.

Felix pulls the duvet higher over his shoulders. She likes nothing more than watching him sleep.

How can something this good be wrong? Love lies at the heart of life; God wants us to be happy and fulfilled in whatever form that happiness takes.

She sits up hugging her knees, drinking in the way his cheeks dip and curve, the sweep of lashes against the freckles. Every time she looks, some new feature reveals itself. That tiny scar under his chin, the curl above his ear that refuses to lie flat, the shape of the shadow where he has yet to shave. It's almost impossible to resist tracing her fingertips across his lips, the endless thrill of touching his skin. Instead, she shrugs back down under the cover and moulds herself against his shoulder, her breath rustling his hair. She kisses the small mole just above where the bone peaks.

How many times have they managed this? Six, at most. An abnormal couple in so many ways. Why does he bother? She knows how he loathes all the concealment, as if she's ashamed of him. When she's alone, she dreams of him pulling her against him, owning her even in sleep. She lays her head back down on his chest, inhaling his biscuity warmth. Just one minute more.

Everything is silent; no consoling thrum of small-hours traffic, no night buses intimating other, less complicated lives.

Felix's foot is dangling over the side of the bed. He turns and mutters something. These nocturnal monologues were disconcerting at first; sudden flashes of his subconscious self. Now she cherishes the unguardedness.

Loving him, feeling so completed in his presence; why should there have to be any conflict with her other world? Sex is the deepest expression of love.

She turns over to face the wall.

Adultery.

She hears him breathing next to her, the comforting rhythm of it.

The pressure is growing stifling. Three and half weeks to Petertide.

It's like being at the twenty-three-mile mark in a marathon. She turns back and absorbs Felix's warmth, tears prickling. Just a minute more.

Lord, I pray that my love for this man, greater than any I have known for anyone, is not sinful in Your eyes. If it be Your will. Amen.

Vic-i-leaks: Scenes from Parish Life, 14 June 2017
Wish the clergy wouldn't go on about cash all the time. What was the point of Jesus throwing the moneylenders out of the temple? I mean, surely a couple of the Care Bears must have a few grand stashed in the drawer under their incontinence pads?

She inhales sharply.

Gwen.

The address is at the far end of Balls Pond Road, a mile or so on from where Arthur used to live. She swallows as the bus passes his old block. They carry on past scrappy front gardens, litter-scattered pavements, a crop of 'for sale' signs. She gets off a couple of stops early to walk the rest of the way. She needs time to prepare herself.

Friends close, enemies closer. Somewhere along the line, Gwen has swapped roles without Margot even noticing the transition.

Fabian, on the other hand, has been a wolf in satin shirts from day one. Felix's insistence that she report him, that she owes it to every other female curate, to every woman who wants to have anything to do with the Church, to all working women everywhere, is all perfectly legitimate. And completely out of the question. March up to Jeremy in the vestry and tell him his favourite fundraiser is a sexual predator who jumped on her in the front of his BMW? He probably wouldn't even believe her.

This morning's visit, however, is different. On this, she has no choice.

She checks the scrap of paper yet again for the address she scribbled down from the electoral roll. A train passes below the fence opposite with an unnerving roar.

She stops again a few feet away, takes a few deep breaths, and then walks off the pavement. up a couple of steps and presses the bell for 40B. Her stomach is roiling with nerves. She shouldn't have come alone.

She bites her lip. Enough. The woman's a 63-year-old do-gooder, not a violent psychopath. As far as she knows.

No answer.

She buzzes again, more firmly. Still nothing. She's starting to retreat down the steps, when a light comes on in the hall and the door opens an inch or two on its chain.

The face peering out at her isn't Gwen's.

Margot stares back down at the paper in her hand.

'Oh, I'm sorry, I must have made a mistake.'

'Hello, love. You must be the girl vicar she's always on about.'

The chain rattles out of the lock and the door opens. David, of course. The husband whose existence Margot so often doubted.

'Come in, Vicar.'

It's such a violent derailing of the scenario she's rehearsed, Margot's at a loss for a reply.

'Gwennie's just popped out to the post office. She won't be long. How about a cuppa while you wait?'

'Maybe I should come back another time?'

'Oh no, she'll only be a minute. She'd be so disappointed to miss you.'

She sleepwalks along the dark corridor, noticing the slight limp, as well as the powerful blend of beef extract and beeswax in the air.

'Give us a sec while I put the kettle eon.'

He gestures her towards an olive-green two-seater covered in home-crocheted cushions. Margot worries she'll snap in two if she attempts to sit down, but forces herself onto the sofa.

She looks round the small room and its commentary on the Gwen. A large collection of royal tat stretching all the way back to the wedding of Princess Margaret, an anaemic watercolour above the fireplace, a scuffed wooden bookcase with two shelves of thrillers and several potted cacti.

Her eyes flit to the other end of the room and stay there, stunned. It's covered wall to wall in photos of six or seven different children at various stages in their development, from babies all the way up to late teens and beyond, hairstyles changing and features maturing as they moved from primary school onwards, dressed as Brownies and Scouts and Guides, sometimes singly, sometimes in twos or threes, gummy, gappy smiles right through to the guarded self-consciousness of young adulthood.

'Sugar, Margot?'

'Oh, no, thanks.'

'That's right. You're sweet enough, aren't you?'

His face betrays nothing as he hands down the Charles and Di mug, the liquid inside a rusty brown.

There's an ancient computer on a small table in the corner, its keyboard concealed under a pastel crocheted cover.

She forces her eyes back to her host.

'So, David, have you and Gwen lived here—'

'She never shuts up about you, you know.'

Her mug is balanced on her knee, the surface of the liquid

trembling.

'Margot this, Margot that. Sometimes it feels like there's three of us in this marriage.' He gives a short laugh. 'She even loves hearing your voice messages. I wouldn't be surprised if she's called you once or twice on the sly just to hear you say you're not there.'

His tone is neutral. She's not sure whether she's expected to laugh.

'Wow.'

He shrugs.

'Gwennie likes mothering people, that's the thing. Always has.'

Margot is sinking out of her depth.

'She's so incredibly generous with her time at St Mark's,' she says, hearing her voice rise an octave. 'The vicar thinks she's a superstar.'

David considers this.

'We all do,' she adds quickly.

'Generous, too.' He drops two lumps of sugar into his mug. 'That massage thingy you two went on, she paid an arm and a leg for it. You have no idea.'

Her cheeks flare. He's right. She doesn't. Of all her responses to that day, all the images that disturb her, the one thing she never dwelt on was the cost. The price to her – Margot – in terms of time and dignity and acute discomfort, she's contemplated that long and hard. But she's never once reflected on what such an expensive outlay would do to this couple's limited budget.

'It was such a kind gesture,' she clears her throat, 'and a truly wonderful day.'

David watches her as he unwraps a toffee. The crinkling is setting her teeth her edge.

'Beautiful photos.'

'The wishing wall, I call it.' He stirs his tea, 'Not to Gwennie of course.'

'Oh, why? What, oh…'

He gives her all the rope she needs. The realisation when it comes fills Margot with an intense sense of shame. All that bravado when she was having her manicure.

'Our nephews and nieces – oh, and a couple of the neighbours' kids.'

Margot pulls at her collar then lets him see her looking at her watch, the coward's way out.

'David, I'm so sorry, I wish I could stay, but the vicar needs me to finish something back at St Mark's.'

He compresses his lips.

'She'll be very unhappy if I let you leave, Margot. This would have made her day, you here in our flat.'

'I'm so sorry,' she says, replacing the mug on the coaster and reaching for her bag as she stands. A fat tortoiseshell cat winds around her calves. 'Very fancy keyboard cover, I must say.'

Her heart is pounding.

'Oh, that. Gwennie made it for me. She knows absolutely nothing about computers. Zilch. Probably thought they need to be kept warm or something. Sweet, though. Typical of her. Told you she likes mothering things.'

Mothering, smothering. She bites the inside of her cheek. The evidence of who, what Gwen is – and what she isn't – bears down on her on all sides. Being pushy and bossy and in-your-face doesn't make her an identify thief: just a sad, unfulfilled woman looking for some meaning to her twilight years.

'Shall I give her a message for you or something?'

'Oh, yes, it was just something to do with the book club. I'll fill her in on Sunday.'

She turns at the door. 'And send her my love, will you?'

The smell of Bovril clings to her as she leans her head against the bus window, humiliated. Above all, ashamed.

Care Bears. How many people know about that? She'd assumed

it was an in-joke in the vestry of St Mark's. But maybe she's wrong. Maybe its common clergy-speak throughout the whole of the C of E?

How is she ever going to prove her innocence? Who of any of them is going to believe her, other than Felix?

Nathan's sitting in the living room in complete darkness when she gets back from the Standing Committee meeting a few days later.

'Oh, sorry, I didn't mean to disturb you,' Margot says, turning the light off quickly. 'I just thought maybe I'd left a file in here.'

'Sit down for a minute, would you?'

Margot drops down into the chair opposite, her eyes adjusting to the shadows.

'Is everything OK?'

'I'm out of ideas.'

She waits but he doesn't say anything else.

'Cyd?'

'Sam found this.'

He holds the foil wrapper out for her to inspect, but she doesn't need to.

'Where?'

'Doesn't really matter where, does it? In here. Stuffed behind one of the cushions.'

Now would be the time to confess. Admit that she's been the keeper of Cyd's secrets for her, a knowing accomplice to underage sex, alcohol and, for all she knows, drugs. She goes cold with shame, looking at the misery on Nathan's face. Because part of the reason she hasn't said anything is her own culpability. That bottle of champagne in the fridge.

Margot was supposed to be the adult in the room.

'I'm out of my mind with worry about her. Some boy called round a couple of nights ago.' He rubs his face. 'Boy? Christ – man, more like. I sent him packing, but there's only so much I can do.

God knows how I can rein her in; I can't even think of the effect this may be having on Sam and Josh.'

He downs the rest of his whisky.

'I feel totally helpless, Margot.'

'Clariss, please pick up. At least text me to tell me you're OK. I understand how mad you are, and believe me, I know why, but at least do this one thing for me and let me know you're fine. Please?'

Lord, I feel so at sea. I've messed up everything. I thought it would be straightforward to live my life in Your service, following Your example of grace and compassion. Even if I make it through the three weeks, which is looking completely unlikely, I don't think I'll ever deserve the trust put in me.

Part IV

A Time of
Reckoning

Chapter 21

Mid-June

It's a sultry day, the banked-up clouds swelling with menace. The Fields are still of people soaking up the warmth of summer's flamboyant arrival. But Margot finds it a headachey heat, the pavements of Upper Street burning beneath her feet, the air torpid and relentless.

Walking into the cool, airy silence of the church this evening gives her a sense of physical as well as spiritual relief. The freesias' sugary greeting an antidote to the sweltering fumes outside.

The oboe ushers in the choral anthem, '*Domine Deus Rex Coelestis*' from Vivaldi's *Gloria*. Its reedy perfection pierces the air, the melody curving like a ribbon around them all.

Kyrie, Kyrie eleison. Lord, have mercy.

The beauty of it brings tears to her eyes. She's loved evensong ever since Cambridge: its quiet, reflective nature, the liturgy both tender and powerful, the sense of solace intense. Never has she needed it more.

Gwen is sitting a few rows over to the right. Margot turns to her and smiles. Gwen looks at her blankly and then turns her head away. She can't have seen her. Margot tries again a few minutes later. Again, nothing. Margot's heart starts to race. Gwen, who until now has hung on her every word, now treating her like the Medusa.

'We heard a few weeks back about Jesus's humanity when He ascended up to heaven,' says Jeremy from the pulpit. 'He was flesh and blood, just like we are. Jesus was one of us. He never claimed to be perfect, just as none of us ever can.' He frowns over the yellow frames and scans the small number of people scattered around the pews. 'I think we'd all say Amen to that.'

This time, Margot does catch Gwen's eye, but she wishes she hadn't. She bites her lip. She'll track her down after the service, find out what's wrong, make amends for whatever slight to Gwen's pride she's delivered this time. She can't have any idea of Margot's Vic-i-leaks suspicions, but she nevertheless needs to atone for them. A friendly chat, a big push on the book club, even an invitation to lunch. Whatever it takes.

'May the road rise to meet you,' says the vicar, his hand held high in blessing. 'May the wind be ever at your back, may the sun shine warm upon your face and the rain fall soft upon your fields and, until we meet again, may God hold you ever in the palm of His hand.'

Gwen is drying sherry glasses in the kitchen when Margot finds her. There's usually half-a-dozen women wielding tea towels in here, eager to please the vicar, but tonight Gwen is rubber-gloved and alone.

'Let me help you, Gwen.' Margot reaches for a tea towel covered in self-portraits of the Kool Gang 1998.

'That's wet,' snaps Gwen, snatching it out of her hand, and turning back to the sink.

Margot bites back her response. She opens the cupboard under the draining board and rummages amongst the Tupperware boxes.

'Did David tell you I popped by the other day?' she asks, pulling out a couple of clean cloths.

Gwen's shoulders hunch further.

'What a lovely man.'

Gwen wheels round, a soapy plate in her hands.

'Why didn't you just phone?'

'Oh. Well, I was nearby, so I just sort of dropped in.'

Gwen doesn't even bother to reply. Margot's head pounds harder.

There's a click behind them. Pamela has just walked in, shutting the door as she does so. The tiny kitchen is clammy and oppressive. The small window above the sink looks terminally shut.

'Margot, I must speak to you.'

Margot places the tea towel over the back of the chair carefully. 'How can I help?'

'In my capacity as head of the PCC.' Pamela's voice has tightened.

Margot glances at Gwen, but she doesn't move. Nor does Pamela ask her to. Instead, she swells her chest and steps closer.

'I'm afraid we have a problem.' She clears her throat. 'You have a problem.'

Margot's knuckles are white from gripping the counter behind her. Pamela licks her lips, places a strand of hair behind her ear. 'It has come to my attention that—'

'We all know about you, Margot,' spits Gwen, throwing the scrubbing brush into the sink, slivers of wet biscuit flying off its bristles. 'Thought you'd get away with it, did you?'

'What are you talking about, Gwen?' Her voice is trembling.

'Gwen, please, if you don't mind,' snaps Pamela. 'Allow me to handle this. It has been brought to my attention, Margot, that you have been involved in – how shall I put it? – an *inappropriate* relationship while serving your title here at St Mark's.' Margot looks up at the locked window above her head.

'I don't—'

'Please don't waste my time by trying to deny it. You've been spotted with him all over the parish.'

'She even brought him here on Easter Day,' hisses Gwen. 'Can you imagine? In this holy place?'

'You're not serious, Gwen?' says Pamela.

'No, no, that's true, I didn't do that.' Margot's eyes are stinging; she's finding it hard to breathe. 'Crying over spilt milk,' sneers Gwen.

'It gets worse.' Pamela holds up her hand to block any more incursions from Gwen, whose face is now right next to Margot's, sweaty with indignation. 'As a magistrate, I always insist on being appraised of all the facts in any infraction of the rules.' Margot's head hangs like unplucked fruit. 'Your,' – a small moue of distaste – '*boyfriend* is still married, I gather.'

The loathing in Gwen's eyes is bottomless. Margot wouldn't be surprised if she spat at her, but instead she takes a step back, wiping her arm against her forehead.

'I had such high hopes of you, Margot.' Gwen lowers her head. 'We welcomed you into our hearts. You and I were friends.'

'Yes, Gwen, we—'

'But you're just like all the rest of them, with your make-up and your earrings and your *waxing*.' Flecks of spittle land on Margot's cheek. 'Likes you all smooth and silky, does he? After you've downed a bottle of *champagne* together?'

'Gwen, I must insist that we retain a—'

'You were so young and pretty, such a lovely change from all those men. I'd have done anything to help your mission here. Anything. I *loved* you, Margot.'

Margot starts to sob.

'Gwen, I must please ask you to desist from—'

'You're just like all those Page Three girls. Disgusting that a floozy like you should be ministering at God's table when you're—'

'Gwen, that's enough!' screams Pamela, grabbing a fistful of Gwen's kaftan and pulling her sideways, away from Margot.

Gwen's face is purple, the mole on her cheek shivering.

'Women have no place at the altar,' Gwen shouts, straining out of Pamela's grip. 'St Paul was right. And Roderick. And Fabian.'

Pamela somehow manages to manhandle Gwen out of the kitchen and slams the door behind her.

The only sound is the dripping from the tap and Margot feverishly trying to control her tears.

'You do realise the severity of your situation?' Pamela asks. '"Engaging in conduct unbecoming and inappropriate to the office and work of the clergy"' quote, unquote.'

A huge crash from outside startles them both. The next moment, rain starts streaming down the glass, punctuated every few seconds by flashes of lightning and more thunder.

'Jesus spoke out against adultery in the Sermon on the Mount, as you, of all people, know. Adultery with a parishioner? I can't think of many graver infringements of canon law, other than embezzlement of church finances. Or murder.'

'I'm so sorry,' Margot whispers.

'Of that, I have no doubt, now that you've been caught pretty much in flagrante. But it's not just me you should be apologising to. So many people have a stake in your career, Reverend.' Pamela lets out a huge sigh. 'All of us here who were involved in the decision to take you on, against wiser counsel from many quarters. Your principal at theological college. Most of all, the vicar. Did you never once think of him?'

Margot's throat is raw from gulping back the sobs.

'We're all tainted by association.'

Tainted. Here it is at last.

Pamela takes out a small notebook and flicks open a page.

'I must tell you that under the provisions of the Clergy Disciplinary Measure, if a lay person – anyone at all – makes a complaint to the registrar of the diocese, your case would automatically come before the archdeacon at a provincial tribunal. There'd be no oral warning or letter of caution beforehand. And that, quite honestly, would be that.'

Margot's knees finally fail her and she sinks down onto the tiles, slumped against the dishwasher. The archdeacon, the eyes and ears of the bishop. The removal of her licence, probably for ever. Everyone she knows aware of her disgrace.

Pamela reaches down to her with a glass of water, merciful at last.

'And Jeremy?' Margot asks, her voice small.

Pamela straightens her shoulders.

'As your incumbent, he wouldn't be part of any investigation, fortunately, though he may be called as a witness.' Pamela pauses. 'If it gets that far. You should get up off the floor, Margot. You're in clerical clothes, remember. For now.'

'What did he say?'

'The vicar? He doesn't know anything about this.' She pats her hair. 'Yet.'

Margot starts to haul herself up as the door slams open.

'Too much alcohol again, Reverend?' The spite spits out of Fabian like hot fat.

'Thank you, Fabian, but this is a private discussion if you don't mind.'

He scowls at Pamela, shoots Margot a look of unalloyed venom and leaves, slamming the door hard.

'Too many cooks,' mutters Pamela.

'Who was it who told you?' she whispers.

'As I said, you've been seen together all over the parish, Margot. I would have thought that, as curate, you'd have been aware that people watch you and notice what you do, even when you're not wearing your collar?'

Margot closes her eyes.

'What should I do now?'

Pamela picks up the glass from the floor and rinses it. 'I suggest you take some time out to consider your own position.'

'I don't need to.'

Pamela stands appraising her, hands on her hips.

The air hums after the brutality of the storm.

Pamela gives a curt nod.

'Out of your hands now, I'm afraid.' She clears her throat. 'And, frankly, out of mine. I'll pray for you, Margot.'

At this moment, there's one person she need to speak to more than any other. The one person who would understand.

'Where are you? Please call me. This is a total emergency. Please, please call me back. I need to speak to you badly.'

It's Margot's fault. All of it. From the moment she sent him that first text. The inevitability slicing through every moment they've spent together like dormant strains of a lethal disease.

She'd always known the risk. Acutely understood where the boundaries lay. Did she think no one would see them? Margot Goodwin, public property number one?

And yet, something was uncorked that day at Somerset House. His insouciance, his laughter – his love – somehow reached through all the layers and plucked out the real her. Her time with him has felt pure and good. Blessed.

But just because she wanted it so badly didn't make it right.

She falls into a claustrophobic half-sleep before being jolted awake by the alarm an hour later. For a few moments, she forgets the horror of the previous day; the recollection hits her like a wrecking ball.

She pulls herself out of bed on autopilot.

Come, follow me.

She slumps onto the chair.

I have failed You on every count. Through Your grace, help me to do what I have to do today. Help me not to hurt him.

He always gets in to work by seven thirty. It's been a running joke between them, the early-bird prize.

She holds her breath as she walks through the playground. She exchanges a few words with the receptionist, who points out the direction without looking up,

The corridor taps out the drumbeat of her footsteps like a death march.

In, out. Unseen, undone.

She owes him this.

'Christ, Margot. You startled me.'

He scrapes back his chair and stands.

'You look dreadful.'

He walks round the desk towards her.

'Gogo? What's wrong?'

Her resolve is already fading. She steps back from him and keeps her eyes trained on the floor, on a paper clip on the rug beneath his desk.

'We've got to stop seeing each other.'

'What are you talking about?'

He moves towards her.

'What do you mean?'

She can't let him hold her.

'Please come here, Margot.'

She shakes her head.

'I mean, have I done something? Because, you know, I don't always know. It's a bit difficult to—'

'Someone's reported us.'

Felix turns away and rubs his hands through his hair. Out in the corridor, a vacuum has been switched on.

'It's my fault, Felix. I knew how dangerous it was all along.'

He wheels round again.

'You're five minutes away from being ordained, for God's sake. You've proved to them all you can do the job.'

'Someone reported us to the PCC.' She's trying to stay calm but the expression on his face threatens to disarm her.

She walks towards the wall. Look back now and she's lost.

'Vicars and priests are allowed to fall in love, right? This is 2017, not the Salem Witch Trials.'

He's chopping the air with his hands, trying to reason away two thousand years of precedent.

'It'll probably go all the way to the archdeacon.'

'Wait, it was that prick who assaulted you, wasn't it?'

'It's all my fault,' she says again, barely audible. 'I should never have dragged you into all this.'

'Stop it, Gogo. You didn't drag me into anything. It's been the most amazing—'

She's out of the room and down the corridor before he can stop her. He won't come after her, she knows that. He wouldn't risk being seen by half the school racing across the playground in pursuit of her.

She rushes towards the gate, eyes blurred, praying that she doesn't slam into Cyd as the final humiliation.

Early-evening sun is slicing into the medieval study, throwing dark shadows into the corners.

'Let me be quite clear, Margot. I'm not angry or incandescent or any of the other blood-splitting states you might have been expecting. It's not my job – or style – to be judgemental. I am, however, bloody furious that you didn't talk to me about all this weeks ago. The whole point here is supposed to be the trust and honesty between us. This is supposed to be your safe house, remember?'

Hadley leans back, arms crossed, wearing an expression Margot has never seen before. She hangs her head in defeat.

Walking here, past the porter's lodge and across the courtyard, every step had rung with menace. The perfect green square highlighting on her own inability to respect the boundaries, the ancient stone implacable in its judgement. *We had such high hopes of you, Margot. You've betrayed us all.*

'Let me tell you something.' Hadley walks over to the window and pushes it open further, encouraging the scent of new-mown grass to pour in. She perches on her desk, next to Margot. 'Ten years as a criminal attorney and twelve as a priest have taught me to unlearn everything I thought I knew about human nature.'

She sighs. Margot's spirits fall even lower.

'So tell me. How would you describe your decision to sleep with a parishioner during the most vital year of your career to date, when so very much hangs on your ability to make it through all the hoops intact? A married parishioner, no less. Chuck me some adjectives here.'

Margot looks down at her hands. A bell is ringing in the chapel outside.

'Ready when you are.'

'Stupid,' she whispers.

'Yup.'

'Reckless.'

'Uh-huh.'

'Dangerous.' Margot swallows.

'That'll do it.'

'Selfish.'

'OK, I think we can stop there.'

Margot glances back up.

'You know you screwed up, Margot. That's why you didn't call me. Because you knew you'd done something off the scale of risky and you couldn't face admitting it. As you said, stupid, stupid, stupid.'

Margot can't think of anything to say in return.

'Look, you meet a guy you're really into. No problem there. Sex in a loving, trusting, respectful relationship. No problem there, either. For me at least, though, as you're well aware, many of our evangelical brethren wouldn't agree with me. Our high-church brethren as well, come to that. To be honest, that's between them and their consciences.'

Hadley reaches behind her for her coffee.

'But a married guy in the congregation? A few months before you're due to be priested? Neither smart nor, to be brutally honest, that helpful to the cause of the clergy sisterhood. Never hand the enemy ammunition, Margot. Unfair as it may seem, women are still seen as the custodians of goodness, and judged on our sexuality, earning ourselves every epithet from virgin to harlot in the process.'

Margot pulls a crumpled tissue out of her handbag. Hadley pushes forwards a box of lavender-scented Kleenex. Followed by a tray of Belgian chocolates.

'I'm so sorry.'

Hadley places her hand on Margot's arm.

'If you love this guy, then I get it. So will God. The heart goes where the heart leads. We both know that.'

'Really?' asks Margot, her voice hoarse.

'Being a rounded human being makes you a better priest, Margot. Take it from me. People identify with our flaws in the way they wouldn't – can't, even – with a paragon. Why do you think they call it a curate's egg? Most of us are a seething mass of insecurities, no matter how together we seem on the surface. No one's perfect and I don't believe God wants or expects us to be. That includes you, Margot. And me. It's about following the Divine will and living with integrity. Though, having said that, if people knew what many priests were really like, they wouldn't come to church.'

Hadley bursts out laughing.

'You're something of a George Herbert buff, if I remember, aren't you?'

Margot nods. Hadley reaches for a book from her shelf, festooned with brightly coloured tabs.

'Quick-ey'd Love, observing me grow slack
From my first entrance in,
Drew nearer to me, sweetly questioning,
If I lack'd anything.'

They both fall silent.

'The principal at Wilhurst used to say that your daily life is as much a sermon as any of the words you preach,' says Margot.

Hadley nibbles at the walnut on top of her caramel.

'Mmm, these are insane.' She smiles. 'The most important relationship is between you and God, Margot. Whatever happens between you and St Mark's.'

Margot shivers at the implied danger.

'God never turns away, no matter what you do or who you love. As for your parish, well, let's wait and see. We have no choice but to be honest. Everyone loves crisis mode. Gives them the chance to show how charitable they are. But we all need grace and humility and none of us is God, even the magisterial members of your PCC. "When I am weak, I am strong." Nine times over, we ask for forgiveness in the liturgy, remember? Grace is a gift.'

Hadley closes the lid on the chocolates with an air of finality.

'So, tell me, what do you think would be the best thing to do now?'

Margot hesitates, dreading hearing the words out loud.

'I've stopped seeing him.'

Her eyes fill up again.

'O-K.' Hadley reaches again for Margot's hand.

'So how about this? Why not put him … what's his name, by the way?'

'Felix,' Margot whispers.

'Felix. Lucky or successful. Nicely chosen. OK, so why not put Mr Lucky and Successful on the back burner for a while, as it were? Just until you're priested and have done your first Mass and settled in. If he cares enough, he'll wait. After that, you can review, the two of you together. How does that sound?'

'I think he'd probably rather be rid of me and all my baggage.' She swallows. 'Or "your bloody Church and its medieval take on life", as he put it one time.'

Hadley chuckles.

'Right. Well, if he does care enough, he'll also be prepared to put up with the medieval bit.' She smiles. 'Though if he's anything like Brad, he'll have a good old whinge from time to time. Do you know, he was even interviewed as part of my application process? Incredible.'

Margot looks over at the family photo, wiping her eyes.

'When was the last time you had a break?' Hadley asks. 'Not counting the weeks off after Christmas and Easter.'

Margot can't even remember.

'Thought so. Disappear off for a few days. Go and chill somewhere. Try and clear your head. You owe that to yourself. And to me and your poor incumbent, frankly. And for goodness sake, enough already with the self-torture. It's usually male curates who unload their guilt trips with me.'

'But surely I can't go anywhere right now?'

'Take it as an order from your spiritual director. I'll speak to Jeremy.'

Hadley smiles. Job done.

'And now, time for us to say a prayer together. God has a path for you, Margot, even if it feels like it's got more roadblocks than the M25. Remember what we know about Divine Providence: there's always a Plan A and a Plan B. You've made it this far, Margot. Hold on for the last push. You can do that for me, right?'

Margot gives a tiny nod.

'Let's just pray that none of your hyperactive parishioners decides to fire off a green-ink email.'

Chapter 22

Third week of June

The line where sea meets sky has always captivated her. Blue, green, grey, the swirl of the colours dependent on the height of the cloud, the depth of the water, the presence or absence of the sun, wind, rain. She loves the blurring of the edges, the way it creates a great blank canvas of space and possibility. The huge sweep of the bay out towards the needles and the Isle of Wight, the polar-bear shape on the cliffs at its southernmost tip.

There's a stiff breeze this morning, sending clouds scurrying across the sky and whipping up ridges of opalescent expanse. Part of her would like to stride out into the waves and disappear.

She takes her time walking along the sand, taking in the dedications on the wooden benches strung along the seafront.

Rachel, 1985–2003. Shine On, You Crazy Diamond

For Andy Browne – Who Always Loved This Place

Betsy Lambert, who passed on in 1999, aged 65 years. On a Clear Day We Can See Forever

She slows down at each one she walks past, humbled at these moving testimonies to the endurance of love.

An unseasonal wind has emptied the beach. Just a few doughty hardcore types behind their stripy windbreakers, a handful of mothers and toddlers kicking balls through the shallows, dogs racing along the bottom of the scarp, finally off the leash. Just like her.

Think of these few days as a retreat, Hadley said. A break in which to regroup spiritually and emotionally. Who'd have thought returning here to Highcliffe could offer her any kind of peace? And yet over the past few days, somehow it has.

She sits down one of the benches, watching the sun emerge, allowing a dancing trelliswork of silver to appear where the beams hit the water.

She's found a small B & B place a couple of streets back. The owner hasn't shown the least interest in who she is or why she's here, providing just the anonymity she's been craving. Sitting on the narrow single bed watching the sun dip into its watery berth though a gap in the trees has given her a profound sense of calm.

Over the past three days, she's walked up and down this shoreline she'd forgotten she knew so well, its contours as familiar as a lover's face.

On the train down from Waterloo, she'd worried that she would end up spending the entire time churning everything over. Yet the moment she walked down here past the multicoloured beach huts and caught the salty tang, heard the terns screeching overhead, saw the lush green woodland of the Chewton valley reserve, she knew this was the only place she could have come to right now.

She strolls along the sand, her toes feeling for the tiny turban shells and stripy bivalves they always used to collect as children, watching children play It with the waves, a father teaching his son how to make his kite duck and dive on the currents, a pensioner wielding a metal detector with the intensity of the true believer; she understands that she's home.

Yesterday, she ended up turning inland for a mile or two and then realised she was on a mission. It had taken her over an hour to walk there because she'd got lost a couple of times on the way.

It probably won't even be open, she'd thought. Most aren't on a daily basis: sign of the times. Then, when she'd arrived outside, at the corner of the nondescript parade of shops and 1930s redbrick houses, she'd had to go and sit in a café opposite to regroup. Then she'd crossed back over and stood outside the door, hesitating for several minutes, but finally she'd lifted the latch, because she knew it was another staging post on this journey. The door opened and with a quiet roar, it all came flooding back.

There are six voicemail messages and eight texts from Felix when she finally disobeys Hadley's orders.

'Margot, can you please call me? Christ, this is insane. I mean, you know, I can speak to your vicar or something? You had nothing to do with me and Patties, nothing. You know that. Please call me back. I need you.'

She swallows. His voice was cracking. She forces herself to listen to the next message and the next and the next.

Then the anger.

'Do you have any idea how this feels? Do you? What a shitty way to be treated.'

She throws the phone across the room and buries her head in her hands.

Nothing whatsoever from Clarissa, hostile or otherwise.

'Jeremy?'

She rocks backwards and forwards on the edge of the bed, all of a sudden queasy with unease.

'Oh, hello, Margot.' His tone is flat. 'How are things? Feeling on the mend?'

The bedroom curtain flaps around the window frame in the evening breeze. The ozone is always the most intense at this hour. Something to do with the tide? She's cradling a pink-and-white netted whelk from the small collection gathered on the ledge. Grains of sand are grazing her palm.

'Much better, thanks.'

He coughs. She can picture the glasses being pushed up his forehead. He'll loathe this conversation as much as she does. 'I'm afraid things are hotting up here, one way or another.'

'Right.'

'But best talk about all that when you're back. We won't disturb your retreat.'

She can't detect anything in his voice, but he wouldn't be human if he wasn't wondering what possessed him to bring such a liability into his parish.

'Whatever you think best, Jeremy.'

'A couple of days won't make a difference at this point. And it's important you regain your strength.'

For dealing with the days to come.

'OK, well, see you Friday, then.'

'Thanks for calling, Margot. Oh, one other thing before you go.' She twists the shell in her fingers, wishing she could crawl inside. 'A lady called Linda rang me yesterday.'

Later, when the sun has set, but the twilight is refusing to cede its place, she reaches for the phone again.

In the end there is only love, Hadley said. That's the whole story. All there really is. Alpha and Omega, the beginning and end of everything.

If I speak in the tongues of men and angels, but have not love, I am only a responding gong or a clanging cymbal.

'Dad?'

'Oh, hello, Margot, love.' He pauses, 'I thought you might ring. Sorry about that call, but she insisted, said she'd do the heavy lifting for you or something.'

It takes her a moment.

'Oh. Don't worry about it, Dad.' No matter how bad Linda's phone call was. 'Listen, Dad. I'm down here in Highcliffe for a couple of days. I wondered if I could get the bus over and come to see you?'

She can see the surprise on his face.

'Well, I'm off tomorrow, as it happens. Was planning a bit of fishing down on the Avon. Season's just started.'

She knows exactly where.

Her mother had probably seen it as another form of abandonment when the three of them went off together for the day, each of the children carrying a small backpack with their lunch inside. Yet, despite the emotional tug of war, Margot remembers them as happy times.

Sometimes he'd fish directly from the beach in Bournemouth with his waders on, alongside all the other evening hobbyist fishermen. But best of all was when he used his permit for the Royalty Fishery here on the river near Christchurch. This was the place Margot always loved most of all. Something about the flatness of the meadows and the angle of the light made it feel as though they were stepping into a medieval painting of villagers working the fields, standing upright from time to time to rub the base of their spine and look southwards towards the church tower dominating the horizon. It had once been an Augustian Priory before Henry VIII unleashed his fury and ransacked its coffers. Margot had climbed the bell tower a couple of times when she was young, counting the steps all the way up to the top, until she and Dan were able to look down over the moss-spangled turrets to the wide-open plains below.

She leans against the grassy bank and takes in the scene. The river has a glassy quality she remembers well, a dark green ribbon meandering through the fields, the weeds below the water yearning seawards, the peppery cow parsley on its banks swaying in the wind.

'Caught anything, Dad?'

She peers into the bucket.

'Right out of practice, I'm afraid. I need to work on my rolling meat technique.'

'Whatever that is.'

'Not so much time these days.'

Their eyes catch. Treacherous waters already.

'Linda encouraged me to get back into it, actually. As long as I throw them straight back in.' He clears his throat. 'Something to do with one of her previous incarnations. Or was it theirs? I can never remember.'

'I see.'

She avoids his eyes. Who is she to criticise the sanity – let alone the sanctity – of anyone's beliefs?

There's what sounds like a light snort behind her, and she turns back, surprised, to see Ricky grinning at her.

'Just kidding, love. I'm not, you know, totally up to speed on all that stuff, but, hey, live and let live.'

She smiles back. The danger has passed.

A bee is working its way up a reedy stem next to her. This was always his favourite, most productive, place to fish. Parlour Pool. An abundance of pike, carp and barbel, the water so clear there, it's black.

'Down here for work, then, Margot?'

'Kind of.' She hesitates, loathe to shatter the mood. 'I need to sort a few things out.'

'Oh?' He looks up from rewinding his reel. 'Not because of Linda?'

'No, no, of course not,'

He stands the rod up against the fence.

'Anything you want to talk about?'

Margot sighs, looking out at the water moving inexorably towards the end of its journey less than a mile away. The smoothness of the surface here is deceptive; she knows that a few metres further on, it becomes a torrent, impatient for resolution.

'Maybe later?'

'Take this bait box, then, and make yourself useful.'

Neither of them speaks for a while amidst a companionable silence of twisting flies onto hooks.

Margot clears her throat.

'Dad, I wanted to tell you, I'd be happy to do your wedding, your handfasting.' She pauses. 'But I'm not sure I'll be able to now.'

He waits. She manages reaches for a pink-and-red fly far too beautiful to be speared on a hook.

'But I will do, if I make it that far.'

'Don't be daft. Why wouldn't you?'

A heron is sitting statue-still on the opposite bank, intent on something it's spotted under the surface. She envies its undiluted sense of purpose.

Ricky watches her watching.

'That guy knows all about patience and biding his time. If he goes in too early, there'll be no lunch for our long-necked friend.'

He reaches over for her arm.

'You'll get there, love. Dead cert. I mean, you've put up with my barracking all these years, right?'

She doesn't dare look at him. This is the first time in eight years he's ever said anything like this.

He squeezes her shoulder.

'Linda will be thrilled about the wedding. The whole thing is a big deal for her.'

'How about you?'

He gives a light laugh.

'I know this hasn't been easy for you, Margot. Even after all this time.'

'Dad, I—'

'For either you or Danny, actually.'

Margot looks down. She can't speak for him on any level.

The wind ruffles the rushes below them. The heron is still on the opposite bank in its elder statesman pose. He'll wait as long as it takes.

Her father sits down next to her.

'Did I ever tell you about the first time I saw your mum?' She breaks off a piece of reed for support, welcoming the breeze across her cheeks. 'She was in a comedy revue. I was working in Bristol and one of the guys dragged me along to this thing. I don't remember anything about the rest of it, just your mum in a couple of the sketches. Hilarious. She was the best bloody thing by far. Standing there in her black high heels, red curls piled on top of her head, hand on hip, looking like she owned the stage. Which she did. She was in her own skin up there.'

Out of the corner of her eye, she sees him run the back of his hand across his cheek.

'You spend years afterwards thinking about all the things you should have said. Done.' He takes a deep breath. 'Or not done.'

She places her fingers on his wrist.

'I know you and Danny were kind of cut adrift afterwards. I was completely bloody useless.'

'Dad, stop. It doesn't matter any more,' she says, not sure she can take much more.

'I just didn't know where the hell to start.'

She squeezes his fingers.

'I had no idea she was so depressed at the time, love. Danny told me years later. When you were at Cambridge.'

Margot carves a hole in the reed she's holding. Danny had to deal with it.

'It was Linda who helped me sort out my head about it all.'

She raises her head.

'She's made me feel whole again. In her own way, she really is a kind of healer, I suppose.'

There's a beating sound as the heron glides into flight, its enormous grey wings drawing a graceful arc above them.

Margot turns back to face him.

'She is,' she says, smiling. 'I'm happy that you're happy, Dad. Really happy.'

The knot inside her shifts a fraction, a tiny loosening of its inner coils.

'I'm sure you and Linda will, you know, click, when you get to know each other a bit more.'

She picks up a second reed and ties the two together.

'Look, I'm already weaving my crown for the big day.'

She watches his line cast out into the farthest reaches of the stream. Christ was a fisherman.

Follow Me, and I will make you fishers of men.

The staircase in Clarissa's student accommodation block on Mare Street is dingy and sour-smelling on a drizzly, unforgiving June evening. Why does she continue to live in these places, Margot wonders, with their overwhelming sense of impermanence and lonely anonymity?

Her heart is thumping hard. This was the first thing she needed to do when she got back from Highcliff. So much to try and heal. So many acres of friendship to try and claw back.

Right from Cambridge onwards, Clarissa's loyalty has been a fixed point in her life. No matter how autocratic, Margot knows that Clarissa would have braved anything – anyone – on her behalf.

She's carrying bricks on her shoulders as she knocks on the door.

Nothing. She's sure she's in there.

Margot knocks again, harder, determined to see it through.

'Clariss. It's me.'

Margot can sense her presence on the other side of the metal door. Someone has scratched their initials near the lock.

'I never had you down as a coward.'

The door yanks open.

'Why didn't you reply to any of my texts?'

'Tell you what, feels shitty, doesn't it?' snaps Clarissa.

'Can I come in?'

'Give me one good reason why.'

Margot bites her lip.

'Because you're a better person than me.'

The hostility radiating from Clarissa is chilling. She braces herself for the door being slammed in her face, but finally Clarissa jerks her head sideways and lets Margot pass.

She's shocked yet again at the prison-like brutality of these rooms. A bed, a desk, a wardrobe, washbasin and that's it.

'Been a while since I was here.'

'You said it.'

'Can we sit down?'

Margot drags the chair out from under the desk. Her breath shortens at the thought of the conversation ahead.

'I know I owe you an apology.'

Clarissa doesn't move a muscle.

'I know why you're mad at me, Clariss. But it was just all so—'

'Don't tell me, passion got the better of you.'

Margot focuses on the fluorescent-green bag in the corner, grubby and coming unstitched in the corner.

'Can you just let me try and explain?'

'Sorry, but you're mistaking me for someone who gives a fuck.'

Margot pinches the inside of her arm for support.

'Look, I'm sorry about all your Soulmates guys and—'

'*My* Soulmates guys?'

'No, what I meant was—'

'Will anything ever puncture that self-righteous little bubble of yours?'

'Clariss, I haven't come here to—'

Clarissa shoves some piles of clothes off the bed and crashes down next to Margot. Her eyes are ringed with black shadows. There's a half-eaten plate of something abandoned on the floor.

'Let *me* explain. Soulmates was a bit of fun to help you, Margot.' She jabs her finger in the air. 'That's how it's always been. Me picking up the little bits and pieces of you and gluing them back together after whatever the latest drama in your life has been. The Eddie obsession, the finals crisis, the shall-I-be-a-priest crisis. Sometime I feel I've lived through it all so closely, it's like these things are my backstory, not yours.'

'You finished?'

'We agreed, no married men. Ever.'

Margot recoils against the wall.

'Have you been stalking me?'

'You've heard of Facebook?'

Margot gapes at her.

'I can't stand hypocrites,' adds Clarissa. 'You've known me long enough to know that about me, Margot.'

Something dislodges in Margot. This is all because she dared to fly solo, the one small area of her life where she has not sidestepped the rules.

She jumps up and grabs for her bag, but misjudges and its contents upend all over the floor.

'You know what? That's pretty funny coming from someone who didn't mind humiliating me just for a laugh,' she says, shovelling everything back inside her bag. 'And anyway, Felix is as good as divorced.'

'Don't tell me you fell for that?'

The metallic clang of Margot's heels bounces off the walls as she charges down three flights of stairs.

It's only when she's back on the pavement that the anger gives way to shock and then to grief.

Her best friend.

Chapter 23

Fourth week of June

The vestry has become the Minotaur's cave. This cluttered, shambolic, familiar space she's worn like a second skin now bristling with menace. Her fears that she might not get to the end of her curacy next week are now taking shape in gothic form. Glances slide, silences are spiked, throats theatrically cleared.

Jeremy is already at his desk when she walks in. He's been doing this often recently, insomnia yet another reward for him putting her on his payroll.

She absorbs the fall of his shoulders, the pile of untouched paperwork.

He gives her a wan smile.

'Jeremy, I'm—'

He holds up a finger, as if the words hadn't already failed her.

'I'm going to collect something from the bookshop down near the Angel. Fancy joining me?'

She nods, miserably.

'Do you think we need a brolly?'

The small café is packed with young mothers balancing toddlers on their laps. The chaos of buggies by the front door almost deters Jeremy, until Margot reminds him this place does the best cupcakes in Islington.

They squeeze in next to a table laden with flat whites, organic muffins and sippy cups. Several of the women glance over and exchange a look with each other.

Through the window, she can see the greasy spoon over the road where she and Roderick met all those months ago. She looks away. This is the conversation she's been dreading most of all.

'You know it's not me who makes the rules, don't you?'

She concentrates on carving her cappuccino froth into small spikes.

'As far as I'm concerned, we don't live in the Dark Ages.' He clears his throat. 'One thing I don't get.'

A sippy cup lands by Margot's foot. She hands sit back, glad of the brief diversion.

'You were so keen to blend in.'

'I was. Am.'

'And then you launch yourself headfirst into a frankly insane relationship with a married member of the congregation.'

She shakes her head. Where does she start?

'No? Well, I know he's married and he's been spotted more than once in St Mark's. In my book, that makes him a regular.'

'He's an atheist.'

Jeremy leans away from her. 'And that's supposed to be a recommendation?'

'No, no, I mean, he's about to get divorced.'

Jeremy sighs, rubbing his eyes.

'Plus, someone saw you going into his flat one night. Don't ask me who.'

At this point, it wouldn't even surprise her if she's been tailed by a private detective.

Jeremy picks up a napkin and swipes at his chin.

'Let's set aside what this guy does and doesn't believe. Each of us has to find our own pathway. And what you get up to in your private life should be your own business, of course. Within limits. But,' – he wipes the side of his cup – 'we're supposed to be setting an example, you and I, unfair though that may seem. Congregations hold us up to different standards, far higher than any they would ever set themselves. They want us to be paragons of virtue, no matter how pockmarked our virtue may be.'

One of the young mothers on the neighbouring table is nuzzling her baby's hair, stroking the skin on his ankle where the tiny sock has rolled down. Margot looks away.

Jeremy nudges the plate of cupcakes towards her.

'Discomfort eating,' he says, biting off a marzipan carrot. 'So, are you going to marry him?' He pauses. 'When, you know, he's free?'

Her cheeks flare.

'We're not seeing each other any more.'

'Ah.'

A commotion over by the door distracts them both. A woman is trying to drag a large buggy outside with a little boy on a scooter in tow. A couple of other pushchairs have got caught up in the tangle. She makes it outside with the help of a couple of young guys who then walk into the café, heads together, sharing a quick joke. They're attractive, slim, both dressed in jeans and button-down shirts. Several heads follow them to their table. But it's not the expressions on the other women's faces that strike Margot. It's Jeremy's.

She waits for him to look at her again. When he does, it's all there.

The space between them shimmers. He gives a tiny shrug.

'No righteous judgement from me, Margot. I've been on the receiving end of it for the past twenty-three years.' He looks down at his plate. 'Endless interrogations about my holiday plans, where was my vicar's wife and all the rest.'

The backstory unspools in her head. How did she never see? He waits a few moments for her to catch up.

'Let me tell you something, since we seem to be doing True Confessions this morning.'

She starts to fold her paper cupcake case into tiny squares.

'When I was in my last parish down in Devon, I met someone. Just like you have.'

He pauses, gathering himself.

'Without wanting to sound like daytime TV, it was the bolt-from-the-blue thing we all crave but very few of us are lucky enough to get. But you know, I was – we were – lucky. He swallows. 'It felt so good that very not long afterwards, he came to live with me. We thought it would be OK, we'd be discretion incarnate and no one would be any the wiser.' He shakes his head. 'How naïve we were. Someone in the congregation got wind of it somehow and that was that.'

She looks up. His face tightens.

'They threatened to expose us unless we, we—'

'You stopped seeing him.'

'The single biggest regret of my life.'

She looks back down, appalled by the implications of this. 'It's too late?'

'It is too late.' There's a catch in his voice.

She pulls her jacket tighter. The happy babble around them in the café is a particularly cruel soundtrack to this story without a happy ending.

Jeremy shrugs and arranges his face into bravery, straightening his shoulders and flicking the crumbs off his jacket. He reaches for the rest of her cupcake.

'Don't misunderstand me, Margot. I've very fulfilled in my life now, serving God and pursuing my ministry at St Mark's in the way I always wanted to. I would never have willingly given that up. It's the life I chose and was chosen for. Just like you. I feel that even more now than I did when I started out.'

She tips her head. 'But?'

'But if it were today, I would fight for him. I know we could have carried on under the radar somehow, come to some sort of accommodation with the parish, if you like. And things have moved on so far now, in any case. In the rest of society. at least.' He bites his lip. 'We just got our timing very wrong.'

They look at each other for a few moments.

'We're all human – even priests,' he continues. 'We all feel fear, rage, lust, love. I don't know how up you are on your Leonard Cohen, but he hit it bang on when he said, "There's a crack in everything. That's how the light gets in."'

'That's beautiful.'

'What's the New Testament if not one long manifesto on forgiveness and compassion? "Let him who is without sin cast the first stone."'

'Hadley said the same thing last week.'

'Did she? I'm looking forward to meeting her at your priesting.'

Margot looks away. She won't make it that far,

'Who you are as a human being – a sexual being included – has no bearing on your role as a man or woman of God. Sin is a state without God. The most important thing is integrity in a loving relationship. You and I are as devoted to our mission as Reverend Bloggs with his wife and his two point two kids and bog-standard existence. More so, even, because we've swum so much against the tide to get here.'

He's right. But he's not the one pronouncing judgement.

'Not everyone sees the world the same way, sadly,' he sighs, reading her mind. 'Some people don't even want a vicar's wife to have a life of her own, let alone the female vicar. St Mark's used to be a live-and-let-live kind of place. I don't know what happened.'

He touches her arm.

'Let's pray that no one makes a complaint to the bishop's office. He tends towards the evangelical on this kind of stuff.'

Why doesn't she just jack it all in now? At least then she'd be in control of the decision.

Halfway through the morning, there's a loud tap of the vestry door, a boisterous statement of intent rather than the tentative tappings announcing the arrival of one of the flower ladies.

Jeremy glances over at Margot and pushes back his chair.

She gasps as a few moments later, two policemen stride inside. The sight of the domed helmets, the Day-Glo vests, the shiny handcuffs and the radios attached to their jackets jars violently in this tiny room. The taller of the two is so bulky, he topples the pyramid of tombolo donations by the door. The other one is younger, skinnier and, she realises with a jolt, familiar. She's seen those ruddy cheeks and the wisps of strawberry blond before.

They give Roderick a businesslike nod and he offers an odd little wave in return. Was he expecting them?

Jeremy pulls on his jacket.

'How can we help, gentlemen?'

'We're here to speak to Reverend Goodwin, vicar.'

Roderick's crooked finger directs them to their target.

Margot somehow feels calm. Something sinister has been lurking on the edge of her vision for weeks now. She just wasn't expecting it to appear in this precise form: two Metropolitan policemen, one of them fiddling the handcuffs hanging from his belt as they wait for her to respond.

'That's me.'

'A private word, madam, please.'

'Reverend,' corrects Jeremy.

A gaggle has formed over by the kitchen door. Tommy, frowning in concern, two of the flower ladies, huddled and scared, and, out of nowhere, Gwen.

'Somewhere private, maybe?' the senior one asks again.

Margot glances over at Jeremy and then steps in front of them towards the hall. Should she have some kind of legal representative with her? Maybe she's not even entitled to that.

'You having a clear-out, miss?' the younger one asks, as they walk towards the Kool Gang Corner.

'A clear-out?'

He frowns. Margot drags one of the playgroup tables across, then a couple of the plastic chairs. The young one grins at the sight of his superior's attempts to squash into one.

'This is as private as it gets, I'm afraid.'

The two of them nod and pause. She waits for the sound of the gavel.

'I believe you know a minor named Cydney Armstrong?'

A rush of adrenaline powers through her. An accident? A hit-and-run? Drugs?'

'Can confirm you know her, please?'

'Yes, yes, I do,' whispers Margot.

An uneven clip-clopping sound starts at the other end of the hall. They all turn to see Roderick stumbling towards them, bearing a tray with two mugs. In the eleven months and three weeks Margot has been at St Mark's, he has never once switched on the kettle.

'Coffee, officers?'

The tray makes a shaky descent onto the table, each mug adrift in a small puddle of brown.

'That's very kind, sir. Don't mind if I do.'

Roderick pulls out the handkerchief, wipes his fingers, stuffs it back in his trousers and stands watching, arms across his chest.

All three men look at each other. The superior clears his throat.

'I'm sorry, Reverend, but we need to speak to Miss Goodwin in private. If you don't mind.'

'Are you sure I can't be of any help?'

'We've got it covered, sir. Thanks all the same.'

Roderick's face creases back into a scowl. They wait until he's shuffled his way back out into the vestry, Margot suppressing a scream.

'Nice bloke,' says the young one, before taking a sip of his coffee and wincing.

'So, Reverend Goodwin, can you confirm how you know Cydney Armstrong?'

Margot takes a deep breath.

'I lodge with her family. At forty-nine Aberdeen Avenue.'

'Correct.'

The younger one jots down something in childish script.

'Is she OK? Has there been some sort of accident?'

'Depends on what you mean by accident.' He pauses for dramatic effect. 'An incident, certainly.'

There's no sound for a few seconds, other than a roaring in Margot's head, as the younger one makes more notes in his pad.

'Can you please confirm where you were late afternoon on June the nineteenth? We're talking between five and six p.m.?'

The Kool Gang's Pentecost paintings are swimming in and out of focus opposite her, scarlet and orange flames twisting before her eyes.

Her mind has turned blue screen. She battles to control the tremor in her voice. 'Two days ago, you said?'

He waits.

'I can look it up in my diary.'

'Please.'

'Can I ask why you need to know?'

The one in charge sniffs, pulls a tissue out of his pocket, takes his time wiping his nose, and stuffs it back in his trousers. Red veins marble his flabby cheeks. She's aware of the younger one watching her, mouth slightly ajar.

'Cydney Armstrong has been charged with aggravated criminal damage. At Highbury High School.'

Margot inhales.

'Smashed up the head's room,' the other one says.

'Deputy head,' the senior officer snaps.

Margot clamps her hand over her mouth.

'Allegedly smashed.'

'Allegedly.'

'Impossible.'

'Nasty business,' says the senior officer in a flat tone. 'Graffiti all over the walls, not nice at all, Reverend. Picture frames smashed, drawers tipped out onto the floor, a right mess, to be honest. It almost looked like a professional job. I've seen enough of those.'

'They even cut some soft toy to ribbons,' says the younger one, excited. 'You OK, miss? You've gone sort of grey. Want some water?'

Margot pinches the skin between her thumb and forefinger hard.

'Can I call you once I've checked my diary?' She hesitates. 'I've left it at home.'

The senior one frowns.

'My vestry diary won't have all my movements in.'

The officers look at each other, then the older one sighs and heaves himself up. Margot takes the card he gives her and leads them to the door.

She watches them marching along the pavement, the world dissolving around her. Cyd's in grave trouble. And she's nursing some violent grudge against Felix.

But where does she herself fit in?

Then, in an instant, she understands. She sets off up the pavement at a run.

'Wait, officers.'

They both turn and stare.

'I'm sorry, I've just remembered,' she blurts. 'Cydney and I were out shopping that afternoon. By the Angel. You know, that indoor shopping centre. I needed a birthday present for a friend and asked her to come along and help me choose.'

The senior officer gives her a long, level look.

'Underwear shopping. You know, officer.'

The younger one blinks.

'You sure about that, *Reverend*?' the older one asks.

She nods, unable to trust herself.

'Sure you don't need to check in that diary of yours?' His voice stays neutral. 'Right, I see. Well, miss, if charges are pressed, we'll have to bring you into the station to make a full sworn statement. You understand that?'

Margot's teeth are starting to chatter.

'Clear?' adds the young one.

She nods again and turns away, almost breaking into a run back towards St Mark's.

This is all her fault. If she'd spent more time with Cyd, really tried to coax the hurt out of her, instead of devoting so much time to just pleasing herself with Felix, they wouldn't be in this nightmare. She was put in that home for a reason. Jeremy as good as told her that.

The image of Felix's room haunts her: his sanctuary, all those things he loved – violated.

Then the final nail.

He's the one pressing charges.

No one's in when she flings open the front door and rushes into the hall. The cavernous house crackles with silence.

In the kitchen, there's a note from Nathan on the table, tucked under a bag of hamster food.

Margot, I've taken Cydney away for a couple of days. She needs a break. The boys are bunking up with friends. Sorry for the abruptness of this.

N

PS Could you feed Arsène and Mauricio?

She tries his number repeatedly, but it goes straight to voicemail each time. She slumps in a chair and buries her head in her hands.

Later – three hours, maybe four – as the late June day bleeds from the sky, gashes of red slashed into the clouds, Margot drags herself up the stairs of this grim sarcophagus of a house, with its leaching secrets and vindictive ghosts.

She drifts from space to space, realising that, only now, is she seeing it properly for the first time, reading its unspoken codes.

She walks into the boys' rooms with their unmade beds and clutter-ridden floors, most of these toys and clothes no doubt chosen by their mother before she ran away from them. A handmade balsa-wood plane twirls dustily on its length of cotton from the ceiling lamp in Josh's room, like a reminder of the cobweb frailty of family life.

She walks on into Nathan's room and stands in the middle of the navy chequered half-moon rug. The former marital bed is covered by a beige-and-brown bedspread, as though to confirm all life has been sucked out of it. Margot catches her reflection in the mirror of the dresser and snatches off her collar. On the side table, Nathan has set out a small orderly parade of aftershaves, two cufflink boxes, a pair of nail clippers, some plastic collar tabs and, on a raised shelf, a recent photo of the four of them in a rowing boat on a lake somewhere. There's no evidence anywhere in the entire room that Elspeth ever existed. Until, that is, she spots, in a small china bowl on the window ledge under a tangle of elastic bands, Nathan's wedding band.

Margot backs out, a somnambulist, fully absorbing the facts of this small, broken family. She stands on the landing in front of the Monet print, at which she's barely given a second glance since the day she arrived. The vase of freesias on the side table, the water cloudy brown inside. All the other details surrounding her in plain sight, present but invisible to her.

She breathes in and starts moving up the stairs to the attic room, an intruder in too far to pull back now.

She stops at the top step, paralysed by the thought of the grief

Cyd has experienced on the other side of this door, alone.

Today would have been Margot's mother's fifty-fifth birthday.

She's been pacing up and down for about ten minutes, looking over at the house down the road, trying to steady herself, afraid she lacks the courage of whatever convictions she still possesses.

In the half-a-dozen times or so she's been inside it, she's never once seen a photograph of his wife. Maybe when she goes over and presses that buzzer, she'll be able to put a face to her guilt at last.

It takes her another five minutes but, finally, she crosses over the road and lifts her hand.

'Hi.'

Her chest feels as though a steel band is being tightened around it.

He stares at her with an expression that contains so much more than shock. Heavy blue bags sag under his eyes.

'Christ. Do you know how many times I've tried to get hold of you? Why the hell didn't you call me back.'

He sighs and lifts his arms towards her.

She doesn't move. She glances up at the window above them then back at him. She must see this through.

He folds his arms across his chest.

'I even picked up the phone a couple of times about to call your vicar, I was so worried.'

The anger in his voice is like a physical slap.

'Can we go for a walk somewhere, Felix?' Even the smell of the hall behind him is pulling her in.

'Why?'

'Please?'

Felix scans her face. She looks down. He does nothing for a few moments, then she hears him snatching his keys off the hook and kicking the door closed behind him.

'OK. Lead on.'

She's rehearsed this endlessly over the past couple of days. But walking alongside him now, with not just his hurt, but the contours, the smell of him a physical fact, her script deserts her.

Their feet are out of step as they walk along the backstreets near his home in spiny silence. A barbeque is in full swing over on one corner, meaty smoke pouring out over their heads. Someone opens a bottle with a defiant pop.

A few steps further on, Felix stops and swivels round to face her.

'How do you think I felt when you wouldn't answer any of my messages?' He swallows hard. 'I didn't deserve that.'

'No, no.' Her nerves are taut with the effort of denying her every instinct. The emotion on his face is so raw, she has to turn her head away.

'There must be some way out of all this?'

She puts more space between them.

'Or maybe you don't want there to be?' He thrusts his hands in his pockets.

She can't afford to do this.

'In which case why exactly did you come today?'

She takes a long shuddering breath.

'I need to talk to you about something.'

'I'm all ears.'

A young couple saunter past. The guy catches Margot's eye and smiles.

'You were saying?'

'It's about Cydney.' Her voice cracks. 'Armstrong.'

He leans in towards her, his lips set in a hard line.

'I know she's in trouble.'

'And? Since when has that been front-page news?'

'With the police.'

He blows out his cheeks.

'She told you that?'

A silent reel is unspooling in her head. The hunched figure in

277

the attic, face pulpy with tears.

'Sorry, let me just check where we are here. You've blanked me for two weeks and now you've pitched up on my doorstep to interrogate me about Cydney.' He blows out his cheeks. 'Jesus, of all people.'

She grabs hold of the garden fence behind her.

'I need to know whether you're pressing charges.'

He lets out a bark of fury.'What, so anyone can stroll in and commit massive criminal damage and we should just say, Oh well, never mind?'

A couple of young boys slice past them on the pavement, doing wheelies on low-slung bikes.

'You should withdraw the charges.' She stops. 'Because, well, I—'

He tips his head.

'Yes?

'It wasn't Cyd.'

'Fuck, what are you talking about?'

'She was with me,' she screams. 'We were shopp—'

He grabs hold of her shoulders.

'Stop it, Margot!'

She twists out of his grip.

'What are you saying?'

She feels like she might pass out.

'You need to drop the charges.'

He rubs his mouth, pushes back his hair. For an insane second, she wonders, if he might be about to hit her.

'My room was completely trashed,' he says very slowly. 'Books torn to pieces, class notes, stuff I'd had for years. All kinds of crap scrawled all over the walls. I actually felt like throwing up when I walked in. She even smashed an engraving my father gave me.'

Margot's shoulders slump.

'She's fifteen, Felix.' Her voice is scratchy. 'Her mother ran away and is having a baby with someone else. Her father's a train wreck.

She's been hanging around with a guy who could easily be ten years older than her.' She grabs his arm. 'Surely you can show her some compassion?'

'*Compassion?*'

'Please.'

'You're not serious? You have no idea how many second chances she's had. How many times I've had her back when other people had completely had it up to here with her.' He slices his finger across his throat. Then he looks at her and the fight seems to leave him. 'In any case, it's not my call. You know that. The head has a policy of zero tolerance for stuff as bad as this. It's my job to enforce it. If we let her off, what kind of example is that?'

'What makes you so sure it was her?'

Something passes quickly across his face. He walks away from her towards over to the curb, then turns back to face her.

'Everyone knows. She was boasting to all her crew about payback time, after I gave her and some of the others detention.'

Margot leans back against the fence.

'You're supposed to be taking care of her, not throwing her to the police like, like—'

'Like a Christian to the lions?' His voice has risen so much, someone looks over, concerned, from the other side of the road. 'You were the one living in the same house. Wasn't it up to you to take care of her – given she was right there under your nose? Isn't that your *job*?'

She can't stop a huge sob escaping her.

Felix runs his hand across his face again.

'Fuck, I'm sorry, I didn't mean that. I—'

'Just drop the charges, Felix. *Please.* Do it for me, if not for her.'

He leans in for her hand, but she pulls away.

'I just told you. It's in the head's court.' He walks back up alongside her 'And what if people found out I'd done something like that for you?'

Margot stares at him. Surely he's not threatening her?

'Along with all the other disgusting stuff, she,' – he takes a breath – 'she scrawled something on the wall.' He bites his lip. 'About you.'

She holds herself very still.

'She didn't name you. But it didn't take much figuring out. And don't ask, because I'm not going to tell you.'

He reaches out again for her hand, but Margot stares at it, then wrenches herself away and charges back along the road.

He calls her name just once.

I feel like I'm wrapped in a sea mist, unable to see any way ahead. Help me to have the strength to get through these last few days with some shred of dignity. I'll never be a priest now, but I still don't want to let You down in the trying.

Chapter 24

Late June

Four thirty a.m. A greasy film of sweat clings to Margot as she turns on the spit. She can't perjure herself. But she knows Felix won't, can't, back down. She feels numb at the thought of him, her loss.

And what does it all mean for Cyd? A young offenders' institution? A permanent criminal record?

What did she write about her on that wall?

And he was right. If anyone should have known the extent of Cyd's pain it was he, above anyone. She has no excuse.

She stares up at the shadows on the ceiling. Her last Sunday as deacon. Her last as part of the Church, ever?

The irony is, though, as she takes her seat at the side of the altar, this feels like a good-energy day. There's a buzz in the air she can't explain. The pews are unusually bursting for early July. She sits with her hands folded, somehow experiencing the resigned calm of one who has accepted her time has almost run out. That green-ink email from a parishioner to the archdeacon could arrive in his inbox any day. If this is her valedictory appearance, the congregation seems to be arranged in their usual seats as if for this exact purpose. The flower ladies in a small posy in the third row below the lectern.

Assorted members of the PCC sprinkled to the left and right of the aisle, ready to take up their assorted roles of reading, serving the chalice, doing the collection or offering this week's prayers. The coffee tables laid up at the back, white tablecloths fluttering in the breeze from the porch. Even Pamela pumped her hand warmly this morning when she walked in. It felt like being handed her last cigarette before the appointment with the firing squad.

The life of this church will continue, exactly as it has for the past 181 years, long after Margot herself is a smudgy footnote in its history.

'Guide Me, Oh Thou Great Redeemer' swells to its boisterous finale. She looks down at the front rows, people's mouths wide in appreciation of the choice of hymn.

Jeremy gives a gruff cough and walks over to the lectern for the notices. It's bread-and-butter business: the final tally from last week's fundraising picnic, the second airing of the marriage banns for a couple no one can quite place, the summer schedule for the Kool Gang, the monthly request for all the bakers to come and reclaim their Tupperware boxes.

'Anyway, saving the best 'til last,' Jeremy says, looking up and pushing his glasses onto his head. 'I hope you all have next Sunday in your calendars because, exactly one year after she joined us, our own Margot is going to be priested by the Bishop of Stepney at St Martin-in-the-Fields. It's a huge celebration for St Mark's and we hope many of you will join us there.'

Sal and Kath grin over. Margot tries to return the smile.

'I'm sure you'll all join me in thanking Margot for all she's done over the past year as curate. Her work with the Kool Gang, the educational talks, the—'

'SHAME!'

Jeremy ducks down as though someone has just hurled a missile at him. There's a second or two when the world stops turning and Margot's breath slows to a whisper. Then a loud clattering on the dias and Roderick appears at the front of the altar. He shuffles forwards and faces the pews, arms stretched out wide, head thrown back. He rips up his order of service with a flourish, jumps off the step and marches down the aisle with a speed and agility that is as shocking as it's impressive.

Here it is, then.

An excited hum rises to a keening ululation as people turn to look at each other. No one else moves from their seat for a few seconds. Then someone stands abruptly and pushes past the rest of his pew towards the central aisle. A woman on the far side does the same. Then another. And another. It's like a tableau of Antony Gormley figures coming to life. Two minutes later and a dozen or so have shoved and shuffled their way to the centre of the church. Margot and Jeremy stare at them in disbelief. But she has just about enough presence of mind to see it's a motley, predictable crew: a handful of Roderick's septuagenarian groupies; that tight-lipped widow who insisted in Margot's first week that canon law forbids the ordination of women; a couple of moth-eaten Roderick lookalikes; the small gaggle of swivel-eyed charismatics for whom it was only a matter of time.

Margot's eye is caught by a movement to the right of the pillar. Fabian is now on his feet in the third row, fingers raking through his hair. He sneers over at her as he marches down to join the rest.

An awed hush fills the church. Margot looks at the faces in the first few rows. Something momentous is happening; they just haven't quite worked out what.

She has. High Noon. The Pied Piper of Highbury seizing his revenge.

The refuseniks have gathered in a half-moon around the coffee table, Roderick standing out in front of them. He's lost twenty years in five minutes. The arthritic stance, the snivelly shakiness, the gloomy torpor: all gone. In their place stands a commanding figure, shoulders straight, ramrod-acked, the assertive naval chaplain of three decades earlier. Cometh the hour, cometh the man. Or, in his case, cometh the woman, goeth the man.

His transformation would be inspiring if it wasn't so catastrophic. She's aware that Jeremy is now staring at her, his cheeks ashen. The entire congregation is staring at her. A couple of sobs break out near the front. A giggle here and there.

Margot drags herself upright and walks with legs of lead to the spot halfway down the aisle where the Gospel is read.

The silence crackles.

'This is about me, isn't it?'

'Self-obsessed as ever, Margot.'

'No, I just—'

'"Let women keep silence in church." One Corinthians, fourteen thirty-four.'

'Wouldn't it be better to talk about this in private, Roderick?' Jeremy asks from far behind her, his voice tremulous and small.

'This is between me and *her*.'

'But, Rod—'

'"A woman should learn quietness and full submission. I do not permit a woman to teach or assume authority over a man." One Timothy two, eleven to fifteen.'

Is he going to work his way through the whole of St Paul?

'I mean, where's it all leading? Our Mother who art in heaven? The Father, Daughter and Holy Ghost?'

'Hear, hear,' bellow a couple of his cohorts.

'You women are trying to pull the Church out from under us. Feminisation, be damned.'

Margot walks further down the aisle. People are now scrambling up onto the pews for a better look. She tries to steady herself.

'Roderick, God's actions in the world are to set all humanity free. Including women. God created mankind as both male and female.' She wills the catch in her voice to subside. 'My calling is no less meaningful than yours.'

Roderick also takes a couple of steps back up the aisle towards.

There's a murmur in the pews around her.

'"Wives submit yourselves unto your own husbands, as unto the Lord. For the husband is the head of the wife even as Christ is head of the Church." There were no female disciples. Your *sex*,' – he purses his lips in disgust – 'makes you unfit to serve and minister at God's Holy altar.'

Unfit. That has to be the cue. She waits for the torrent to start, bracing for the catcalls.

But nothing comes. No one else speaks. And all of a sudden, she feels a charge of energy coursing through her.

'There were no non-Jewish disciples either. And Jesus displayed a shockingly liberated treatment of women. The first person to whom the risen Christ revealed himself was Mary Magdalene.'

'A whore.'

A heartbeat.

'A disciple and a believer.'

'A mistake.' His voice has risen an octave. 'Male-to-male representation is the only faithful one. Two thousand years of tradition can't be wrong.'

He grins at his followers.

'You're the one who's wrong!' It's her mother's voice she can hear ringing out now, clear and commanding. 'There are no gender connotations in the symbol of bread and wine. And we're in Highbury in 2017, not Palestine in AD 75.'

'Moses. Isaiah. David. Elijah. The Pope and all the Holy Fathers. Male. All male.' There are flecks of spit on his chin.

'Ruth? Priscilla? The prophetess Huldah? The judge Deborah? Phebe, Tabitha?' A row of coffee ladies nod in the pew next to her. 'The ordination of women bishops was approved two and a half years ago, Roderick. Did you miss it?'

Roderick snorts.

'Oh, and the head of the Church of England also happens to be female.'

He swats this away as well.

'A women's role in church is as backstage helper.'

So much fury been stored up inside him for years. One enormous liturgical sulk since 11 November 1992. Every ordination, every photo of a smiling incumbent outside her new parish church, a dagger to his left ventricle. And then Margot comes along in his home patch, to add insult to the injury.

'It's a matter of hermeneutics, Roderick.'

'Herman who?'

'The theory of interpretation. The word "spirit" was feminine in the Hebrew so—'

'You and your poncy Cambridge pretentiousness,' he spits. 'We've had enough of experts. What everyone here wants is plain English. Lessons for life. Simple stuff. None of your ologies and your isms and thinking you're so much better than the rest of us. Put all that into your blog of yours, didn't you, Margot?'

Margot gasps, shaking her head.

'That was nothing to do—'

Someone starts clapping. She moves her head a fraction. Gwen. Margot holds her breath. Surely any second now the whole story will come raining down on her head in front of them all. But Gwen's clapping peters out as she walks down to join the rest of them. Still no public denunciation.

All of a sudden, Roderick starts to move towards her, slowly at first, then breaking into a charge. He stops right in front of her, stubble held up to her face. She can hear his lungs creaking. She reaches for the end of the pew for support.

'The moment you arrived here, Margot Goodwin, it all started to go belly up. With your Ph.D. and your polysyllables and your bloody nail varnish. You're like a cross-dresser, playing the part of a man. Why don't you go and get married and pop out some babies just like St Augustine said, there's a good girl.'

'Twenty-first century, Roderick. Time you—'

She feels the sting a moment before the screams of those around her. She's not fast enough to reach him. A sweep of his cassock and he's hurried out through the porch, followed by his ragbag of support. The door bumps on its hinges and squeaks to a halt.

No silence could ever be deeper than this.

Yet she's throbbing with adrenaline. If Roderick was bottling up that explosion, so, she realises, was she. All those years of good behaviour and biting her lip.

Hundreds of faces are watching her, eager for Act Two. Margot slowly turns to look behind her. Jeremy is clinging to the lectern as though he's just survived a Force Eight. His hand is shaking as he beckons her towards him. He steps back and points her to the lectern. He's inviting her to speak, but she doesn't have the strength. He motions at it again, insistent.

She steps up and positions herself behind it, just like that very first time all those months ago. That first sermon, when she was so full of hope, as well as terror, about what lay ahead.

'I'm so sorry you had to witness that, everyone.' She stops, biting back the tears now. 'I'm well aware that I've fallen short of your expectations in so many ways.' She stops again, swallowing. 'You, all of you, entrusted me with this most precious of roles in your church, in your lives, and I've managed to make a complete mess of it. I can only apologise for having let you down.' She pulls out a crumpled tissue and waits. 'For having set such a poor example of what a priest can and should be.' She blows her nose hard and lifts her chin. 'But thank you for welcoming me into your community in the way you have over the past year. And now, if anyone else would like to join those who have just voted with their feet, please follow your conscience. I know I have.'

She steps back from the microphone and closes her eyes.

There's not a sound in the church. Then a light tapping sound starts, like rainfall on forest leaves, gaining momentum. It takes her a moment to realise. Applause, growing more and more thunderous.

She opens her eyes. The first person on her feet, leading the ovation that follows, is Pamela.

One of the last of her Christmas candles is flickering in a jam jar at the side of the bath, its powdery scent only adding to her sense of nausea.

Gwen and Roderick. Guilt is what consumes her most of all. She knows now that all Gwen wanted was a friend, some purpose and meaning to fill the emptiness in her life. How much would that have cost her? And she knows the same was true of Roderick. Even though he'd have happily tied her to the ducking stool given the chance, he was a crouched, scared old man who didn't recognise his world any more. St Mark's was their home. They've exiled themselves because of her.

A visceral need for Felix sweeps through her. For his humour and wisdom, his acceptance of her exactly as she is: his tireless efforts to try and understand the universe into which she'd dragged him.

Surviving the rest of today without Felix. Surviving all the rest of her days without Felix.

Salty tears slip down into the lukewarm water. She slides below the surface and holds her breath.

It's very late, pitch dark, when her phone flashes on the rug next to her. She flicks on the bedside lamp.

Jeremy's voice is thick as he confirms that he's lost a fifth of his flock: his prized congregation built up over decades, decimated in the course of a single hour. Gone for good, all thanks to the black sheep in their midst.

She's quiet after he's finished. She's entirely in his hands.

'Who'd have thought that St Stephen's, Finsbury, would be more exciting than us?'

She shudders.

'St Stephen's also happens to be where that famous nephew of

Fabian's pitched up, so my spies tell me.'

The fey-faced weasel with the iPad under his arm. She stares at the wall. Of course. Vic-i-leaks is probably his handiwork as well. Not that that matters now.

'Roderick's been planning this since the start of Lent, apparently. People have been calling me all afternoon to tell me they suspected something. Quite why they didn't think to say anything before, you may well ask. Seems it was a very professional job. Flyers, phone calls, emails, undercover Twitter, the whole works to encourage people to defect. Fabian's nephew again, no doubt.'

'I'm sure.'

Roderick and Fabian. The ultimate odd couple, Mr Groomed and Mr Grime.

'Even the evangelicals have gone to St Stephens?'

'Not them, no, they've scarpered to that Alpha place at the back of Holloway Road. But both ends worked together on this – an unholy alliance of high and low, with the common enemy of St Mark's. We're far too liberal and easy-going for either camp.' The bitterness of his laugh is new to her. 'Seems we underestimated Roderick, Margot. There was plenty of Pentecostal fire left in that ancient belly.'

'I'm so sorry, Jeremy.'

'For what?'

Being a woman. Being the wrong kind of woman. For daring to imagine she had what it takes.

'Funny old world,' he mutters.

There's another pause.

'Do you know what, Margot? Gutted as I am to lose so many parishioners – it's a big dent in our annual income, one or two were amongst our biggest standing-order givers – I somehow feel it's for the best. That level of bad feeling will always burst out sometime, showering everyone in stinking pus.'

'It wouldn't have happened if I hadn't been here.'

'Maybe not. But the next curate might be female too, or the one after that. In any case, for Roderick, it wasn't just about you being female, but also you being a much better priest than he is. Well, bugger off, Roderick, you foul-breathed old bore. St Stephen's is welcome to you.' He bursts into a quieter version of the familiar chuckle. 'You know what William Booth of the Salvation Army said, don't you? "My best men are women."'

Her turn to laugh now. But the relief is brief.

'I'm sorry Fabian's gone, though Jeremy.' She stops. 'I know how much you valued his help.'

'Well, since you've brought that up, there's a story there. Two, in fact.'

Her skin prickles.

'He came to see me a week or so ago.' Jeremy clears his throat. 'About you.'

Margot looks down at her hands.

'Claimed you'd made some sort of lunge at him. Said you were probably a nymphomaniac, given all the other goings-on, but that he hadn't told me earlier because he didn't want to destabilise the congregation. He also said he was sure his nephew could be parachuted in to help if need be.'

Margot looks over at her reflection in the mirror on the back of the door.

'Ridiculous, of course. But is there anything you want to tell me?'

So she does. The whole tawdry tale. She even mentions Arthur's early warning.

'Just as I thought. That's why I laughed and sent him away with a flea in his ear. But I don't understand, Margot. Why didn't you tell me?'

'Golden-Boy Fundraiser's word against mine.'

'You know me better than that.'

'I'm sorry.' Yet another miscalculation.

'Anyway, the second story is just as lunatic. Pamela tells me that

Fabian was hatching some plan to turn St Mark's into a high-end nightclub-cum-casino money-spinner. They had a huge row about it a few days ago. That's the real reason he walked, I suspect. Business plans not on track. He must been hoping to cream off some serious money from it. All his "big I am, finger-in-every-pie" routine, was just that – a routine. And I completely fell for it.'

He clears his throat.

'I had heard something about the nightclub idea. Lunatic.'

'Turns out he was already talking to contractors and so on. The bloody cheek of it. I know we all obsess about funding around here – needs must in a building as old as ours – but there are limits. Sexing-up St Mark's? He was planning to change the name to Marky's Place, Pamela said. Can you imagine?'

Margot can. 'Well, he and his nephew will have many happy hours slagging off St Stephen's.'

'Exactly.'

They fall silent for a moment. She can hear him yawning.

'Jeremy?'

He grunts. She closes her eyes.

'Has the bishop been in touch?'

'No.'

'I thought that maybe Gwen or Fabian or even Pamela – you know?'

He pauses, apparently refilling his glass with something.

'Fabian was too busy trying to turn us into Stringfellows, Margot.' He sighs. 'Someone like Gwen would never criticise St Mark's in public, no matter how much we'd disappointed her, and Pamela, well, it seems she's now your number-one fan.'

'Really?'

'She liked your gutsy rejection of the loadsamoney scheme. Fabian told her during their big showdown.'

Perfect Pamela.

'And Roderick?'

'My hunch is that Roderick was too preoccupied with plotting his coup d'état to expend any effort on your love life. He had you down as a hussy from day one, so you didn't have far to fall.'

Another light chuckle.

She allows herself a small smile.

'Now that Roderick's legged it to the lacy end of things, the church flat is free, of course. Let me know when you want to move in.'

Her heart leaps for a second before reality kicks back in. She's nowhere near out of the woods yet.

'Do you mind if we leave things as they are for now?'

'You're kidding? I thought you'd be biting my hand off for the keys, after all your whinging.'

'Can I let you know in a day or so?'

'Oh, there is one other thing. Went out of my mind with all this other stuff happening. He coughs. 'I did hear from the bishop's office, actually. As did all the north London incumbents with a female curate. About that website.'

The sense of safety had lasted five minutes, at most.

'There are only six female curates in the diocese. Unfortunately, the other five are all in their mid sixties. There are rumours of a full-blown investigation. We may not be Roman Catholic, but we do love our inquisitions.'

'I understand.'

'Chin up, Margot. We're a team, you and I.' He pauses. 'But it would help if we come up with a head for their platter.'

She's making coffee just before midnight a few days later when the house phone rings. She hesitates, then decides to answer it.

Nathan's voice is tight.

'Sorry to call so late, but we've got a problem, Margot.'

Margot sinks onto a stool.

'It's Cyd.'

Her heart starts to race.

'I left her with my sister in Lincoln while I went off to a work meeting for a few hours. She's done a runner.'

Margot gasps.

'I've no idea whether she has any money on her or where she is or who—'

'Tell me how I can help,' she says quickly.

'I haven't called the police yet. That's all we need right now.'

'Shall I try and contact some of her friends?'

She swallows. She could ask Felix if he could help.

'None of them know anything. Or claim not to.'

'What about her mother?'

'You're joking.'

She bites her lip.

'She took some of her clothes with her, so at least we know some pervert didn't just lift her off the street. Not yet, anyway.' His voice has started to crack.

'She'll be safe, Nathan. I'm sure of it.'

He blows his nose.

'I'm not sure I can share your faith in happy endings. I'll keep you posted.'

The line goes dead.

Please, please may she return home safe. Help her to understand that whatever pain and hurt she's feels now won't last for ever. That her mother still loves her even if she can't see it right now. That we all love her. That there's always hope. Please, God, may she come home safely.

The next few hours are the most harrowing of her entire life, every possible threat that Cyd might be facing parading at some point through her mind.

At one point near dawn, she falls into a fitful half-sleep, in which she's on her hands and knees crawling towards a finishing line, but each time she's almost there, the tape is pulled further and further away. She wakes with a jolt, dry-mouthed, heart pounding.

The shame she feels at her inability to help is beyond words.

Camden Market is echoing when she arrives mid morning the next day. Most of the stalls are locked up and there's hardly anyone walking around, compared to the boisterous, teeming atmosphere when she was last here.

Margot has no idea why she's come or what she's expecting to find here. The chances of bumping into the boyfriend are virtually non-existent. She just felt drawn here as the last place, the only place, she and Cyd visited together, and because, as she told Jeremy, she had to be doing something, somewhere, rather than just waiting at the other end of the phone.

She wanders around the Stables Market and on through the warren of Asian food stalls to the section next to the canal, most of which is boarded up. The whole exercise is pointless.

She's close to tears by the time she walks into the Proud Gallery, just in case. She snatches for her phone the second she hears the bleep.

'I need to speak to you.'

Margot has to double-check, she's so taken aback. She holds the phone up to her ear, dreading this conversation as well.

'Sun, moon, whole entire universe. It all revolves around you, doesn't it, Margot?

'No, no, I—'

'The rest of us, like some supine Greek chorus, watch you weep and wail and wring your hands before we shepherd you towards your happy ending. Margot Goodwin, a masterclass in self-obsession.'

Margot's mouth fills with bile.

'Please, not right now.'

'I've quit my Ph.D.'

'Don't be stupid.'

'Fait accompli.'

Margot slumps back against the wall, next to a row of photos of 1960s' psychedelia.

'But it was going so well.'

'Was it?' A sharp bark of laughter. 'How would you know?'

Guilt upon guilt.

'Well, how about taking some time out to regroup?'

'You don't get it, do you?'

Margot lowers her head.

'No, I don't, Clariss. You're right. I'm sorry.'

She listens in silence. The writer's block on the post-doc. The six months of swelling panic as she realised she was losing the thread, the deadline looming like an obstacle in the fast lane, threatening everything she'd slogged so hard for over the past eight years. Exactly the same time it's taken Margot to get here.

Her eyes are hot with tears. The slow-motion derailment Clarissa is describing could so easily have been – still be – her own. No wonder she became so fixated on Soulmates. Then, in that instant, she sees with absolute certainty what she's always known.

'It's you, isn't it?'

Silence on the other end of the phone. The barman glances over as he wipes down the optics behind the counter.

'Vic-i-leaks? It's you.'

Margot's arms are stippled in goose pimples.

'What are you talking about?'

'You need to be honest with me.' Margot swallows. 'My head's on the line. It's really serious.'

She can hear a huge intake of breath on the other end of the line.

'It was meant to be just a bit of fun, M.'

Everything falls into place like a child's Slinky toy snapping back into its coils. Margot had confided all sorts of things in those first few months and Clarissa's insider knowledge, of course, allowed her to fill in the rest.

'A bit of light relief from all the feminist theology.'

'You think it's *funny*?'

Disgust churns inside Margot. 'You could have trashed my entire career.'

'Sounds like you don't need my help on that front.'

Margot holds the phone away from her.

'Margot? Are you there? Hello? Look, I'm sorry, OK?'

Margot leans back against the wall.

'You're right. I'm sorry. It was a shitty thing to do. It just sort of ran away with itself. I guess I got carried away.' She clears her throat. 'I was angry, OK?'

'*Angry*?' She swallows. She knows the answer.

'You just disappeared off the radar. One minute we were mates, the next you'd sort of pissed off into your own cosy parish universe. I suppose I thought the Soulmates stuff was a way of having some fun together.' She pauses. 'And then that obviously didn't happen either.'

Margot closes her eyes.

'They're about to wheel in the diocesan heavies, Clariss.'

'OK, don't worry, I'll sort it.' Clarissa pauses. 'I miss you, M.'

'I really have been a crap friend, haven't I?'

'So much worse than that.' Clarissa blows her nose on the other end of the line. 'But in a spirit of extreme, entirely selfish generosity, I'm prepared to forgive you and try again'

'I miss you too,' Margot says.

The weight falls back on her shoulders the second she comes off the phone.

Twelve o'clock. Not a word from Nathan.

She arrives back at Aberdeen Avenue half an hour later to find the front door unlocked. She steps inside slowly.

'Hello?' She walks forward a few steps. 'Hello?'

'Fuck, why aren't you at church?'

Margot sags against the wall in relief.

'I've been sick with worry about you.'

She steps forwards to hug her, but Cyd's too quick.

'What the fuck are you doing?'

She looks dreadful, her hair unwashed, grooves and shadows as though she hasn't slept for weeks.

'Does your dad know you're here?'

Cyd tries to shove past Margot up the stairs, but Margot gets the better of her this time.

'Does he?'

Cyd shrugs.

'Call him right now. Or I will.'

'Still issuing orders in spite of everything?'

Margot turns pale. Thirty seconds ago, seeing this pinched, furious face was a moment of pure joy.

'I hate hypocrites.'

'What are you talking about?'

Cyd's face twists into a grin.

'Porter will make a great vicar's wife. Or would, if he didn't already have one.'

Margot gasps.

'Did you think it was a secret?' She laughs in Margot's face. 'Even the twins saw you out together. Oh, and the champagne in the fridge.' Cyd leans in closer. 'A boy in my year even caught you in the toilets. How gross.'

Cyd tries to push past again, but Margot whips her arm out and pins her to the wall.

'Ow, that hurts.'

'Your turn to listen to me, and you're going to listen properly – got that?'

Cyd jerks her head away.

'You're right, Felix Porter and I were seeing each other.' Her mouth is parchment. 'He and his wife are getting divorced, not that it's any business of yours. But we're not together now and you want to know why? We had a huge row and all because of you.'

Cyd cocks her head and smiles.

'I'm flattered.'

Margot just restrains herself.

'Because you thought it was so clever to go in and trash his room – don't even bother denying it – I had to tell the police that it wasn't you, that it couldn't have been you, because, because—'

Cyd's eyes are wide. Margot is breathing hard and fast.

'I told them you were with me.'

Margot drops her hands, anger draining out of her.

'Except I think they don't believe me and the school won't drop the charges.'

She sinks down onto the rug, burying her hand in her hands.

Much later – she's lost all sense of time – there's a knock on Margot's door. She drags the duvet higher over her head.

'Margot?'

She can't move a muscle.

'Can you open the door?'

She turns to face the wall.

'Please can you?'

She hesitates, then forces herself to unpeel the covers.

Cyd shuffles from one foot to the other like a ten-year-old. 'You look terrible.'

Margot closes her eyes, swaying.

'I wondered, you know, if you wanted to, like, get something to eat?'

Margot opens her eyes and stares at her.

'I guess I kind of owe you.'

Margot's head is throbbing, her legs made of pipe cleaners.

'Please?' Cyd asks. There's a tiny flicker of something in her eyes.

Margot sighs.

'I know somewhere we can go, Cyd. It's a bit further away, but it's worth it.'

Neither of them attempts to talk as get off the bus and walk down

Gray's Inn Road, as though they're both holding something in reserve.

They continue on into Sidmouth Street and then Tavistock Place. A few minutes later, Margot stops outside an unprepossessing red-brick building set amidst a terrace of Georgian houses. There's a large glass frontage, through which they can see tables and chairs arranged inside.

'OK, this is it. We're here.'

Cyd looks down at the board next to her on the pavement.

'Fuck, no, you're joking. Why have you brought me here?'

'Relax, Cyd, no one's going to drug your coffee and convert you when you're under the influence. That would be a waste of decent drugs.'

The scowl's going nowhere.

'Look through the window. You can see people in there drinking coffee. Do they look like they've been brainwashed?'

Margot peeks in again, just in case.

Suspicion radiates from Cyd, but she gives a tiny shrug of submission. Enough to work with.

'Only because I owe you.'

They step in through the automatic doors. Cyd steers to the left but Margot touches her arm.

'Just a sec. I want to show you something first.'

Cyd steps back.

'Cross my heart and hope to die, I'm not going to kidnap you and pack you off to some Midwestern cult. I just wanted to show you something that I think is very beautiful and serene. I think we could both do with that right now.'

Cyd's eyes narrow.

Margot smiles to herself. Another tiny victory.

She reaches behind her for Cyd's arm.

It was a freezing day, a day bleached of colour, when she first came across the Lumen United Reform Church the first time.

Walking into this space, being drenched in light, took her right back to that first afternoon in New Milton Community Church, that same sense of being dazzled by possibility, of bathing in radiance.

She leads Cyd forwards into the interior of the building. It's a modern, free-flowing space, stretching all the way through to a simple black-and-white stained-glass window at the far end. In its sinuous simplicity, it's one of the most serene places Margot has ever encountered.

'Come and look at this, Cyd.'

She points upwards to where a huge white cone has been sculpted at the centre of the space, slanting all the way up to the roof, as though a solid shaft of light has been beamed down from the heavens. She tugs Cyd forward slightly, towards an opening in the cone and they step together into the tepee-shaped area inside. There are a few beanbags scattered around, a handful of plastic children's chairs and, right at the very top of the soaring structure, a good ten metres above their heads, an iridescent circle of light, a window onto the sky.

She turns to her right. Cyd is leaning back against the wall, arms folded, staring upwards, the start of a smile.

An hour later, they're still in the café. 'You know that evening I came up to your room?' Margot pauses. 'When we were all watching the movie together?'

Cyd continues to dab her finger into the brownie crumbs.

'I was just trying to say – very clumsily – that I understood how you felt.'

Cyd keeps her eyes on her plate.

'What, because your dad's dumped your mum and is marrying Linda instead?'

Margot winces, but holds it in check.

'Not exactly.'

She pushes her mug to one side.

'Let me tell you something. About my mother. About me. About everything.'

The café owner comes up for a second time to their table, J-cloth in hand.

'Sorry to have to hassle you, ladies, but we're shutting in ten.' He grins at them, one after the other, and walks back into the kitchen.

Cyd is still threading her scrunchie through her fingers, in, out, out, in.

'So I sort of know what it's like to feel as though your insides have been shredded on a cheese grater, Cyd. You can't really know if you've never been through it.'

Clarissa did understand, though. So did Felix.

Cyd stops fiddling.

'I remember how it is when all you want to do is curl up and lock yourself away to make the pain disappear.'

Cyd still won't look up, but she gives a tiny nod.

'Either that or running away as far as you can possibly go. In my case, when I was your age, to a happy-clappy church, which, to be honest, at the time offered me a real sense of escape.' She smiles. 'In yours to, well, whatever, wherever you've just been.'

Again, a barely detectable movement of the head.

'It won't always feel this raw. I promise you. Of course, no one or nothing can just somehow magic away the hurt of it all. Not even prayer, before you ask. But where there's love, there's always hope. And.' She stops, hesitating. 'A new baby has to be the most powerful symbol of hope there is, right? Just wait and see.'

Margot pulls her bag towards her.

'We should let these guys close up.'

'What about your dad and Linda, then?'

She stands and pulls on her jacket.

'Margot?'

She sighs.

'Same thing applies. It was my problem, not theirs.' Cyd waits for her to say more. 'And, against all the odds, Linda has helped heal us a bit, I think.'

Cyd drains the dregs in her glass.

'Thank God for Linda.'

Margot smiles as she waits for Cyd to slide off the bench. They walk out onto the pavement together, into the warmth of the early evening.

'I still don't get why you did it, though. Why you were prepared to tell such a big fat lie to save me?'

Margot stops to do up her laces to buy a little time.

'I mean, I never would have in your shoes. Fuck, no.' Cyd drags her hair back into the scrunchie. 'Was it because you felt guilty?' She gives a light laugh. 'Or because you're so Christian?'

Multiple answers shimmer between them.

'Well, I could say that our way of life is our belief.'

Cyd's eyes roll upwards.

'That religion is about doing things that change you, rather than just going on and on about them. If you're a practising Christian, you're practising just as much as you are Christian.'

'You haven't got the hang of it yet?'

Margot smiles.

'But why did you?' Cyd stands still, while Margot walks on a few steps. She stops and turns around.

'Do you know what, Cyd? I just think everyone deserves a break. A second chance. That's all. I don't think you've had too many of those.'

Cyd wraps a stray strand of hair around her finger. 'You won't go to hell or anything?'

'I'd have thought you'd have happily bought me a one-way ticket.'

'I guess I do owe you.'

'Actually, I think it's me who owes you.'

They carry on walking up the street side by side.

'Sorry about your sex life, Margot. Though I think he's a twat.'

Margot bites her lip.

'Thanks for the drink. And, yeah, the sermon.'

Margot smiles. First steps.

They're halfway home when Margot hears the beep from her phone.

Vic-i-leaks: Scenes from Parish Life, 29 June 2017

Finally, after all the moaning, the Big Day's here! Tomorrow's my ordination, people. This is what it's all been about! Sure, all the old bags will still be present and correct when I come back here newly priested on Monday morning, but, hey, I can live with that. They come with the territory. I can't tell you how much I'm looking forward to this next stage in my career. Priest? Me? What a high! And then I'll be taking my very first Mass next week. Can't wait. And so, because I'm about to become a proper grown-up responsible member of the C of E, I've an announcement to make. Time to say cheerio to this blog. It's been fun, but as Bugs Bunny says, That's all, folks xxxxx

Chapter 25

Sunday 2 July 2017

Powdery light filters in around the curtains. Margot lies completely still, cupped by the mattress, the warmth of the sheet across her legs. Is this how some women feel in the hours before labour starts? Some say they have an intuitive sense of the imminence, irrespective of whatever else they've been told. She looks down at her watch. Six and a half hours until she's kneeling at the altar of St Martin-in-the-Fields, the bishop's hands on her head. She feels slightly sick.

She leans over to release the window catch. The sky isn't quite festooned with shafts of gold, but a sweet tang still pours into the room, the generosity of a warm midsummer day.

Sunday 2 July 2017. Petertide. Her last day as just a deacon.

She catches sight of herself in the mirror and rubs at her cheeks. Four days from now, she'll be conducting her first Mass, performing the Eucharist, offering absolution and taking the blessing.

She flops back down on the bed, a broad smile creasing her face.

When she pitched up at Mildmay Grove a year ago, with two suitcases, a box of books and a head and heart full of naïve good intentions, she had no idea who she really was. It's taken some of the toughest months of her life for her to understand that she's someone else entirely.

If blisse had lein in art or strength,
None but the wise or strong had gained it:
Where now by Faith all arms are of a length;
One size doth all conditions fit.

Herbert's words have never felt more right.

Everything, all of it, has been leading right here to this momentous morning with its subtle assurance of heat and light. The golden thread of deep conviction reeling her in like a bream on her father's line.

She got back late on Friday night from the priesthood retreat: three days in an old house in Docklands run by nuns, along with eleven other deacons from the diocese, many of them the POTTY lot. They'd spent most of the time in prayer and contemplation, including two days of complete silence, preparing for the leap from servanthood to ministry.

Being away in that completely sealed environment had given Margot the peace she needed finally to be ready. To understand the sacrifices she will continue to have to make —and to run towards them with a willing heart.

And whatever reservations the bishop may have had about her, he confined himself to a wry observation that, while life can sometimes veer off onto a Plan B, God is in it, wherever it leads.

'It's only by facing up to who we are, Margot, that we fully learn all that we might do and be. God bless you and you will go on to achieve in your ministry.'

She flicks on the bathroom light and slips the collar into her black shirt.

Is anyone really sure they're right for this, ever? No. But, she realises, the grace, the delight, lies in the unknowing and still striving towards being the best you can be.

I thought I'd never get to this point. You knew that more than anyone. Thank You for believing in me, for repeatedly instilling in me greater strength and purpose. For letting fresh air blow through my faith, for letting me question and probe and explore – and understand that we're not entitled to certainty, because Jesus rarely answered, but instead said, 'What do you think?' Thank You for letting me get so much wrong before I finally started to get a few things right. I lost my faith in myself, but I never once lost my faith in You. Your love and grace are present in my life more powerfully than they've ever been. I know my sense of calling as a profound privilege and blessing. Help me to act on that blessing every day from this day onwards.

A text beeps from the bedroom.

Breakfast! Plenty of carbs!

Quintessential Hadley. Fourteen of them being ordained this morning. That's a long wait until the celebratory lunch.

When she steps out of the shower, something shiny is sitting on the carpet outside her door: a large silvery square shape shouting out purple sparkles. There's a card on top: *MAGGOT.*

Spangles disco in the morning light as she sits on the bed to open it.

A day of gifts. Starting with the text that came through just after midnight.

Gogo, the head's decided not to press charges against Cydney after all. Or go ahead with suspension either. It took some arm-twisting, but he accepted that zero tolerance isn't always the way to go. Hope that also applies to me one day. Good luck for today. So proud of my beautiful girl.

Whatever ends up happening, this – this – gives her enormous joy.

She pulls at the corner of the envelope on her lap.

Happy Ordinashun, Maggot. Sam and Josh xxxx :-) It's written on the back of a postcard showing a grinning 1950s housewife, with a speech bubble reading, *Bless him, he thinks he's the boss.*

The package sits lightly on her knees. The bow needs a couple of tugs and inside is another layer, tissue-wrapped this time, with a Post-It note attached.

Go get 'em, Margot. Cyd xo

She carefully pulls back the tissue paper to find a small canvas inside. No title or other explanation.

The solid cone of light tapering up towards heaven.

The kitchen is empty when she walks in. Nathan has probably told them all to give her some space. She'd ended up confessing her nerves last night over a glass of his very-special-occasion malt.

'Excited and a bit shit-scared, just like the day before your wedding day,' he'd said, refilling her glass, then stopping, bottle by his shoulder. 'Sorry, bad analogy. You've made a much better choice than me. And you know what, they're lucky to have you.'

He'd clinked her glass.

'Thanks, Margot. Your presence has worked a quiet magic in this house. More, I suspect, than I'll ever know.' He raised his glass to her again. 'We're going to miss you.'

She's dressed an hour too early. Prowling up and down her room isn't going to help, so she flicks open her laptop instead.

Every time she lifts the lid now, Gwen comes into her mind. How could she ever have suspected her? Sad, unfulfilled Gwen, with her food parcels and her mothering and her jackhammer offers of help. Gwen and her Wishing Wall. She feels another hot wave of guilt. She could have done so much more to make her feel appreciated. It wouldn't have taken much. One day soon, she'll write to her, try to make amends somehow. But she knows it won't bring her back to St Mark's.

She gets up and walks to the window for a few moments to steady herself, then comes back to her bed and clicks opens her emails.

There's an email from Clarissa, with the subject line *Female Priests: The Final Frontier.*

We might not get the chance to chat later, M, after you've moved over to the Serious Side. I've been to a couple of these things before. The battle for the grub makes David's tussle with Goliath seem like a conker game. So I thought I'd send love and luck and all the rest of it via e-pigeon. I may not have found your Soulmate but you've still got your Bestmate. ROFL.

Thanks for your support last week over the dearly departed thesis. You know what? Thesis schmesis. The future lies in Vic-Lit. Guess who told me to get writing a novel? A healer called LINDA!!! Her card must have fallen out of your bag that day you flounced out of my room. She's the BEST. I know you're not into any of that whacky stuff, but then the stuff you are into is whacky enough anyway, right?!

Mucho hugs

Laters, Vicigator

P.S. A woman's place is in the House of Bishops

She takes a last look in the mirror, makes a tiny adjustment to her collar, adds a slick of lipstick. She looks down at her handbag on the floor: time to invest in a new one. She hooks it over her shoulder and walks out of the door.

What's the collective noun for a cluster of about-to-be-priested deacons? A batch? A jelly? A breath-hold?

The impression here in the robing rooms of St Martin-in-the-Fields is, of course, overwhelmingly male. But she's here, isn't she? One of a small clutch of female curates, together with Hadley and the half-a-dozen women incumbents amongst the group of clerics from the candidates' home churches: the touchline team here to cheer them on.

She exchanges 'do-they-mean-me?' glances with a few of the POTTY lot, all of them, she's sure, experiencing the same churning mix of terror and exultation. This is the most important, magnificent day of her life.

Being Christ for the people.

She flicks through the service sheet to distract herself, reading the abbreviated CVs of all the candidates. Rupert, that Anglo-Catholic with the nice line in tweedy waistcoats. Rob, the chirpy Mancunian who used to ask her out at the end of every POTTY session. John-Anthony, the Nigerian evangelical always up for a joke, even though they disagree on virtually every theological and philosophical point in existence. Tallulah, the Belfast bombshell who, Margot's thrilled and envious to see, has donned pink satin heels under her surplice.

They all start to process up the aisle, the bishop toweringly resplendent in his gold brocade cope and mitre. It feels, looks, like a coronation ceremony. She glances up at the chandeliers above their heads, the dark wooden upper balconies, full of friends and family cheering them all on. They're being crowned and anointed. Prepared for the greatest privilege of all: taking their places at the communion table and performing the full sacramental role, acting directly *in persona Christ*.

She sneaks a look at the pillars on both sides of the church, just in case Roderick is hiding for a last hurrah. She pulls her eyes back towards the altar. This is her moment.

She glances up at the window high up behind the altar, where a slanted white egg sits at the centre, distorting the steel fretwork within which it floats. It's unlike any other church window she's ever seen, as though someone has pushed their way through it to heaven.

The bishop's voice is sonorous and slow, full of ancient certitudes.

'Today is an important threshold for all our young curates here this morning.'

She catches the eye of the sixty-something woman standing next to her, who winks.

'In this beautiful place of worship, we've gathered together to watch a kind of miracle: new priests being made. In just a few moments, I and this great company of priests here behind me will act on behalf of the whole Church by laying hands on the candidates and praying for the Holy Spirit to enter them as they begin their sacramental priesthood.'

Margot looks down at her hands.

'Fourteen people, at least one of whom you'll know personally, about to assume an entirely new identity. It's something both thrilling and, as I remember myself, intimidating, in equal measure. As those who love and support these young people, we pray for them in this moment of transition, hoping that their new worlds will bring blessings as yet unimagined.'

They approach the altar for the laying-on of hands one at a time, each candidate shepherded by his or her small posse of supporters. Jeremy steps up alongside Margot and Hadley joins them on the other side, squeezing Margot's elbow under her surplice.

Three, two, one, in front of her. It's her turn to kneel down on the red cassock.

She feels the light pressure of the bishop's hands on her head. Just a few seconds, that's all, and it's done. She stays kneeling a few moments longer and then rises back to her feet. A ray of sunshine strikes the carpet beside the altar. Jeremy turns to her with a grin.

She makes her way back to her seat. Somehow she's managed to dodge all the bullets and stay alive. Never more alive than this.

Her calling fulfilled.

As the rest of the priesting line continues to shuffle forwards, Margot looks to her left and spots Nathan and the boys over by a pillar, waving at her wildly. She had no idea they were planning to come. Then she realises that several members of the congregation are here, too. Sal and Kath, Tommy, most of the choir, several of the flower and coffee ladies, five Kool Gang families, plus every remaining member of the PCC, including, resplendent in a hat brim so wide that she's cancelled out half the row behind her, Pamela.

Margot is humbled at the loyalty of their support. All these people she's grown to respect, like, love, even, realising that whatever their foibles and quirks and imperfections, they're all so less significant than her own. They've welcomed her and accepted her into the very heart of their community, no matter how grievous her faults.

And what felt like intrusion and prurience when she first arrived, she now sees, in most cases, as genuine interest and care.

She looks towards the front again. Clarissa sitting in the middle of the second row: she's always prided herself on her mosh-pit skills. She looks transformed. Who knows how much stress has been lifted from her shoulders by her decision to, at last, be true to herself.

'Dad?'

They're hovering over by the drinks table, looking slightly as though they've somehow stumbled into the wrong party.

'I wasn't sure you'd want to come.'

They share a long look between them.

'How often does your only daughter get herself made into a vicar?'

He smiles and leans over to hug her.

'My turn,' shrieks Linda, shoving him aside and throwing her arms around Margot. A newly minted priest and his parents glance over. Linda's hugs have the power to crush Margot's spine into something snortable, but she doesn't care. Linda is wearing head-to-toe white, from the feather boa to the towering platform shoes, perhaps working a Holy Ghost theme, but there's no doubting the warmth of her embrace.

'Welcome to the noble line of priestesses stretching all the way back to Phoebe the moon goddess and beyond.'

'As it happens, Phebe was also the only female called "deacon" in the New Testament.'

Linda giggles, delighted.

Give and you will receive.

'Congratulations, love.' Ricky raises his glass. 'Is that what you say at these things?'

She was wrong, Clarissa was right, as in so many things. Linda does have healing powers.

He clears his throat. 'Danny sends his apologies.'

A brief shadow passes over them, then she smiles, appreciating the kindness of the lie. One day, she prays.

'We've decided to postpone the wedding, love,' says Ricky.

'Oh?'

'We've moved it to the autumn equinox,' adds Linda. 'The planet alignment's much better then. Saturn was way too much to the left of Jupiter before.'

Margot nods.

'Gives us something to look forward to in October,' he adds, lightly. 'And maybe by then, you'll be able to help us out?'

'You bet, Dad.'

She's moving across to talk to the cluster of flower ladies now inspecting the enormous centrepiece of freesias and lilies when an arm grabs her from behind.

'Yay, you. Having a moment, M?'

The pleasure on Clarissa's face makes Margot's cheeks tingle.

'You smashed it, M. All that "should I, shouldn't I?" diva stuff at Cambridge. I knew I was right. I always am.'

Margot hugs her again.

'So, anyway. Look who I spotted lurking behind a pillar.' Clarissa stands back to give Margot a better view. 'I'll just go and get us some refills, shall I?'

Margot is afraid to breathe.

Felix looks to either side of him and takes a small step forwards.

'You look different, Gogo. Luminous.'

He goes to move forward again, but checks himself.

'It must be an ontological thing,' she answers, her voice shaking. He laughs and leans in towards her.

'You don't mind that I came, do you? I wasn't going to, but then I woke up this morning and thought how much I'd love to be here, that it would probably be OK if I stayed hidden from view. But then Clarissa—'

She steps forward and reaches for his hand, just for a second. The familiarity of his fingers.

'I love that you came.'

'You really nailed it. I'm so proud of you. Next stop, the House of Lords. They won't know what's hit 'em.'

She laughs. Hadley is looking over at her from a group of incumbents in the centre aisle, smiling broadly.

'You're very special, Margot. I knew that right from the start.'

He lifts his hand as though to touch her face, but lowers it again.'

'You are,' she whispers. 'Thank you for what you did for Cyd.'

He searches her face for something.

'You know you can't get rid of me that easily, don't you, Reverend?'

He kisses her fingertips, taps the end of her nose and walks out of the crypt without glancing back.

They're all packed onto the main steps of the church, hundreds of them, priests old and new, the bishop, incumbents from all over the diocese.

Tourists milling around Trafalgar Square gather in bemused knots, their phones raised high, a crop of one-eyed flowers. Nearly two hundred feet above them all, the bells are sending liquid peals into the summer air.

Margot is standing at the end of one of the rows and feels a sharp tug on her stole.

'Excuse me, hello, please?'

A tiny Japanese woman is staring up at her, wielding a large black and gold fan.

'Is this the movies?'

Margot bursts out laughing.

'Kind of. It's a celebration for people who have just become priests.'

'You too?'

Margot nods, understanding the disbelief.

The woman giggles behind her hand. Margot delivers a tiny bow. Tokyo will soon be awash with this confirmation of English eccentricity.

Another hand rests on her shoulder and squeezes it.

'You did it, Margot.'

'Too right,' adds Hadley, leaning around Jeremy laughing.

'We did it,' she corrects.

'Never a dull moment,' says Jeremy.

Margot looks down at her feet.

'I know this year you'll do an even better one,' he continues.

Hadley reaches across and gives her a high five.

'I've never been wrong about a curate yet,' chuckles Jeremy.

A sudden rushing, beating sound breaks out by the fountain. A flock of pigeons, hundreds of them, takes to the air right in front of them. Margot shades her eyes to watch their ascent. Some carve back around to return to the rich pickings in the square, but the rest continue to soar, dipping and rising on the currents and moving higher and higher into the sky, up and over the roof of the National Gallery and on to whatever lies beyond.

Jeremy points at the flock, squeezes her shoulder and turns away to talk to someone on his left.

Margot fingers graze her collar.

This is it, then.

Margot Goodwin.

Priest.

Glossary of terms

Acolyte – someone who assists the priest by performing ceremonial duties, such as lighting altar candles

Andocentric – centred on or dominated by males and masculine interests

Anglo-Catholic – the traditional, 'high church', end of the Church of England

Biretta – a square cap with three flat projections on top, worn by Roman Catholic clergymen

Canon law – Church law

Chasuble – an ornate sleeveless outer vestment worn by the priest when celebrating Communion

Church Commissioners – the body which supports the work and mission of the Church of England

Clerestory – the upper part of a large church, containing a series of windows

Clobber texts – slang for passages of the bible wielded as weapons by the anti-women-priests camp

Cope – an ornate cape-like garment worn by a bishop

Cotta – a type of surplice

Deacon – ordained clergy, part of the threefold order of bishops, priests and deacons